Heath... MacQua... lives in Belf........ ...and, but ... .o spends a good deal of her time in the Algarve reg... .n of Portugal. Happily married to Ross, she is a mother, grandmother and former teacher. Since leaving the classroom behind in 2012 Heather has enjoyed reinventing herself as a writer of contemporary romance and mystery fiction.

Double Cheque is her fifth novel.

Also by Heather MacQuarrie

A Voice from the Past
In the Greater Scheme of Things
Blood is Thicker
Broken Cups

www.heathermacquarrie.com

Thank you to the team at Matador, especially Heidi, Emily and Andrea, for their professional services and friendly advice in managing the production of this book.

Thank you to my husband, Ross, and to the rest of my family, for their unwavering support and encouragement and for their guidance in all things technical.

And thank you to all those who continue to buy and read my books. I hope you enjoy this one.

Heather xx

DOUBLE CHEQUE

Heather MacQuarrie

Matador
9 Priory Business Park,
Wistow Road, Kibworth Beauchamp,
Leicestershire. LE8 0RX
Tel: 0116 279 2299
Email: books@troubador.co.uk
Web: www.troubador.co.uk/matador
Twitter: @matadorbooks

ISBN 978 1789013 849

British Library Cataloguing in Publication Data.
A catalogue record for this book is available from the British Library.

Printed and bound in the UK by TJ International, Padstow, Cornwall
Typeset in 12pt Aldine401 BT by Troubador Publishing Ltd, Leicester, UK

Matador is an imprint of Troubador Publishing Ltd

Part One

Chapter 1

Jasmine remained in her hiding place behind the coat-stand in the darkened hallway until her mother went back upstairs and closed the bedroom door behind her. Only then did she dare to breathe as the horror of what she had just overheard began to sink in. She slipped furtively into the now empty kitchen and slouched down into the nearest chair, holding her head in her hands as she went over it again in her mind. Dougie. Who on earth was Dougie? And Grant Cartwright. She recognised that name. She just couldn't place it but it was definitely familiar. Something from her childhood. Yes, it was slowly coming back to her. Visits to Mum's friend, Cathy. A girl called Rebecca and a baby. A baby with a boy's name even though it was a girl. Robyn; that was it. The baby was called Robyn. And they had a big brother about the same age as her own brother, Sam. Grant. Grant Cartwright. Jasmine knew that her mother had remained friends with Cathy but it had ceased to be a family thing once they were all old enough to forge their own friendships outside the family circle. She hadn't seen any of them for years.

Several minutes passed while Jasmine tried to digest the information that was now flooding her brain. Why was her mum speaking to this man, Dougie, in secret? Who was Mr Ferguson? One thing was for sure; she didn't want her mum to know that she had overheard her phone call so she tiptoed out to the front door, opened it as quietly as she could and then slammed it shut quite noisily, hoping that her parents would hear her and think that she was just arriving home. She was pretty sure that they hadn't heard her clocking in for real twenty minutes earlier. Her plan worked perfectly. As Jasmine mounted the stairs and made her way to her own room, she heard the muffled greeting from her parents' bedroom.

"Is that you, Sweetheart? Night night! Sleep well."

"Night Mum," she answered as though on autopilot. "Night Dad."

It felt surreal. She was just exchanging pleasantries as normal. But things were not normal. They were anything but normal. She had heard enough to know that her mum was having an affair with someone called Dougie. She was cheating on her dad.

Jasmine lay awake for a long time, staring at the ceiling. She didn't know what to do. And she couldn't believe that this was happening. Phenomenons like this presented themselves in other families, not in hers. Her parents' marriage was rock solid and always had been. She missed her brother and her sister. Sam was living with his girlfriend, Tania, at Tania's parents' house until they could afford somewhere of their own. They had a little baby, Stevie, just nine months old. It wouldn't be fair to burden Sam with this disclosure; he had enough problems of his own. And Molly was in Australia, probably arranging her next sky dive or parachute drop to add to her gap year experiences; she wouldn't be able to help either. With a heavy heart Jasmine realised that she had no allies. She alone was aware that her parents' marriage was in jeopardy. But what could she do about it? She closed her eyes in an attempt to stem the tears but with little effect. Maybe it would all turn out to be a bad dream.

★★★

Breakfast on a Monday morning never was the cheeriest of occasions in the Campbell household so nothing appeared to be amiss until Patricia dropped the bombshell that she might have to work over the coming weekend. Her boss wanted her to attend an exhibition in Scotland, she announced; it was apparently an excellent PR opportunity for the company. Jasmine froze, her coffee cup suspended half-way between the table and her lips, a piece of toast wedged in her throat.

"You didn't mention it yesterday," Kenneth said, a look of puzzlement on his face.

"Do you know, it completely slipped my mind," his wife replied nonchalantly. "It was only mentioned briefly as a possibility but I just had a text message confirming it. While you were in the shower."

Jasmine coughed to dislodge the toast and took a sip of her coffee. She would have to think quickly. She could not let this happen. She had only heard one side of that conversation last night but she had definitely witnessed her mother arranging to spend the weekend with someone called Dougie and admitting to being in a relationship with him. And her mother's phone had been sitting on the shelf behind them, plugged into the socket in the wall, the whole time that her dad had been in the shower. She hadn't been near it.

"Can you take an early flight out and get back the same day?" Kenneth was asking.

"I'm afraid not," Patricia answered without batting an eyelid. "The exhibition runs for two days. I'll need to stay over."

Kenneth gave her a funny look, which started Jasmine thinking.

He knows. I'm sure he suspects something. This isn't the first time Mum has gone off on her own for the weekend but she usually says it has something to do with her friend, Cathy. She doesn't often use work as an excuse. But Dad knows that things have cooled a bit between Mum and Cathy in recent weeks so she has had to come up with something else. But that look he gave her. I think he's beginning to catch on. Surely it isn't too late to stop her. I have to do something.

"Why don't you go too, Dad," she blurted out on an impulse. "Mum won't be working the whole time. You could have a romantic mini-break in a nice hotel and you'd have time to do a bit of sightseeing while she's at the exhibition. I know how you love your museums and art galleries."

"That's not a bad idea, Jasmine," Kenneth agreed, nodding his head.

Jasmine almost found it funny as she watched her mother squirm at this response until she remembered the seriousness of the situation. She complimented herself on her resourcefulness and breathed a sigh of relief. If she could at least thwart her plans for this weekend, there would be more time to come up with a permanent solution. But then Patricia spoke again.

"I'd rather do that another time when I'd be free to go sightseeing with you," she said. "Your birthday is just a couple of weeks away. We could do it then. Have a real mini-break together."

"Or you could do both," Jasmine put in, desperately.

Patricia glared at her daughter. "Stop telling your dad what to do, Jasmine," she bristled. "He can make up his own mind. What's it got to do with you anyway?"

"The birthday treat sounds good to me," Kenneth affirmed, bringing the conversation to a close. "Now look at the time. We're all going to be late for work if we don't get a move on." He finished his coffee in one gulp and left the table.

Jasmine wasn't so sure now that her father had twigged what was going on. But she had no doubt about her mother's guilty secret; the look of self-satisfied smugness on Patricia's face said it all. Well, it wasn't over yet; she still had four days to stop this rendezvous from taking place.

★★★

The Cartwright children hadn't entered Jasmine's thoughts for many years but hearing Grant's name mentioned last night had evoked memories from her childhood which refused to go away during her day at work. Jasmine was a dental receptionist in a large modern practice. She spent her working hours checking patients in and out as they arrived for appointments, sending reminder emails to cut down on the number of people who fail to turn up at the given time and answering the phone. Today was particularly busy and she hardly had time to breathe or dwell on her parents' problems until her coffee break at eleven o'clock. As she sat in the small staff room and poured hot water onto the spoonful of instant coffee in her blue mug, her mind reverted to those far off days when she had played in Auntie Cathy's garden. She wasn't really an aunt but that was how she had been taught to address the woman. She was her mum's best friend. Sometimes her real nephew was there too as well as her own children. There had been a big party to celebrate the millennium but after that Jasmine couldn't recall seeing much of the Cartwrights or their cousin. She would have been about eight at that time.

One of the hygienists came in for her break and started chatting to Jasmine about her holiday. Emily had just returned from a fortnight in Lanzarote and was sporting a healthy tan. She proceeded to display pictures on her phone, everything from busy and colourful beaches and swimming pools to lively bars and restaurants and cycle rides on lonely country roads. Jasmine enjoyed the distraction but her mind returned to the past as soon as her colleague left.

The millennium party was held at Cathy's parents' house. There was the baby, Robyn, and the girl, Rebecca, who would have been about six, same as Molly. Sam and Grant would have been teenagers and there were two other boys about their age. One of them couldn't walk very well and could hardly speak. What was his name? Alastair. That was it, Alastair. He was Grant's cousin. And his friend was called Bradley. Molly and I thought he was gorgeous! And Rebecca's grandfather organised all sorts of games for us to play. Gosh, that was sixteen years ago! I wonder where they all are now.

Jasmine shook herself from her reverie. Her break was over and she would be needed back at the desk. Those people weren't in her life anymore; it didn't matter where they were today. Except for Grant. Her mother had said something in that phone call last night about passing on a message to Grant Cartwright and something about someone called Ferguson. She couldn't remember exactly what had been said but it was clear that there was some kind of connection between Grant Cartwright and her mother's lover, Dougie, and she was determined to get to the bottom of it. She would have to enlist the help of her brother, Sam, after all.

Chapter 2

Tania Hopkins was at her wits' end. Here she was still living with her parents at the age of twenty-five, complete with a nine month old baby and a boyfriend who didn't really love her and didn't really want to be there. His discomfort with their living arrangements was tangible and it was getting worse by the day. Tania was well aware that Sam still hankered after his first love, still held a torch for her, a girl called Imogen. She was convinced that he still regretted not opening up to Imogen when she phoned him one evening last November, shortly before Stevie was born. Tania had witnessed the conversation and much as she respected him for his loyalty to her, she understood that it came at a price. Sam didn't love her. They had only stayed together because of the pregnancy. And she had to be honest. She wasn't sure whether she loved him either. He was a nice enough guy, good fun to be around in a casual manner. But she couldn't imagine marrying him, not that he had proposed to her anyway. So why was she still with him? Especially when he was obviously so unhappy.

The doorbell rang. Tania was annoyed. It was one of the rare occasions when she had the house to herself. Her parents were at the cinema, Sam had gone to the pub for a few pints with his golfing friends and Stevie was fast asleep. She considered ignoring the interruption but the caller was persistent, ringing the bell for a second time. Tania went out into the hallway and opened the door.

"Hi Tania." It was Sam's sister, Jasmine. "Is my brother at home?"

Tania shook her head sadly and then suddenly, without warning, she burst into tears. Jasmine was alarmed.

"Whatever is the matter?" she asked, as she stepped inside and closed the door behind her. "Have the two of you had a row?"

Jasmine gently shepherded the young mother back into the lounge and sat down with her on the sofa. Tania hadn't yet answered her question. She repeated it.

"Is everything all right between the two of you? Where *is* Sam?"

"He hates living here," Tania now disclosed. "He feels trapped."

Jasmine was shocked. "Has he moved out?" she faltered. "Where has he gone?"

Tania shook her head. "Not yet," she sighed, "but it's coming to that. He's just gone out for a drink with some friends but he's doing that more and more and staying away longer each time. We're coming to the end of the road."

"Oh no! I can't believe it. What about Stevie?" The baby wasn't even a year old yet.

"Stevie's fine," Tania reassured her. "We both love him to bits but we don't have anything else in common and my parents are driving Sam round the twist."

Jasmine had forgotten her reason for calling by now. She could fully understand that living with Tania's parents was not an ideal situation for her brother by any means. He had a strong independent streak, liked to do things his own way. "Don't let it get you down," she soothed. "Surely you'll be fine once you have a place of your own."

"He doesn't love me," Tania said resignedly. "He's only ever loved one person."

Jasmine stared at her. Surely not. Surely not after all this time. But deep down she sensed that it might be true.

"Imogen," they both said together.

The door opened and Sam himself materialised in front of them. "Hi Sis," he slurred, evidently a bit intoxicated. "What are you doing here?"

"Well, thanks for the warm welcome," Jasmine answered with a scowl, hoping that he hadn't overheard them. "At least Tania was pleased to see me."

"It's a fair enough question. You don't often come to visit in the evenings."

"How would you know?" Tania retorted. "You're hardly ever in."

"Well I'm in now. And it's only nine o'clock. Give me a break, Tania!"

Jasmine stood up and tried to pretend that she hadn't detected the animosity between them. "Well I'll be off and give you some time to yourselves," she said as cheerily as she could muster. "I just thought I'd pop in because I was in the area."

"Everything all right at home then?" quipped Sam. "Have you heard from Molly?"

"She's having the time of her life," Jasmine replied. "I don't know how she'll settle down to study next year after all this excitement."

"And is Mum behaving herself?"

Jasmine was momentarily confused by the question. "What do you mean by that?" she quizzed her brother.

"I just wonder sometimes about all those weekends away with Cathy. Do you never think that there might be something more to it than meets the eye?"

Jasmine was wrong-footed by the unexpected remark but pleased to see that Sam had now gone over to his wife and was giving her a cuddle and a kiss on the cheek. Maybe things weren't so bad between them after all. Perhaps she should admit why she had called in the first place. "What are you suggesting?" she asked.

"Look, I'm sorry. I shouldn't have mentioned it. I've had a drink too many. It was just something that Dad said to me one time."

"There's Stevie awake," Tania suddenly said, hearing the soft cries coming from the baby monitor. "I'll just go and check that he's OK. I think he might be coming down with something. He was very restless all day."

"I'll go," Sam offered. "You stay here and chat with Jasmine."

"No, I think you should have a chat with your sister," Tania riposted. "I'll see to Stevie. But thanks for the gesture; you're a good Dad."

"But not such a good partner," Sam mumbled, as she left the room.

"It can't be easy for you, living here," Jasmine comforted him. "You should have moved on by now. Are there no decent flats on the market? Have you not asked her to marry you?"

"Leave it, Sis. You don't know the half of it."

"I like Tania."

"I like her too."

"Like? What about love?"

Sam remained silent. The only sounds in the house were Stevie's soft cries and Tania's soothing voice coming from the room above. But the atmosphere was loaded and they could both sense it. Jasmine decided to take the bull by the horns. She sat down again and took off her coat.

"I'll tell you why I really called round here tonight," she began, "if you tell me what's going on with you two. And let's start with a cup of coffee. It might sober you up a bit."

Sam retorted that he was not drunk but then admitted that he would like a coffee. They both moved into the kitchen. "You first," Sam insisted, as he turned on the machine.

"There's not much room in here," observed Jasmine, taking in her cluttered surroundings. "It must get a bit cramped with two families trying to share."

"You first," he reiterated, more vehemently.

Jasmine paused to gather her thoughts. "It *is* to do with Mum," she then admitted. "What was that you were saying about Dad telling you something?"

"He told me one time that he thinks Mum just uses Cathy as an excuse to explain her absence when she might actually be with someone else."

"He actually said that?"

"I didn't believe him at the time but a few weeks later Mum said she was at a show in Dublin with Cathy and I know for sure that she wasn't because I met the woman in Tesco's. At least I spotted her at the checkout; I didn't actually speak to her or let on that I had seen her."

"Are you sure it was Cathy?"

"Hundred percent. We used to know her quite well. Do you remember we used to play in her garden with her kids? She always gave us jelly and ice-cream, even when I was in my teens!"

Jasmine laughed. "I was just thinking back over those days myself," she told her brother. "Do you remember the millennium party at her parents' place?"

"Yes, that was awesome."

"We never saw much of the Cartwright children after that. I suppose there comes a time when you start making your own friends. After all we only knew them because Mum and Cathy were so close. They didn't go to our school or anything."

"Or maybe Mum deliberately kept us away. If she was starting to use Cathy as an alibi."

The two siblings frowned at one another, sharing a sad understanding, and then Sam spoke again.

"You've discovered something too. That's why you're here. Am I right?"

Jasmine nodded her head. "She's planning to spend the weekend with someone called Dougie. But this time she's pretending that she has to work. In Scotland."

She told Sam the whole story about the conversation she had overheard and the comments that had been made at the breakfast table.

"So there's still some sort of connection with Cathy."

"And with Grant. Mum said something about delivering an important letter to Grant Cartwright. So this guy, Dougie must know both Cathy and Grant."

Sam scratched his head. "I used to know Grant quite well but I haven't seen him for a few years. The last time I met him he was with a lovely girl called Zoe. I think they were engaged."

Jasmine took a sip of her coffee. "Anyway, I've kept my side of the bargain," she proclaimed, changing the subject. "Now what's going on with you and Tania? You both seem to be a bit down in the dumps."

"I think we're growing apart," Sam answered with a sigh.

"You have a baby together," rejoined his sister.

"That's only part of a very complicated scenario," Sam told her over the sound of the washing machine, whirring loudly on its spin cycle. "We are both exhausted. We never have time to have any fun anymore. Judy and Eddie are so damn through-other. I'm really beginning to detest them. I mean, look at the place." With a wide sweep of the arm he drew his sister's attention to the basin full of underwear macerating in some kind of pink detergent next to the sink, the tubs of soiled bed linen lining the wall behind them and the bulk purchase of about two hundred toilet rolls stacked up in the corner.

As though on cue, the door opened and Tania's parents breezed in, enthusing about the film they had seen and bustling about the house, dropping coats and handbags, phones, wallets and keys on every available surface. Edward reached up to the wine rack and selected a bottle of Merlot, muttering only the briefest of greetings to Sam and Jasmine, as he poured two glasses for Judy and himself. Then he returned to the lounge where he turned on the television at top volume, sank into his favourite armchair and proceeded to scroll through the channels, choosing something to watch. Checking her phone and noticing that she'd had a couple of missed calls, Judy phoned her friend back and started to talk and laugh loudly over the sound from the lewd reality show that was now on the TV. She reminded Jasmine of Sybil Fawlty.

"Welcome to my world," Sam said to Jasmine. "This is fairly normal."

"You need to get away from this," Jasmine agreed. "You and Tania need a place of your own." As she spoke, Tania ran down the stairs and yelled at her parents.

"Do you have to have that so loud? I had just got Stevie back to sleep and now he's crying again. Thanks a lot!"

Judy immediately apologised and admitted that she had forgotten about the baby. Edward said nothing but did turn the volume down a bit, though not enough to make much difference. Tania threw Sam a look of exasperation as she deposited the wet nappy she was carrying in the bin and turned back towards the stairs.

"We'll be outside," he mouthed. "I won't be long." Then he turned back to his sister and suggested that they should continue their conversation in his car. He fetched her bag and coat from the lounge and led her out through the back door.

Thankfully, being mid-September, it was quite a balmy evening and they were comfortable enough as they scrambled into Sam's silver Volvo.

"I can't take much more of this," he declared with a grimace.

"I don't blame you," Jasmine concurred. "I can't understand why you agreed to move in here in the first place."

"Believe it or not, Judy is actually brilliant with the baby. Tania depends on her a lot."

"Other couples manage," Jasmine retorted.

"I know."

"I think Tania needs a break. Why don't you take her away for a holiday, even just a weekend? Have a bit of time on your own, a bit of fun."

"I'll think about it. It's not a bad idea. Anyway, I need to get back in and help her with Stevie. Tell me more about the situation with Mum and Dad. Has she really got a lover?"

"I suggested that Dad should go with her to Scotland this weekend but she put him off and she got really rattled with me for pushing it."

"You're sure it's this weekend? In Scotland? I wonder whether Tania would enjoy that."

"Seriously?"

"Why not? Two birds with one stone and all that."

"It's not really putting Tania first."

"I think she'd enjoy it, the subterfuge. I can combine that with a bit of romance. Can you find out what flight she's taking?"

"It's not a joke, Sam. This is about our mother sleeping with another man, cheating on our dad."

"Sorry, Sis, I know it's not a joke but it hasn't really come as a shock to me. I've suspected it for some time. Text me the flight details and leave it to me."

Jasmine smiled at her brother and then gave him a big hug. "Say 'night night' to Tania for me," she told him, as she got out of his car and into her own with her fingers firmly crossed for a solution to at least one of the two big problems facing her family. She drove home feeling apprehensive but hopeful.

Chapter 3

"There she is," whispered Sam, as he spotted his mother talking on her mobile outside the bookshop at Belfast International Airport on Friday evening. He steered Tania away from the area so that they wouldn't be observed and waited until Patricia had finished her phone call. He watched as she put the phone back into her handbag and walked over to the screen displaying the departure details of outgoing flights, before marching purposefully towards one of the gates.

"The gate number must be up," Sam said, just as confirmation of this was announced over the Tannoy system. "Let's wait a few minutes so that there'll be plenty of people in between us. I hope she isn't seated too close to us."

"You'll have to change tactics if she is," Tania replied, "or if she spots us in the queue."

"Keep that hat down over your eyes," he told her, as he wrapped his own scarf loosely around his neck so that it covered the bottom half of his face. "We'll have to take these off for security but we can put them on again afterwards."

"This could be quite good fun if it was someone else we were trailing," Tania observed, "but I do feel a bit guilty snooping on your mum. There's something very sleazy about it." Sam had been perfectly honest about the purpose of the trip but had also convinced her that they needed the break themselves. That bit had come as a pleasant surprise.

"I know. So do I but needs must. I don't want my parents breaking up. I'll do anything I can to stop that happening."

"Sometimes it's for the best," Tania cautioned, "if two people really aren't happy together anymore. Maybe we shouldn't interfere. Fewer and fewer couples are staying together these days."

"It might come to that," Sam agreed, "but I have to try."

They strolled over to the screen and double-checked the gate number for their flight, taking in the bustling atmosphere around them, then spent a few minutes browsing in the duty-free shopping area. "OK, let's go," Sam ventured at last. "That should be enough of a head start. We don't want the plane going without us."

Passengers were already boarding and there was no sign of Patricia. Good, she must be already on the plane. Sam and Tania removed their hats and scarfs as planned and went through security, showing their ID and boarding cards, then replaced their partial disguise before mounting the steps and making their way towards their allotted seats near the back of the plane. Sam hoisted both their bags into the locker above their heads and sat down beside his girlfriend.

"Can you see her at all?" he hissed.

"I think that's her about five rows in front of us, on the other side."

Sam took a furtive glance in that direction. "You're right," he confirmed, recognising his mother's blue coat and blonde hair. "We'll have to be careful getting off. I don't want her seeing us until we get the chance to catch her red-handed. This Dougie bloke will be sure to be waiting for her in the arrivals area."

"What if she walks past us to go to the toilet?"

"It's a very short flight. I don't think that's likely."

Sam sent a text message to his sister before they would be instructed to turn off their mobiles.

On plane. Mum is a few rows in front. Hasn't spotted us.

Jasmine answered immediately.

Good. Keep me informed. Make sure you two have some fun in spite of the reason for your trip!!

Sam showed the text to Tania.

"I like your sister," she said.

"She likes you too."

An air stewardess was now going through the safety procedures and telling everyone to turn off their phones and buckle their seat belts. Tania felt a sudden and overwhelming surge of relief and freedom. "I like you as well," she told Sam with a smile.

"I love you," he replied without hesitation.

Tania held her breath, hardly believing her own ears. How long had she waited to hear him say that? Long enough to convince herself that he didn't love her and worse still, that she didn't love him. But now he had said it and that changed everything. Her whole body was tingling with excitement.

"I love you too," she whispered, as the plane taxied along the runway and rose from the ground.

"Marry me," Sam breathed in reply. They were now soaring above the clouds and Tania had a fleeting wish that they could stay up there for ever. But then she had a vision of little Stevie and she came back down to earth with a thump. Would anything really change if they were married?

"Please," Sam persisted. "I've been doing a lot of thinking these past few days. I want us to be a proper family, Tania. You, me and Stevie. Marry me, and let's get as far away from your parents as possible."

Tania was momentarily offended. "My mum has been very supportive," she countered. "I don't know how we could have coped without her."

"I'm not disputing that," Sam reasoned. "But I can't live in her house any longer or I will go mad. I mean it, Tania. I can't go back there."

She didn't reply but she understood his reserve. Their current living arrangements were anything but ideal.

"You haven't answered me, Tania," Sam said after a few moments. "Will you marry me?"

"I thought you were still in love with Imogen." She could have kicked herself for saying it but it just came out. She couldn't help herself.

Sam started at the name of his first love. How could he blame her for thinking it? He had been deeply in love with Imogen and had lost her because of a stupid fling with her friend, Holly. It had been nothing more than an infatuation and he had regretted it almost as soon as it started but he knew that he couldn't expect Imogen to take him back. He had begun a relationship with Tania on the rebound. When Imogen had phoned him one night and had said she still loved him, Tania was already pregnant. With a heavy heart Sam had done the honourable thing. But he had eventually managed to put it all behind him. He did love Tania now. He really did want it to work.

"I don't love Imogen," he said simply. "I love you and I love Stevie. I want us to be a proper family."

"Then yes," Tania whispered.

"Yes?"

"Yes, I'll marry you. And yes, we'll live somewhere else. Just you and me and Stevie."

They shared a kiss. Luckily there was no-one in the aisle seat so they had a fair amount of privacy.

"I think Jaz should be the first to know," suggested Sam.

"OK," agreed Tania, bursting with happiness, "followed by Lawrence and Maggie."

"Fair enough." Lawrence was Tania's older brother and Maggie was his fiancée. They had been engaged since April but had delayed their wedding plans due to Maggie's dad being very ill. He had died just last month.

Sam took hold of Tania's hand and held it lovingly for the rest of the flight. Jasmine had been right. All they needed was to get away for a romantic break. And it was only beginning. They weren't even there yet. Tania was over the moon. He had said those four words that she had longed to hear, ever since she had known him. He had said it at last. *I don't love Imogen.* She could scarcely believe it. And they had a whole weekend ahead, just the two of them. Bliss! That is, once they get things sorted with Sam's mother.

The plane landed on schedule and most of the passengers stood up and started to put on coats and retrieve their hand luggage from the lockers. Sam and Tania sat on, looking out of the window, disguised again by their hats and scarfs. They squinted sideways from time to time and were aware of Patricia passing by and exiting the plane. Only then did they stand up and follow her down the steps and into the arrivals area, keeping a discreet distance behind.

"I don't know whether she checked in any luggage or not," Sam said, "but I wouldn't think so. She's only here for two days like ourselves."

As expected, Patricia bypassed the baggage reclaim carrousels and made her way towards the exit, trundling her green cabin bag behind her. And suddenly there he was, rushing up to her and taking her in his arms. They kissed on the mouth, long and passionately. Sam felt sick. His mother and another man! "Come on," he said to Tania. "This is it."

Sam and Tania quickly caught up with the older couple and shadowed them as they walked out of the airport, hand in hand, and made their way to the short-term carpark, the stranger now trundling the green bag. Stopping beside a black BMW, the man took a key from his pocket and activated the lock. The lights flashed and he opened the door.

"Hi Mum," Sam said clearly, as other people who had arrived on the same flight continued to walk past in search of their own cars. Patricia recognised the voice immediately. She swung round in panic.

"Sam!" Then she caught sight of Tania by his side. "What are you two doing here?"

"We could ask you the same question. Aren't you going to introduce us to your friend?"

"Oh, this gentleman is just giving me a lift to my hotel," she bluffed. "I'm working at an exhibition tomorrow. Didn't your father mention it at all?"

"So you snog all your taxi drivers then," Sam said sarcastically. "I saw the two of you greeting each other in the arrivals area just now."

"Have you been following me?" Patricia now accused him crossly and very red-faced.

"Yes," Sam admitted. "I have."

"Hello Sam," the gentleman now intervened. "Douglas McKendrick. It's nice to meet you at last." He held out his hand in friendship. Sam ignored the gesture.

Patricia was horrified. "What are you doing?" she hissed at her companion.

"The game's up, Patty. We might as well come clean. It was going to happen sooner or later."

He turned back towards the young couple. "And you must be Jasmine."

"I'm not Jasmine," Tania said.

"Let's not have this conversation here in the car park," Mr McKendrick suggested. "Where are you two heading? Can we all go somewhere and have a civilised drink together?"

"There's nothing civilised about you sleeping with my mother," Sam scoffed. However, he was equally reluctant to have a bickering row in front of other passengers who were going to and from their cars so close to the airport entrance. Begrudgingly he told the man the name of the hotel they had booked and agreed that they all go there. "And by the way, this is Tania, my fiancée," he concluded, as they climbed into the back seat.

"Fiancée?" Patricia exclaimed. "Since when? It would have been nice to have been kept informed."

"Since about an hour ago."

Tania hissed in Sam's ear, reminding him that they had agreed to tell Jasmine and Lawrence first but she didn't really mind. She could sense that Sam wanted to give more weight to his argument that loyalty and faithfulness within the family is important. Unless that was the only reason he had proposed. She began to doubt his motives. Meanwhile they were receiving congratulatory comments from the front seats.

Not another word was spoken until they all arrived at the hotel.

"We'll wait for you in the bar," Douglas proposed, "if you want to check in and leave your bags in your room."

Sam just nodded. He didn't trust himself to speak. Tania went with him to reception, where it only took a few minutes to organise their accommodation. In under ten minutes they had gained entry to their room, deposited their bags, and freshened up. "Right, let's get this over with," Sam said firmly.

Patricia and Douglas were seated in a fairly private alcove at the far end of the bar. Douglas stood up politely as the younger couple squeezed in opposite them. "What would you like to drink?" he asked them.

"Just water," said Sam. This was going to require a clear head.

"Sparkling please," added Tania.

Douglas gave the order to a passing waiter and then they all eyeballed each other, not sure how to begin. In the end it was Patricia who spoke first.

"This is none of your business, Sam," she cautioned. "You are not a child any longer. I do not have to be answerable to you in all my dealings and you should not have followed me over here."

"You're cheating on Dad," he replied, incensed at her attitude. "Am I supposed to just sit back and let that happen?" Before she even had the chance to respond, he spoke again. "If he even is my dad! How can I be sure of that if you are sleeping around?"

"Of course Casey is your father!" Patricia said emphatically and in an angry tone of voice. Kenneth had long been known as Casey by most of his close friends by virtue of his initials, KC.

"Jasmine and Molly too?"

"Absolutely! How could you begin to think otherwise?"

"You're being very disrespectful towards your mother," Douglas now put in, admonishing the younger man.

Sam was tempted to thump him in the face but he managed to keep his cool and just shot him a withering glance. Tania squirmed in her seat, feeling very uncomfortable. The waiter arrived with the two glasses of sparkling water.

"I love them both," Patricia now confided. "It really is possible to love two people. You just have to believe me on that."

"I do believe you," Sam said without hesitation as an image of Imogen flashed through his mind. "But you still have to choose one of them."

"And let the other one go? No, I can't do that."

"You have to."

"Don't make me do that, Sam. I can't believe that my own son is grilling me like this! Can't you see that I am happy with things the way they are. No-one is getting hurt. No-one is losing out. Your father and I are perfectly content."

"You're kidding yourself, Mum. Dad is not content. He knows about this."

"He knows that you followed me here?" The trepidation was obvious in her panic-stricken face, which was reassuring to Sam. She must at least care about her marriage.

"No, but he has his suspicions. How long has this been going on? How long have you and Cathy Cartwright been hoodwinking my dad?" He addressed this question to Mr McKendrick.

Douglas looked bewildered. "I don't even know Cathy Cartwright," he revealed. "I met her once, about thirty years ago."

"You're lying," Sam accused him but he didn't want to get his sister into trouble and expose her as an eavesdropper, so he didn't elaborate.

"I'm not lying," Douglas insisted. "I don't know the woman although I did meet her son recently."

"Grant?"

"Yes, is he a friend of yours?"

"He used to be, years ago. How do *you* know him?"

Douglas wasn't sure whether the truth was out in the open or not but he wasn't going to jeopardise his own relationships by protecting someone he hardly knew so he told Sam exactly what had happened.

"It turns out that a friend of mine is Grant Cartwright's father. He came over here looking for him and I was able to put them in touch."

Then he turned to Patricia. "Actually, Cameron Ferguson phoned me again this morning," he told her. "He's still very anxious about that letter he wrote to the boy, the one he gave to me to pass on to you. Apparently he hasn't had any reply."

"Well, I definitely gave it to Cathy and she was seeing Grant the very next day," Patty repeated. "I told you that on the phone. Sure it's not even a week yet. How quickly is he expecting a reply?"

"I think he anticipated that the lad would get in touch right away. He sent him his mobile number and email address."

"So why doesn't he just phone Grant himself?"

"He doesn't have a number for him or an address."

Whilst all this seemed to confirm what Jasmine had related concerning the overheard phone call, Sam was now getting frustrated that they were digressing. He was anxious to get back to the point. "All right," he said, "so I was wrong about you and Cathy being in this together but you still haven't answered my question. How long has this been going on? You and my mother."

"We've been friends for years," Douglas now told him, "since our student days."

"Have you ever met my dad?"

"No."

"Not friends then. Lovers."

"No, Sam," his mother interjected. "Just friends for a long time. Dougie's wife, Lucinda and I were very close. Casey met *her* several times."

"So you've also put *your* marriage on the line!" Sam was utterly scathing and almost spat the words at him.

"Lucinda died ten years ago. We sort of drifted into a relationship after that."

"Right."

Sam was increasingly aware of Tania's discomfort as his side. He took her hand and mouthed an apology. "This isn't a very nice introduction to the family for my fiancée," he said aloud.

"Then you shouldn't have engineered it," Patricia said cuttingly. But then she softened her approach. "You're not going to tell Casey, are you?"

"No, I'm not."

She relaxed and smiled. "Thank you," she breathed gratefully.

"I'm not, but *you* are," Sam retorted caustically. "That is if you still want to be part of Stevie's life. Now enjoy your weekend and make sure it's your last one with this man. We have an engagement to celebrate so we'll say goodbye." As he spoke, he led Tania away from the booth towards the busy restaurant.

"I hope we're not too late for dinner," he enquired as the maître d' approached them.

"You're just in time," the man replied. "A table for two?"

"Yes please," Sam answered. "A table for two and a bottle of Champagne."

"I'm not dressed for a nice dinner," Tania fretted as they sat down. "I'm still wearing the clothes I travelled in."

"You look beautiful," Sam told her. "We'll have another Champagne dinner tomorrow night and you can dress up for that one if you like. We'll make it a proper celebration."

"So you do still want to marry me? It wasn't just a ruse to make a point to your mother?"

Sam was genuinely shocked. "Of course I want to marry you. I love you and I should have asked you long ago. This has nothing to do with my mother."

"I saw your face when she said that it's possible to love two people at once. And you didn't disagree with her."

"What about my face?"

"You were thinking about *her*."

And then he said it again, filling her heart with relief and joy. "I don't love Imogen. Not anymore. I love *you*, Tania. Now, are you going to send that text to Jasmine and Lawrence or will I do it?"

"I'll do it," she said happily as a smart young waitress approached the table with a notebook and pen, "just as soon as we order our meal."

Chapter 4

Maggie Redpath was exhausted but elated. She had just completed the first week in her new job and she loved it. Just knowing that those twenty-six nine-year-olds were her responsibility for the whole year was at once scary but so satisfying. It was quite different to the exhaustion she had felt after a week's subbing where she had covered for an absent teacher who was on sick leave or attending a course. This was her own class. She would really get to know these children properly, get the chance to appreciate their individual personalities and needs, find out what makes them tick. You could do that to some extent when teaching on a temporary basis, but this time she would be able to guide her pupils through a whole year and hopefully see the progress they made at the end of it. It wouldn't be easy. There were several challenging characters within the group. But Maggie's own experience of an unhappy childhood stood her in good stead to understand others and the impact that extraneous factors can have on school performance. Not that it had been all bad, by any means. Her mother had been a tower of strength, taking on both parental roles when her father had walked out on them and her Uncle Bill had been very supportive, still was to this day. Indeed he had helped her to get this job through his sound and friendly advice. It was almost a month now since her father died. Maggie felt a bit guilty about admitting it to herself but she was happier without him. She shook the bad memories from her mind and took a sip of her Pinot Grigio. Lawrence was finishing off in the kitchen, tidying up after their meal of spaghetti arrabiata and rhubarb crumble. She heard the buzz of a text message coming through, then a second buzz from across the room, indicating that, in all likelihood, they had both received the same text. Maggie picked up her phone and took a look.

We just got engaged!! Just thought you'd like to know. Tania and Sam xx

"Lawrence," Maggie called out in excitement, "there's a text for you here from Tania. She sent it to me too."

"I hope it's about her finding somewhere else to live," he quipped in reply.

"Not quite," Maggie smiled as he joined her on the sofa. "Look!"

Lawrence read his sister's message for himself. "I didn't see that coming," he admitted. "I thought Sam was going to leave her."

"Are you pleased?"

"I think so."

There had been a lot of tension in the family when Tania had discovered that she was pregnant. She was only twenty-four and hadn't been with Sam for more than a few weeks. None of them had even met him. But give the guy his due; he had stood by her and was turning out to be a doting father to wee Stevie. However, Lawrence had sensed that he wasn't happy, that his relationship with Tania was on the rocks. In a drunken stupor one night he had revealed that he was still in love with a girl called Imogen. Lawrence remembered meeting Imogen the day that he and Maggie were celebrating their own engagement. Maggie had come across a journalist she knew in the restaurant, a girl called Jillian, who was enjoying a girls' night out with a couple of friends, both of whom turned out to be amongst Sam's exes. He had only dated Holly for a very short time but Imogen had been the love of his life, or so he had thought at the time. Hopefully that was all in the past.

Maggie keyed in a reply.

Really pleased with your news. Congratulations! Maggie xx

Lawrence followed suit.

Great news, Sis

He never had been one for extended text messages.

The doorbell rang, heralding the arrival of Maggie's mother, Greta. Lawrence led her into the lounge and offered her a drink.

"A glass of wine would be lovely," she said as she gave her daughter a big hug.

Maggie mentioned the text from Tania and Sam and Greta told them to pass on her congratulations. Then they chatted about the week they had all just had at work, especially Maggie since she was the one in a new job. Greta was a bit reserved, appearing to lack interest, as though she had something else on her mind. Maggie tried to be understanding. After all it was only three weeks since the funeral.

"There's something I want to tell you," Greta intimated at last, twiddling nervously with the tassels hanging from her green silk scarf which she cradled comfortingly on her knee.

Lawrence stood up. "I'll give the two of you some privacy," he said thoughtfully.

"You should probably hear this too," Greta countered, but hesitantly.

"Maggie can fill me in later." He gently patted her arm and left the room. Greta breathed a sigh of relief, indicating that she would indeed prefer to talk to her daughter alone in this instance.

"I wasn't ever going to tell you about this," Greta then began somewhat mysteriously, "but it's preying on my mind and I've decided that you do have the right to know about it."

Maggie remained silent, allowing her mother to organise her thoughts, to turn them into words.

"It's about your father."

Maggie sighed. "Is it something Granny told you?"

Greta was not long back from a visit to her mother-in-law in England. The older woman was too frail to have attended the funeral and Greta had made a courtesy call to her home as a mark of respect. They hadn't had that much contact over the years due to the marital split and the physical distance between them.

"No, your granny doesn't know anything about this. It's something your father told me himself."

"I remember you saying that he had opened up to you a bit before he died, that he had told you he never stopped loving us."

"That's right."

"Too little, too late," Maggie retorted, but with a sadness of heart. "I don't really care what he told you, Mum. He had years to put things right between us, opportunity upon opportunity to make a new start and show some interest in my life but he never bothered. He never even tried." She could not have anticipated her mother's next words.

"He killed someone, Maggie."

"What!"

"He killed someone. It was an accident. But he never owned up to it. He felt so guilty."

Maggie felt a cold shiver run through her whole being. She couldn't speak. She just listened as her mother continued.

"It was a man, a young husband and father. And Dennis got it into his head that he didn't deserve to have a happy marriage when he had destroyed someone else's. And he didn't deserve to be a father when he had left a little boy without his. So he distanced himself from us and started to drink and gamble and ..."

Maggie started to cry.

"Well, you know the rest of the story." Greta put an arm round her daughter and allowed her to grieve.

"How do you know he wasn't making this up?" Maggie sniffed after a moment.

"He kept newspaper clippings about it. He showed them to me."

"So you know who this man was, the man he killed?"

"Yes, he was an American citizen. His name was Henning."

"And when did this happen?"

"The newspaper was dated 1990."

Maggie gasped. "I would have been four."

"We were a happy family up until then," Greta reminded her.

"I know. I have some vague memories and I've seen the photos." She remembered showing those photos to her friend, Jillian, just a few weeks ago, when she called to offer her condolences.

"I could never understand why he changed."

"You're taking it all very calmly, Mum," Maggie observed, the tears still rolling down her own cheeks.

"Only because I'm cried out by now. I've shed bucket loads since he confessed to me. It was just a few days before he died and he knew he wasn't going to make it this time. He made me promise to send the evidence to the police so that they could let the Henning family know that he had died."

"And are you going to do that?"

"I already have."

Maggie looked aghast. "So this is going to be all over the papers, the fact that my dad was a murderer!"

"No, I kept his name out of it. I sent it anonymously and posted it in England for extra security. But it might give that poor family some closure."

Greta closed her eyes and took a deep breath. Then she spoke again.

"Don't call him a murderer, Maggie. He did something wrong, something very wrong, but it was an accident. He regretted it every day of his life. I hope I've done the right thing in telling you about it."

"Can I tell Lawrence? We don't have any secrets from one another."

"Of course. But other than that ..."

"I won't say a word."

"Thank you."

"I don't know how I feel about it."

"I know. I felt like that at first too."

"And now?"

"Mixed feelings. But I just thought you should know. I'll go now and let you talk to Lawrence. I'm sorry for spoiling your evening, especially when you had something to celebrate."

Maggie walked her to the door and they embraced on the doorstep.

"Life could have been so different for both of us," Greta mused as she said goodbye.

"Sure we always knew that," Maggie riposted wisely. "Nothing much has changed in reality."

She waved as the car drew away from the house and went back in to talk it over with her fiancé. Another cold shiver ran down her spine. Everything suddenly made sense.

Chapter 5

Imogen Tomlinson and Grant Cartwright had never been happier. They were very much in love and basking in the delight of Imogen's pregnancy which had only just been confirmed. Nobody else knew about it yet. They had first met nearly a year ago, when Imogen had taken a fall whilst shopping in Grant's store and had been brought to his office as a precautionary measure. It had been love at first sight. Although several complications had combined to thwart their relationship in the beginning, it was now stronger than ever and they were planning to marry within the next few weeks. After work on Monday they strolled together through the aisles of their local supermarket, selecting items for their joint trolley.

"I'll just have a look at the books if you don't mind," Imogen said to Grant, passing the trolley to him. "I'll meet you at the fruit and veg."

"OK, anything you want in particular?" he asked.

"Carrots, celery, tomatoes, grapes. Anything else you fancy. I'll only be a few minutes."

Grant headed off down the aisle and turned towards the fruit and vegetables. As he reached out for a pack of bright red cherry tomatoes still on the vine, he spotted a face he recognised. The other man noticed him at the same time.

"It's Grant, isn't it?"

"Sam! Long time, no see."

"Gosh, I can't get over meeting you today of all days. We were just talking about you over the weekend, Jaz and I. We were reminiscing about that millennium party at your grandparents' place. Do you remember my wee sister, Jasmine?"

"Sure I do. She was a few years older than my sister, Rebecca. And yes, I remember that party. We had some fun that night."

"Well how are you Old Chap?" Sam chuckled. "It never fails to amaze me. You don't see someone for years and then your paths cross the very day after you think about them. How is the lovely Zoe? I suppose the two of you are married by now with a couple of kids."

"I'd forgotten that you met Zoe," Grant replied with a lump in his throat.

Sam immediately detected that something was amiss. Maybe they weren't together anymore. "Have I said something out of place?" he enquired.

"Zoe died," Grant told him. "We did get married but it was only for a few months."

Sam wished that the ground would swallow him up. "Gosh, I'm so sorry, Mate. I had no idea."

"It's OK. I've been to hell and back. But you learn to cope. I'm with someone else now. We just got engaged."

"Really? Me too."

"Here she comes now, my fiancée."

Imogen popped the two books she had chosen into the trolley and then looked up to see who Grant was talking to.

"Imogen, Sweetheart," he was saying, "this is an old friend of mine from years ago. We used to keep each other company while our mums were getting together for a chat."

Sam and Imogen were staring at one another, hardly aware of what Grant was saying.

"Imogen?" he breathed.

"Sam?" she echoed.

"Do you two know each other?" Grant asked innocently, not yet having made the connection.

"You never told me Sam was an old friend of yours," Imogen murmured.

"You mean this is *your* Sam?"

Imogen just nodded, looking embarrassed. "He was my Sam at a time," she then conceded.

"Gosh, I never even thought of you," Grant said addressing the other man. "It's not as if it's an unfamiliar name. I know a few people called Sam."

"What a coincidence," Sam uttered, smiling at them both. "It's lovely to see you, Imogen. So you are engaged to Grant. Wow! That's amazing. I just got engaged myself."

"To Tania, I hope."

"Yes, to Tania." He looked surprised that she knew his girlfriend's name. "We have a little boy."

"I know. Holly has kept me informed."

Sam winced. "I didn't treat you or Holly very well," he admitted, looking a bit abashed.

"Never mind, it's history now. Things have worked out for the best for all of us. Tell me about your son."

Sam reached into his pocket for his phone and scrolled down through his photos, selecting a couple of shots to show them.

"He's gorgeous," Imogen trilled, "and Tania looks nice too. I'm glad you're happy."

They smiled at one another, briefly reminiscing over old times and both privately thinking of what could have been. Imogen felt a bit light-headed. After a moment she left the two men chatting as she moved along the aisle picking up other fruits and vegetables at random.

"So I believe you've been in touch with your father," Sam suddenly said to Grant.

Grant threw him a puzzled look. "How on earth do you know about that?" he exclaimed before adding, "Oh yes, of course, it was your mother who helped us find him. I wasn't sure whether she actually knew the whole story."

"No, my mother didn't tell me anything. Sorry, maybe I shouldn't have mentioned it."

"He hasn't been a father to me for twenty-nine years and he's not going to start now," Grant said scathingly. "He's a tosser." Then he scratched his head and looked even more mystified. "But if your mother didn't say anything, how did you know we were in touch?"

"Tania and I were in Scotland for the weekend. We met a guy called Douglas. I can't remember his other name. Mum has known him for years."

"McKendrick."

"Yes, that was it. Douglas Mc Kendrick."

"Imogen and I have met him too. We liked him."

Sam had a vision of his mother kissing the man at the airport, his arms all over her. "We weren't so keen," he snarled.

"But you talked about *me*?"

"Not directly. I just heard him say that your father had sent you a letter and was surprised that he hasn't had a reply yet. He was talking to my mum, who had apparently delivered the letter to your mum because he didn't have your address."

"Yes, I got it. He won't be getting a reply."

"None of my business, Mate," Sam conceded hurriedly. "I'm sorry if I've offended you by bringing it up. I just got the impression that there was something urgent about it because it was also mentioned in a phone call that Jaz overheard last weekend."

"Urgent?" Grant drawled bitterly. "Well, if he wants a kidney or something he can go and jump."

They all moved out of the way to let other customers reach the tomatoes and Sam was glad of the distraction. Imogen put the items she had chosen into the trolley and, picking up the general drift of the conversation, she spoke softly to Sam. "Grant's father wasn't very welcoming when we met him. He doesn't want anything more to do with him. He didn't read that letter. He burnt it."

Sam nodded. Time to change the subject. "I'm looking for somewhere to live," he told them, "so if you hear of any nice flats going on the market ..."

"Seriously?" Imogen grinned. "I've just vacated one but I haven't given it up officially yet. I thought my brother was going to take it on but apparently he's found somewhere else."

Sam looked confused. "You don't have a brother," he intoned.

"Long story," Imogen chuckled, "but I do, actually. Would you like to see the flat?"

"I don't think so", Sam responded bluntly. "Tania might not like the association with you."

"Sensible decision," Grant advised. He wouldn't like it any more than Tania. After all, Imogen would still be spending lots of time over there. Her best friend was still living upstairs.

"But Jaz is also looking for a place of her own." Sam was now thinking aloud. "She might be interested."

Imogen gave him the details just in case.

"So how come you suddenly have a brother?"

Grant was beginning to feel irritated. This man used to sleep with his fiancée. He didn't really want them spending any more time together or sharing family secrets. "Like Imogen said, it's a long story. Some other time," he enjoined.

Sam took the hint and they chatted more casually for a few more minutes before going their separate ways. As they headed towards the bakery section Imogen couldn't help turning round for another glimpse of her former boyfriend and found him doing the very same thing. They smiled at one another somewhat wistfully.

Chapter 6

The week passed with very little being said in the Campbell household about Patricia's exhibition in Scotland. She had blithely reported that it had been a roaring success and that her boss had been very pleased. Luckily for her there were lots of other topics of discussion that took precedence over work issues. Sam and Tania had got engaged. Jasmine had found a flat that she liked and could just about afford. Molly was continuing to enjoy her travels; she had just posted a series of pictures from the Great Barrier Reef so that all her Facebook friends could ogle them with envy.

Sam had kept Jasmine fully informed about the situation regarding their mother and the threat he had made. True to his word, he had not brought Stevie with him when he and Tania had arrived to announce their good news. Patricia had been forced to feign delighted surprise because Kenneth was hearing it for the first time with no inkling that the pair had met up with her on their mini-break. Sam had visited again, with Stevie, at a time when he knew that his father would be in the house on his own and had deliberately left some evidence of their presence in the form of a soft toy and a rattle as a pointer to Patricia. She had been devastated to think that he really had denied her access to the baby. They hadn't spoken about the matter since the showdown in Scotland.

Now it was Saturday morning and Jasmine was moving into her new flat, recently vacated by Imogen Tomlinson. She had met Imogen a couple of times when she was dating her brother, Sam, but had never really got to know her very well. By a strange coincidence she had also known Imogen's fiancé in the past because he was none other than the same Grant Cartwright, in whose garden she had played while her mum and Auntie Cathy were having their tea parties. How strange that his name should crop up again so soon after hearing it mentioned in that phone call a week ago. She had found the flat through Sam, who had come across Grant and Imogen in the supermarket, and it was exactly what she required. It was modern and clean and came already furnished with the main necessities because she had met with Imogen during the week to discuss what she should leave behind. Imogen was now living with Grant.

Jasmine stood in her new living room and took a deep breath. This was paradise. If it wasn't for the worry over her parents' situation, life would be pretty perfect. She went back outside to bring in another couple of bags from the boot of her car.

"You moving in downstairs?" enquired a friendly voice. A girl with lovely reddish-brown hair was just getting out of her blue Yaris, parked beside her own car. "I'm Jillian. I live in the apartment above you."

"Hi Jillian. Yes, I've a few more runs to make but I should be in by tonight. I'm Jasmine by the way. It's nice to meet you."

"I feel as if I should already know you from somewhere," Jillian replied with a puzzled expression.

"I was just thinking the same thing," replied the new tenant. "You do look familiar."

"So, is it just you moving in on your own?"

"It is indeed. My own space at last. What about you? Do you share with someone?"

"Yes, my fiancé, Bradley. I used to live in your flat actually until I moved upstairs with him."

"Oh, you would know Imogen, then."

"Yes, she's my best friend, has been for years."

"That's where I've seen you before, then. Imogen used to go out with my brother."

"Oh, you're that Jasmine!" Jillian exclaimed. "Of course, I remember now, you're Sam's sister. Does Imogen know that it's you who's moving in?"

"Yes, she organised it for me."

"Really? Wow! She never said anything to me."

"Probably just didn't have time. It's been very quick. Sam only met the two of them on Monday and it's been all go since then."

"So Sam has met Grant?"

"He sure has. Turns out they were buddies years ago."

"No!"

"It's true. Look, I'd better get this stuff inside before it rains. But it was lovely chatting to you. I look forward to us being neighbours."

"Me too. Come up for a coffee if you feel like a break."

"Thanks, I will. Give me half an hour."

Jasmine took the bags inside and smiled to herself. She was going to enjoy living here. The flat was perfect. It didn't even need painted. She sat down on the burgundy-coloured sofa, which she had bought from Imogen, and took out her phone, in two minds as whether she should interfere or not. Something had been on her mind all morning. Last night, while Patricia had been in the bath and Kenneth had been engrossed in a film on TV, Jasmine had come across her mother's phone, once again plugged into the socket in the kitchen. She had felt guilty doing it, but she had picked it up and had scrolled through the list of contacts. Family names were there of course and she recognised known friends like Cathy, along with work colleagues she had heard of but, not surprisingly, there were several other names which meant nothing to Jasmine. Who was Mia for example? Probably someone new at work. But in amongst all the names there were a few abbreviations. And one of them was DM. She had taken a note of that number.

During the week Tania had talked to Jasmine about the confrontation with her mother in Scotland, including the threat Sam had made about not letting Patricia see her grandson. Tania felt uncomfortable with the whole situation; it was not the best way to forge a good relationship with her future mother-in-law. But she wanted to support Sam in any way she could. She appreciated the fact that he had been open and honest with her about bumping into Imogen in the supermarket and had given her a full account of their conversation. Tania had subsequently told Jasmine about Grant Cartwright destroying the letter he had received from his father, unread.

Jasmine looked now at the piece of paper where she had scribbled that number. DM. It had to be him. But just to make sure, she entered the digits into her phone and selected the call function. A phone began to ring. Then a voice spoke to her.

"Hello? Douglas McKendrick here."

Jasmine ended the call. It was him all right.

She sent him a text message.

Please leave my mother alone. We are a happy family. Jasmine Campbell

Then she keyed in another message.

Can you please tell your friend that Grant Cartwright has not read his letter. He burnt it unopened. JC

A few moments passed and then Jasmine received a reply. He made no reference to her first text but thanked her for the second one and asked whether she could supply him with a phone number for Grant. Jasmine was uneasy. Why had she started this? She just had a feeling that Grant might regret what he had done. There seemed to be something important about that letter. She did have Grant's number. Both he and Imogen had liaised with her over the exchange of the apartment and she had added the two of them to her contacts. She hesitated for a moment and then, what the hell, forwarded the number to Mr McKendrick. He sent a brief text to thank her. Jasmine was on edge. She didn't know whether she had done the right thing or not but she justified her action by telling herself that nothing is really private nowadays. If the man was determined to get in touch with his son, he could probably do so quite easily through social media sites or Google. She would put it from her mind and go upstairs for that cup of coffee.

★★★

Grant heard the message coming through whilst he was driving to the golf course. Having rekindled his friendship with Sam this week, he had agreed to play a round with him and was really looking forward to it. On arrival he parked his car behind the clubhouse and took his clubs from the boot, totally forgetting that he had received a text. The weather was ideal for golf, bright, sunny and dry and both men enjoyed the game and the companionship. It was only as he was getting back into the car, almost three hours later, that Grant remembered to check his phone. He got a bit of a shock.

Hello Grant. I am aware that you destroyed a letter sent to you recently by your father. I don't know what was in it but I do know that he is very anxious for you to get in touch as a matter of some urgency. Please confirm that you will do so. If I don't hear from you within the next two hours I will go ahead and pass your number on to Cameron myself. Douglas McKendrick

Grant looked at his watch. 4.15. He looked at the time against the message on his phone. 12.48. And he yelled at Sam across the car park. "Did you give that man my phone number?"

Several people glanced disapprovingly in his direction. Raucous behaviour in the carpark was not what they were accustomed to. Sam hurried over. "What man?" he asked.

"McKendrick." He was still shouting.

"Of course not," cried Sam emphatically. "I wouldn't give that bastard the time of day!" The two men had chatted a lot during the game. The course had been busy so they had been obliged to wait for quite a few minutes before playing each new hole. Sam had ended up telling Grant about his reason for the weekend away.

Grant apologised. "Sorry, it must have been Mum. She's given it to your mum. That's how I found him in the first place."

"What does he want?"

Grant showed him the text. "I've missed his deadline by a long chalk."

"Would it really be so bad to speak to him, your father I mean?"

Grant gave him a withering look but admitted, "Looks like I might have to."

"He mightn't have done it yet. Give McKendrick a ring. But let me get well out of his hearing first." Sam went back to his own car and drove away. He just wished that Douglas McKendrick would disappear off the face of the earth.

Grant sat in his car and activated the call function. Douglas answered almost immediately. "Am I too late?"

Grant asked him. "I've only just got your message. I was playing golf."

"Give your dad a ring, Son. He's desperate to hear from you."

"Why?"

"I don't know."

"You didn't do it yet, give him *my* number?"

"No, I figured you'd call me sooner or later. I'm not trying to cause trouble, Grant. I liked you and young Imogen. But Cam is my friend too."

"I have nothing more to say to the man. I don't need him in my life. Did he tell you what happened that second night after you had introduced us?"

"Not really. Just that the two of you hadn't hit it off. But he wrote you something in a letter and he's desperate for a reply before this weekend."

"This weekend?"

"Give him a ring, Son. I'll send you his number."

"Instead of sending him mine?"

"That's right. Ball's in your court."

"Thank you." It was on the edge of his tongue to add *but stop fucking my friend's mother* but he managed to contain himself. It wasn't really any of his business.

A text message came through straight away so his biological father was now just a number away. But would he call? He'd go home and talk to Imogen first. What on earth had his mother been playing at anyway, passing on his phone number to that man? But he didn't want a row. He would just let it go.

★★★

Sam was still living with Tania's parents. He had to get out soon. Grant had offered him an escape route by suggesting Imogen's apartment but he couldn't expect Tania to accept that. The two of them sleeping in the same bed that Imogen had just vacated! No, that just wasn't appropriate. But it was good to have Grant back in his life. He had really enjoyed his round of golf with him today. And it was the perfect solution for Jasmine. She had wanted her own space for some time now. Sam worried about Jasmine. Molly seemed to have more get up and go than Jasmine who was two years older. Molly was out there, seeing the world, meeting people, broadening her horizons. Had Jasmine ever even had a proper boyfriend? He didn't think so. She was probably still a virgin.

Judy and Edward had suddenly announced that they were taking a week's holiday. Would that be a problem? Would they be able to manage without them? Sam had been ecstatic. "No problem at all, of course not," he had said, assuring them that they would manage. And now they were finding that it wasn't easy. But it was good. The only downside was that they had no fall back, no-one else to rely on for support since they had alienated themselves from Patricia. But they had the whole house to themselves. All they had to do now was find their own accommodation where they could continue to be independent.

Lawrence and Maggie called round on Saturday evening. Maggie had spent the week trying to come to terms with the news Greta had given her concerning her dad's state of mind in his dying days. She was glad of the distraction caused by little Stevie and enjoyed bouncing him on her knee and making him giggle whilst Sam chatted to Lawrence about his afternoon on the golf course, suggesting that he might like to join them next time. They all heard Tania answer her phone in the kitchen and speak to someone in an excited voice.

"That was Hugo, one of my colleagues from work," Tania announced as she breezed into the room, still clutching her phone. "One of his friends has a flat to rent just round the corner from the salon. He says we could view it now if we're free." Tania worked with five other stylists in a modern hairdressing salon not far away. She looked at Sam for approval.

"Any chance you two would look after Stevie till we get back?" Sam asked.

"Please," added Tania, addressing her brother with a pleading grin.

"He'll be asleep in no time," Sam assured a horrified looking Maggie. "You won't have to do a thing. Just keep an eye on him."

Maggie laughed, realising that her expression had given her away. "Go ahead then. It's just that I'm not used to babies."

"Neither was I until I had one," quipped Tania. "You soon pick it up."

"Thanks," chorused Tania and Sam.

Tania returned Hugo's call. "We're on our way," she told him cheerfully. "Meet you at the salon."

Two hours later they had signed the lease.

Chapter 7

Imogen and Grant had been living together in their own little love nest sharing the intimate secret of her pregnancy for two weeks now. She hadn't suffered any sickness that might have given it away to others, just an excessive tiredness which could easily be explained away as a result of moving house. She was so glad she had moved in with Grant. They had put it off for too long. Imogen knew that Grant had been afraid of her feeling uncomfortable around things that had been Zoe's but she didn't, not in the least. And there wasn't much anyway; their short marriage had ended so tragically before there had been time to gather up very many possessions.

What a year it had been. Imogen sat in her small but homely kitchen with a cup of coffee and a ginger biscuit and she began to reminisce. It was a ginger biscuit that he had offered her the very first time they met, the time she took a fall in his store. The spicy flavour was conjuring up an image of the two of them sitting in his office that day and she remembered being mesmerised by him right from that first moment. Such a lot had happened since then. There had been misunderstandings and secret fears which had conspired to tear them apart but they had survived the heartache and the trauma and had come through unscathed in the end. She had discovered a brother she never knew she had. Grant had discovered a father.

Imogen now recalled the gathering at Grant's grandmother's house just two weeks ago. Gertrude had called them all together to read them a letter that she had received anonymously, via the police. Well, it was Gertrude who had read the letter to them but it was actually addressed to her daughter, Grant's Aunt Thomasina, whose husband had been killed in a hit and run accident years ago. The letter purported to have come from someone called Marguerite who claimed to be the wife of the driver in that incident. She said she had known nothing about it until very recently and that the man was now dead. It had been a very emotional occasion and both Gertrude and Thomasina had been very forgiving. Imogen shivered involuntarily. For quite a few months she had been plagued by the erroneous belief that her own parents had been involved in that incident. Even now she was extremely embarrassed to think about it. She quickly brushed that thought from her mind. But another thought refused to go away, something else that had happened that same day at Gertrude's house. Grant's mother, Catherine, had handed him a letter from his father in Scotland and he had immediately set fire to it, insisting that he wanted nothing to do with the man.

What if it had been something important? Imogen hadn't dared voice her concern to Grant because she knew his strength of feeling on the matter but Catherine had only told him how to find his father because she believed that Imogen was worried about potential genetic factors. This had been due to a complete misunderstanding but now that Imogen was pregnant, it was beginning to take on a new significance. She couldn't help wondering what had been in that letter.

She was aroused from her reverie by the sound of Grant parking the car outside and coming round the back with his clubs. How wonderful that he had struck up a friendship with Sam. And what a coincidence that they had known each other as children and even into their teens. Imogen would always have a soft spot for Sam. After all he had been the first man she had loved. It was sort of comforting to know that it was his sister who had taken over the flat, who would be sitting on her sofa and sleeping in her bed. So much better than some stranger she had never heard of.

"Hi, I've missed you," she cried, flinging her arms around Grant as he came through the back door and expecting a spontaneous kiss. "How was the golf?"

"Good," he replied but with a somewhat distracted air and no sign of that kiss.

"What's up?" Imogen knew him like the back of her hand. She could tell that something had upset him.

"We should never have gone over to Edinburgh that time," he now blurted out. "I have coped perfectly well all my life without that man. I didn't even know he existed."

"What's happened?" Imogen asked, somewhat alarmed. "You always knew you had a father out there somewhere. You couldn't have been born without one."

"You know what I mean," he chided. "My mum has always insisted that she didn't know who he was. I had accepted that. I didn't expect to ever meet him."

"I'm sorry," Imogen mouthed. "That was my fault. But has something happened? Has he been in touch again?"

Grant took out his phone and showed her the text message from Douglas McKendrick and Imogen burst into tears. Grant was at once baffled and worried.

"I'm sorry," she sniffed, "but I've been worrying about that letter. What if he was warning you about some illness in the family, something that might be passed on to our baby?"

"Don't be daft," Grant told her, "sure I'm perfectly healthy."

"But there are diseases that skip a generation or two."

"Like what?"

"I don't know! But there are things that can happen. I've read about genetic defects that are inherited. It could be anything."

"Imogen, calm down," Grant said firmly. "It's probably nothing of the sort."

"So what then? Why did he write you that letter? Why is he so worried that you haven't replied?"

"I've no idea. But I suppose I had better find out if it will give you peace of mind."

"So you'll ring him? Have you got his number?"

"Yes, Douglas sent it to me. I'll do it tonight. Let's have our dinner first. Better still, let's go out for dinner. I promise you I'll phone him as soon as we get back."

Four hours later Grant and Imogen arrived home after a lovely meal in one of their favourite haunts in 'ballysnackamore'. There were so many super restaurants in that area these days that they were always sure of getting in somewhere, even when they hadn't booked. Imogen had assured Grant that she was perfectly happy and that the issue of his father's letter was the one blip on the horizon. She had just panicked because it had been on her own mind today before he had arrived home and shown her the text. She had blamed it on her hormones. Grant had kissed her and promised that he would make the call. What harm could it do? And now he was ready to do it. He selected the number and nervously activated the call function. He heard a phone ringing.

"Hello? You're through to Cameron Ferguson."

He took a deep breath. "Hi."

"Who's calling please?"

"It's Grant."

"Grant! Oh, at last. I'm so glad to hear from you. Thank you so much for calling. Can you come on Saturday, you and Imogen?"

"Saturday?"

"Yes, the party. It's this Saturday."

"Look, I'm sorry, I don't know about any party. I'm only phoning you because I had a message from your friend, Douglas. He said you were anxious about something. He asked me to ring you."

"But you got my letter? It's all in the letter."

"I'm sorry, I didn't read your letter. I burnt it."

There was silence from the other end of the phone. And then eventually,

"I've been waiting for your reply for over two weeks but you haven't even read it?"

"No."

"I suppose I deserve that. I'm sorry for the way I treated you when you searched me out. It was unforgivable. I realise that."

"Is that what you said in the letter?"

"Yes, but there was more, much more."

"Tell me now then."

"I can't. I can't say it over the phone. I took so long to put that letter together, to organise what I wanted to say to you."

Grant began to feel a bit guilty. The man did sound apologetic and even despondent. "Was it handwritten?" he asked, "or would you have saved a copy?"

This brought about a more animated response. "I saved it, yes."

"Email me a copy then. I'm sorry for destroying it."

Grant proceeded to give him his email address and Cameron thanked him and wrote it down.

"I'll do that right away," he said. "I'm so glad you got in touch. Thank you."

Grant disconnected the call and turned on his computer. In less than five minutes a buzz alerted him to an email coming through. He opened it, clicked on the attachment and selected the print option. And the letter he should have read two weeks ago began to materialise in front of his eyes. He took it from the machine and sat down on the sofa with Imogen beside him. "Right, here goes," he grimaced. "Let's see what was so important about this."

***

Jasmine had made three more runs from her family home to her new apartment transporting her clothes, her books, her painting equipment and all sorts of toiletries and household goods. She couldn't wait to spend her first night under her very own roof. Kenneth and Patricia had called to view the accommodation and had given it the thumbs up. They appreciated her desire to have her own place but commented that the house was going to feel very empty now with just the two of them rambling around what had once been the home of three lively, young children.

"You two can have a second honeymoon now," joked Jasmine, "at least until Molly gets back."

"She won't be staying for long either," Kenneth reminded her. "She'll be off to university across the water."

Jasmine was glad to see her dad smiling. "So where have you decided to go for your birthday weekend?" she asked.

"Spain. Your mum is taking me to Barcelona."

"Wow! Lucky you! Make sure you take plenty of photos."

Nobody mentioned last weekend in Scotland and Jasmine had no idea whether her dad suspected anything. With both Sam and herself warning him off, she really hoped that Douglas McKendrick would get the message and steer well clear of their family.

Kenneth and Patricia were just leaving when two young men got out of a silver BMW and headed towards the building.

"You must be Jasmine," one of them said to her, extending his right hand in a friendly greeting. "Jillian told me about you moving in."

Patricia did a double take. "I know you," she said hesitantly, addressing the other man. "Aren't you Cathy's nephew? Alastair?"

"Aunty Patty!" Alastair exclaimed in surprise.

"I'm Bradley," the first man now put in, also recognising Patricia. "I remember you too. We used to know your son, Sam."

"That's my brother!" Jasmine cried and then she too did a double take. "You're Bradley!" Jillian had said her fiancé was called Bradley. The heart-throb she had worshipped as a child was living upstairs! She stared at him. Yes, that was him all right. Older and just as handsome, even more handsome.

"We were just leaving," Patricia said after reminding her husband how she knew the two young men. "Give my regards to your mother and your grandmother, Alastair."

"Small world," muttered Jasmine, shaking her head in disbelief.

The older couple drove off and Bradley invited Jasmine to come up for a chat.

"Jillian will be sick of the sight of me," Jasmine replied. "I was already up for a coffee earlier."

"Don't be daft," he insisted. "We can talk about old times. Come on, it'll be fun." Jasmine didn't need any further persuasion. *Wait till Molly hears about this,* she thought to herself, wondering at the same time what Rebecca was up to these days. Well, she would soon find out. What a day it had been. Little did she realise then that this was indeed one of those life-changing days that would stay in her memory for ever.

Chapter 8

Grant was speechless. He handed the letter to Imogen and sat back against the cushion with a huge sigh. Imogen started to read.

Dear Grant,

Let me first apologise to you and your lovely girlfriend for the unfriendly reception you received from me in July. I can only excuse myself on the grounds that I was taken completely off guard and did not have sufficient time to think rationally about the situation. It has probably come as an even bigger shock to me than it did to you because you would obviously have known that you had a father out there somewhere whereas I had no inkling that I was missing a son. But it is no excuse in reality. My behaviour was abominable and I am very ashamed.

It's hard for me to put this into words. There is something I have never spoken about except with Lauren but we have decided that, in the circumstances, you have a right to know. Before Lauren and I got married fifteen years ago, she was in a brief relationship with my brother, Scott. He didn't know that she was pregnant with his child when he emigrated to Canada and by the time James was born Lauren was with me. We just passed James off as our own. He even looks like me which isn't surprising since Scott and I are twins. If Scott ever suspected anything he didn't say. He wasn't interested in having a family.

In May 2003 Scott came home for a holiday and played a cruel joke on us. On his last night we both had too much to drink and I fell asleep on the sofa. Scott crept up to the bedroom and pretended to be me. Lauren was initially taken in and you can guess what happened. He swore afterwards that he wouldn't have let things get out of hand but that she had taken the lead and had seduced him. Lauren herself admitted that it had been wholly consensual. When Henry was subsequently born in February we had to accept that he too was Scott's son. Lauren certainly hadn't been pregnant prior to that night and we didn't have relations for at least a month or two after it.

Not long after Henry's birth Lauren suffered a serious illness which resulted in her having to undergo a hysterectomy. Thankfully she fully recovered in every other way and is in good health now but obviously it meant that she couldn't have any more children.

I love James and Henry as my own and we are a happy family. But can you even begin to imagine how I feel, knowing that you are out there but estranged from me? You are my very own flesh and blood, my one and only biological son. I was so confused when I met you and Lauren felt extremely threatened but we have talked and *we have let it sink in and I know one thing for sure – I want you in my life, Grant.*

I know that your life is with your mother over there in Ireland and that you probably have brothers and sisters, aunts and uncles, cousins of your own. My friend, Dougie, was able to tell me that your mother recently got married so you even have a 'father'. But you came searching for me and that gives me hope. Please give me another chance.

My father (your grandfather) will be eighty years old on 30th September. We are having a party for him on the Saturday, that's the following day, 1st October. I would be thrilled if you and Imogen could come and meet everyone. I have enclosed a card with my contact details and address. Please let me know one way or the other. I await your reply with hopeful anticipation.

Once again I apologise for the poor welcome I gave you before. I hope you will give me the opportunity to make it up to you.

With love

Cameron Ferguson

Ps I hope you will accept the enclosed cheque to cover your expenses if you do decide to come.

Imogen finished reading and handed the letter back to her fiancé. "Wow!" she said.

"I have a grandfather," murmured Grant.

Imogen knew that Grant had been very close to his maternal grandfather, who had died from a sudden heart attack about seven years ago. He had spoken about him often.

"I still have a grandfather," he repeated now. "I never even thought about that. It was just the guy, Cameron, with his wife and kids. I never pictured a whole family in the background."

"It's a pretty sincere apology," Imogen ventured timorously, not wanting to influence him.

"It is," Grant agreed.

"He's been very honest. He didn't need to tell you those things."

"I'd like to go. To the party. Will you come with me?"

"Of course I'll come with you. I'll support you whatever you decide to do."

Grant looked again at the sheet of paper in his hand. "Gosh," he exclaimed, "it's just a few days away. To think that I should have had this two weeks ago but just tossed it in the fire!"

"You've burnt the cheque," Imogen added with a chuckle. "I wonder how much it was for."

"And the card he mentioned with his address and so on."

Grant took a few moments to quietly reflect on the revelations he had so carelessly cast aside. And he pictured the man waiting anxiously, day after day, for some kind of acknowledgement that his apology had been accepted. He felt a bit of a heel.

"The friend that he mentions, Dougie," he suddenly blurted out. "Do you remember we met him?"

"Yes, of course. We went to his house and he arranged the meeting in the pub. I liked him."

"He's having an affair with Sam's mother. Sam told me today during the game."

"Patricia?"

"Dougie knows her as Patty, the very person who led us to him in the first place."

"So your mum's friend, Patty and Sam's mother, Patricia are one and the same person!"

"Yep."

"And she's sleeping with Douglas McKendrick?"

"Apparently so."

"Well, I suppose it's none of our business," Imogen mused, bringing Grant back to their own dilemma. "Are you going to contact Cameron?"

"I don't know what to say to him."

"Just tell him we'll come to the party and get the address."

"Should I talk to Mum and Mark first?"

"I don't think you should spread what was in that letter, not yet anyway. I think it's probably private."

"I promised them I'd have nothing more to do with Cameron Ferguson."

"Just tell them you've changed your mind. The man *is* your father. It won't change anything between you and your mum. Mark will understand."

Catherine had married Mark, the father of her younger daughter, Robyn, just three months ago.

In the end Grant sent an email. He did want to become acquainted with his father now, and meet his grandfather, but he wasn't quite ready to put his thoughts into coherent words. He simply thanked Cameron for the letter and the invitation and asked for the address, adding that he and Imogen would be pleased to attend.

★★★

Jasmine had the most wonderful feeling of contentment as she lay in her new bed listening to the unfamiliar sounds around her and staring into the darkness which enveloped her at a touch of the lamp on the little chest of drawers by her elbow. So many mixed emotions vied for pride of place in her mind. She had warned off that Scottish man. Surely he would see sense and leave her mother alone. Sam had also warned him off and had made it clear to their mum that he expected her to end the affair forthwith. Sam himself had just phoned to say that he and Tania had found a flat and would be moving in before the end of the week. And Molly was having a ball. So, harmony in the family all round. But most of all Jasmine was revelling in a sensation she had never before experienced in her twenty-four years. Her heart was fluttering, her whole body tingling with excitement. It had been so sudden, so unexpected. But she had just spent a couple of hours in the company of someone very special. She wanted him with every bone in her body, she wanted to feel his kiss on her lips, his hand in hers, his body wrapped around her own. She longed to give herself to him with wild and reckless abandon. Never mind that a major stumbling block lay ahead if she were to pursue this goal; she would just have to overcome it. Where there's a will, there's a way and after tonight she was determined to have him, no matter who thought otherwise or tried to advise against it. Jasmine had fallen in love.

Chapter 9

Both Grant and Imogen managed to clear their weekend schedules so that they could travel to Scotland on Friday night, attend the party on Saturday and return home on Sunday afternoon. Although he hadn't admitted it, even to himself, Grant had in truth been gutted by his father's rejection when he searched him out two months ago. He was very excited about subsequent developments. Catherine and Mark had been shocked at first but had assured him in the end that they would not be offended and that he had every right to get to know his father if that was what he wanted. He had their blessing. So Friday evening found them both at the airport, boarding a flight for Edinburgh.

★★★

Back in Belfast Sam and Tania were having an engagement-cum-housewarming celebration with Sam's sister, Jasmine, and Tania's brother, Lawrence, and his fiancée, Maggie. Judy and Edward, just home from their holiday in Lanzarote, had willingly agreed to keep Stevie overnight so that the young people would be free to have a few drinks and enjoy themselves. Whilst Tania was in the kitchen preparing some snacks and the two men were chatting about what was happening in the world of sport, Jasmine and Maggie were getting to know one another and finding that they had a lot in common.

"I love painting too," Maggie enthused when Jasmine told her she was using her spare bedroom as a studio. "I mainly do landscapes and seascapes."

"Portraits and still-life are more my type of thing," Jasmine answered, "but I have done a few landscapes."

"Do you sell your pictures?"

"Hopefully some day," Jasmine laughed. "What a super way to make a living, but no, not at the moment. I just do them for family and friends. I work as a receptionist in a dental practice. What about you?"

"I've sold a couple but same as you, really. It's just a hobby. I'm a teacher for my real job."

"What age-group?"

"Year 6. Nine and ten year olds."

"I don't think I'd have the patience for that," Jasmine admitted. "Children are all right one at a time."

Maggie talked a bit more about her teaching and mentioned the fact that she had only just secured a full-time post. Up until now she had done temporary work, subbing for absent teachers, and had also taken some adult evening classes in aspects of literacy. Her friend, Jillian, had actually written an article about her classes for a magazine she produces and Maggie was convinced it had helped her get to the top of the queue.

"I just moved into a new flat last weekend," Jasmine revealed quizzically, "and my neighbour upstairs is called Jillian. *She's* the editor of a magazine."

"Could be the same girl. Jillian's best friend lived in the downstairs apartment. Her name was Imogen."

"Yes, that's her. I'm in that apartment now. Imogen has moved in with her boyfriend."

Maggie nodded her head and smiled.

"Small world," they both said in unison.

For a few moments Jasmine's mind remained on Jillian's flat and the wonderful evening she had spent there the very day she moved in, the overwhelming sensation of lasciviousness and desire that had filled her dreams ever since. Then she shook herself back to the present.

"Well then, you know where I live," she said to Maggie. "Pop in anytime."

"I will," Maggie replied. "I can't wait to see your studio. I'm so jealous."

Tania appeared at that point and beckoned them all towards the kitchen where she had set out various hot and cold tapas dishes. "Help yourselves," she instructed, handing out plates. The food looked delicious and smelt amazing. They all tucked in hungrily.

★★★

Meanwhile, in Edinburgh, Grant and Imogen were checking in to their hotel.

"I can scarcely believe this is happening," Grant proclaimed.

"I'm really happy for you," Imogen smiled as they trundled their bags along the green and black tartan carpeted floor towards the lift and up to the second storey. "I know it hurt you more than you were letting on when we came over here the last time."

"I still find it hard to fathom. I mean, he said he had never told anyone else those secrets about the two boys. He didn't make it clear whether they themselves know about Scott being their father or whether Scott is aware of the truth or not."

"Or whether Scott is travelling home for the party," Imogen added. "It is *his* father's eightieth too."

"Canada's a long way off."

"Not really. Not in this day and age. Not for a special occasion."

Grant unlocked the door to their room and they both gasped. It was enormous and kitted out with every luxury imaginable. Their eyes were drawn to a bottle of Champagne sitting in an ice-bucket on a central table along with two flutes and a welcome card. Imogen picked up the card and opened it.

Welcome to Scotland, Grant and Imogen.
Since my original letter got destroyed, I am assuming that the cheque I sent you to cover expenses also went up in smoke. I hope, therefore, that you will accept this room upgrade and dinner tonight in the restaurant as a gift from me. Everything has been paid for in advance.

I can't wait to see you both tomorrow.
Thank you for coming.
Cameron

"How did he even know where we were staying?" Imogen mused as she handed the card to Grant.

"Well," her fiancé reasoned, "he knew that we stayed here the last time so he probably just assumed we'd come back to the same place and then checked at reception."

"And made sure we didn't lose out on the missing cheque."

"Yes, we've been double checked."

"Ha ha, that's double chequed," grinned Imogen, spelling it out. "It's a very kind gesture."

"It is," Grant agreed appreciatively. "Let's freshen up and go down for that free dinner. We'll have the Champagne afterwards."

"Or a glass now and another one afterwards?"

"Why not? Good idea."

Grant popped the cork and poured the cool, bubbly liquid into the two flutes. Imogen stopped him when hers was only a quarter full. "A few sips won't do me any harm," she reminded him, "or the baby. But certainly not a full glass."

Amidst all the excitement and anticipation of meeting his father and grandfather the next day, Grant realised that he had momentarily forgotten that he was on the brink of fatherhood himself. "Of course, sorry," he answered, shamefacedly but then redeemed himself by adding, "It's just that you look so healthy and so beautiful. And it is early days. There's nothing showing yet."

Imogen laughed. "Don't worry, I'm not offended," she assured him. "This weekend is all about you and your dad and that's the way it should be. I'll stay in the background. No-one needs to know about this yet." She patted her tummy as she spoke.

"Our secret," he agreed, "just like our plans for next weekend."

She just smiled and nodded.

"You haven't changed your mind? It's not too late if you want to do it the traditional way like Jillian and Bradley."

"Absolutely not," Imogen reaffirmed. "We'll just go away on Thursday and come back married on Monday. I don't want any fuss."

They shared a passionate kiss. It was the way they both wanted to do it.

"Let's have dinner now," Grant said happily as the kiss ended and they continued to smile into one another's eyes, their expressions full of love. "I'm starving."

Imogen insisted on taking a few minutes to freshen up and get changed and then they headed down to the restaurant where they were treated like celebrities. It was becoming clear to them that Cameron Ferguson had left nothing to chance in ensuring that they would have a night to remember. And that's exactly what they had. It was perfect.

Chapter 10

Kenneth and Patricia should have been on their way to Barcelona. The flights were booked. A five star hotel awaited them. Their cases were packed. Kenneth would be fifty-five on Monday and they would celebrate his birthday in style. Until he dropped the bombshell. "We're not going. I just cancelled the taxi."

Patricia stared at him dumbfounded. And then she noticed that he had her phone in his hand. She bit her lip and started to tremble.

"I called in at your office today," Kenneth divulged, struggling to keep his voice from shaking. "I congratulated your colleagues on the success of the Edinburgh exhibition. They didn't know what I was talking about."

Patricia felt the blood rush to her head. She knew that her face must be bright pink. She had to think quickly. "It's not what you think, Casey," she blundered.

"No? Well then, maybe you could explain why you have been lying to me."

"It's Cathy," she bluffed. "Cathy asked me to deliver a letter for her, to a friend in Scotland."

"Don't be ridiculous," Kenneth thundered. "Is that really the best you can come up with?"

"It's true. It has something to do with her son, Grant. His father lives in Scotland but it's very hush hush. That's why I didn't say anything about it to you."

"You've used Cathy as an alibi once too often, Patricia."

"What do you mean by that?"

Kenneth just held out the phone. "This started to ring while you were upstairs. Who is Mia?"

"Mia?"

"Yes, Mia. You're just stalling for time but there's no point. I already know who she is."

"Well of course you do. You met her when she was a little girl. She's Lucinda's daughter. You surely remember my friend, Lucinda, who died."

"And why would Lucinda's daughter be ringing you now, years later?"

"Why not? We've kept in touch. She's a grown woman now and we've become friends. We talk about old times."

"Are you going to ring her back then?"

"Yes, of course, but I'll do it later. There's no rush."

"I think there is, actually."

Now Patricia was becoming even more nervous. He wasn't buying this even though it was partly true. And she couldn't think why Mia would have been ringing her anyway. But obviously her name had come up in the caller display so there was no point in denying it.

"Casey, you're making a mountain out of a molehill," she protested. "I'm sorry for telling a few white lies but Cathy just didn't want anyone to know about her private family business and I promised her that I'd keep it to myself. I happened to bump into Mia while I was over there. She did say she would give me a ring. End of story. I don't know why you're making such a fuss."

"She sent you a voice message when you didn't answer."

Alarm bells were really ringing at this revelation, loud and clear. Patricia could tell by the look on Kenneth's face that he had already listened to the message. Surely the girl would have had the sense not to say anything incriminating.

"I wouldn't normally listen to your messages but I think that, given the shock and embarrassment that I felt in your office this afternoon, I had the right to do so on this occasion."

Patricia couldn't very well contradict his point of view, in the circumstances. But she was still livid. And scared.

"Let's listen to it again, together. I'll turn on the speaker phone."

Kenneth activated the 'hear again' function and Patricia crossed her fingers in the hope that Mia would have been diplomatic. She almost collapsed onto the sofa with tears in her eyes as the unexpected voice spoke into the silence of her living-room.

Patty, Darling, I am using Mia's phone just in case my call would be intercepted. What are we going to do? Surely Sam and Tania will not carry out their threat and keep your grandson away from you. Your daughter, Jasmine, has also contacted me and asked me to stay away. I love you Patty.

I never wanted to hurt your family but I can't live without you. I know that you love me too. There is a home for you over here if you ever decide to leave. How did they find out? Maybe this is what we needed all along to bring things to a head. Ring me when you get the chance. I need to hear your voice.

Kenneth now handed her the phone and left the room before she could even speak. She heard him lift his car keys and go out the front door. Moments later she was aware of his engine starting up and the sound of wheels spinning over the gravelled driveway. And then silence.

Patricia sat, rooted to the spot, for a long time, too stunned even to cry. Her double life was common knowledge. Not only did Sam know about it but Kenneth too and even Jasmine. Tania and Stevie might be lost to her forever. How had they all found out? Obviously through this phone-call in Kenneth's case but what about the other two? She and Dougie had been so careful. For almost seven years they had carried on their clandestine affair without anyone getting hurt. She had her life with Casey and their three children; he had Mia and happy memories of Lucinda. Every few months they had met, sometimes for a couple of wonderful hours in a Belfast hotel, sometimes for a whole weekend at his home in Scotland. Mia had resented her at first but had eventually come to accept her, knowing that the relationship made her father happy.

So why now? Something told her that it did indeed have something to do with her delivering that letter to Cathy's son, Grant Cartwright. Cathy must have let something slip and Grant has passed it on to Sam. They played a round of golf together last week. Sam had mentioned it to Kenneth when he dropped in with the baby. She missed seeing Stevie. Sam had been so cruel, leaving toys behind on purpose so that she would definitely know they'd been in. She felt angry with him for that but also sad. And what would happen to her marriage now?

Suddenly the tears came thick and fast, rolling down her cheeks in salty torrents. The house seemed so empty. Sam and Tania had found a new home; at least they wouldn't be living with those awful people, Tania's parents, any longer. Even Jasmine had moved out, her lovely, sensitive daughter. She worried about Jasmine being on her own. She was young and vulnerable, had never really had a boyfriend. How was she going to cope in the big, wide world? Molly wouldn't be back for some months yet. And where had Kenneth gone? Would he come back? Patricia wiped her eyes and took a huge breath. The time had come for her to decide. Whom did she love more, Kenneth or Dougie?

Getting up from the sofa, Patricia's gaze landed on her black and red suitcase, packed ready for her romantic city break in Barcelona. Kenneth would be fifty-five in three days' time. She walked out into the hallway and there was his case, sitting upright at the bottom of the stairs. She touched it lovingly, wishing that she could conjure up a happy scenario where they were together again and the last hour would become a figment of her imagination, a nightmare that hadn't really happened. Her phone started to ring.

Please let it be Casey. Please don't let twenty-eight years of marriage end like this.

She checked the caller display. Mia. The perfect time to chat to her lover while she had the house to herself. But she didn't know what she wanted to say to him. She turned her phone off. Watching the clock on the wall with an aching heart, she waited and waited for the sound of the car returning, but nothing. Eight o'clock, nine o'clock, half past ten, midnight. At two-thirty she went to bed, her head pounding with anxiety. Where had he gone? But when Patricia eventually closed her eyes and imagined those strong arms around her, that manly fragrance stirring her passion and those sensuous lips kissing her, it was Dougie that she clung to in her dreams, not Kenneth.

Chapter 11

Sam rolled over and squinted at his phone to check the time. He must have imagined it. It couldn't possibly be the doorbell ringing that had jolted him from his deep slumber. But it was. Tania had heard it too.

"Who on earth is that?" she mumbled groggily. "So much for a nice lie-in when we've left Stevie with Mum and Dad. What time is it anyway?"

"Six-thirty," Sam yawned drowsily, replacing the phone on the bedside table. "Go back to sleep. Someone's got the wrong house." But just to make sure, he eased himself out of bed and looked out of the window. Even in the early morning darkness he recognised his father's car parked across the road. He tiptoed out of the room, closing the door gently behind him so that Tania could hopefully sleep on. He threw on a fleece which was hanging in the hallway and opened the door. Kenneth stepped inside. His dishevelled appearance and the fact that he was dressed only in a cotton shirt and was obviously shivering with cold immediately alerted Sam to an impending crisis.

"Has Mum told you?" he blurted out. "I warned her

that she had to end it. I told her she'd never see Stevie again if she didn't. Are you all right, Dad?"

"I've been sitting in the car all night. I don't want to see her."

"You must be frozen. Here, take this." Sam gave him the fleece and put the kettle on to make a hot drink.

"Tell me what you know, Son."

Sam was starting to shiver himself now. He had never seen his father look so dejected and it really unnerved him. "Just let me get some clothes on," he faltered, as he flew into the spare room and pulled on a pair of jeans and a sweater. They'd only moved in here a couple of days ago and most of their belongings were still piled up in what would eventually be Stevie's room, waiting to be organised into drawers and cupboards. He found a pair of trainers and some socks in one of the cardboard boxes on the floor and then rushed back to the kitchen to make them both some coffee. "Tania's still asleep," he explained. "We had a bit of a house-warming last night and didn't get to bed until about two."

"What about Stevie?"

"It's OK, he's with Judy."

Kenneth wrapped his hands round the coffee mug in an attempt to gain some warmth and took a sip of the welcome drink. "I'll kill that bastard if I ever get my hands on him," he then declared. "How long have you known that something was going on?"

"I don't blame you. If I ever see him again, it'll be too soon," Sam said in support but his father glared at him and pounced on his words.

"See him again!" he thundered, his eyes blazing. "Are you telling me that you've actually met this man?"

Sam nodded sheepishly. "You'd better tell me what Mum has owned up to."

"Your mother hasn't told me anything. She tried to deny the whole thing."

"So how did you know that I was aware of it?"

"A bloody phone call. He mentioned you and Tania. Jasmine too. How you'd all tried to warn him off. So thank you for that at least."

"He actually had the nerve to phone you?"

Kenneth felt embarrassed, mortified even, but somehow he managed to relate the gist of the phone message he had intercepted to his son. Sam, in turn, told him what had taken place during the weekend in Scotland.

"But Jasmine hasn't met him," he concluded in puzzlement. "I don't understand that bit about her warning him off. It was Jasmine who put me onto him in the first place but he wouldn't know that. Tania and I never mentioned her."

"Jasmine put you onto him?"

"Yes, that's right, and then Tania and I caught them red-handed."

"So how did Jasmine know?"

"It was just something she overheard. She was suspicious. I promised her that I'd check it out. But she didn't have any details about who he was or anything."

"I want to know his name."

"McKendrick. Douglas McKendrick."

"So it is Mia's father, after all."

"I don't know anything about that. He didn't mention having a daughter."

"That was her name, McKendrick. Lucinda McKendrick. She and your mother were friends years ago until she died."

"Yes, that's when it started."

Kenneth gasped and went quite pale. "It's been going on for years?"

"Apparently so."

"Well he is one dead man! Just let me get at him."

"I'm on your side, Dad, and Mum knows that, but let's see what she does now that she's been exposed. It's her fault too, not just his."

"But he must have manipulated her, telling her some sob story about how lonely he was without his wife."

"Well, it's out in the open now. She'll have to choose one or the other."

"Too late for that, Son."

"You're going to split up?" Sam felt wretched; this is exactly what he had tried to pre-empt.

Kenneth didn't give a direct answer. "Can you get her out of the house for an hour or so? I need to gather up some clothes and things. I don't want to see her."

Sam nodded. "I'll pick her up about ten. But don't do anything rash, Dad. Maybe it's not as bad as it seems."

"You'd better tell Jasmine, since she's already in the loop. But say nothing to Molly. Not yet anyway. She's on the trip of a lifetime. Let her enjoy it."

"Where will you go?"

"Can you get me that man's address?"

"Imogen and Grant have been to his house. I could ask them. But is that wise, Dad? What are you going to do?"

"Imogen? Your Imogen?" His voice was now reaching fever pitch. Did everyone know about this, bar him?

"She's not mine anymore. But yes, it's the same person. That bit that Mum told you about McKendrick helping to put Grant in touch with his father – that bit is true. They didn't know anything about an affair between him and Mum."

"Forward me the address. Don't say why you want it. I'm sure you can come up with some pretext." Kenneth stood up to go. "Ten o'clock then. Thanks. Mind if I hold onto this?" He indicated the fleece which he was still wearing.

"Of course not." Sam looked really worried. "Don't do anything stupid, Dad. Do you want me to come with you?"

"No."

"Well keep in touch. Let me know where you are."

Kenneth gave him a sad look and shuffled back to his car, just as Tania emerged from the bedroom, rubbing the sleep from her eyes and wondering what was going on. "You're up very early for a Saturday," she yawned, "especially when we were so late getting to bed."

Sam told her what had happened. Then he phoned Jasmine and gave her an update. "But what was that about you warning him off?" he quizzed his sister. "Have you really been in touch with him?"

Jasmine had to admit that she had searched through their mother's phone and had found the number listed under DM.

"And you phoned him?"

"No, I just sent him a text." She paused and then added, "I also told him about Grant burning that letter. I'm sorry. I felt awful asking a favour from him but I just have a feeling that the letter was important and I think Grant deserves another chance to bond with his father. I think he might regret what he did so I asked Mr McKendrick to pass on the message. I gave him Grant's number. I shouldn't have interfered."

Sam was impressed. "Grant thought it was his mother. Actually he blamed me at first. We never thought of you. So you still have McKendrick's number?"

"Yes."

"Can you get his address so we can leave Grant and Imogen out of this?"

"I can't just ask him for it!"

"Why not? Tell him you want to send him something. Don't let on that Dad has twigged although Mum might have told him already, of course."

"I don't think I like the idea of Dad turning up on his doorstep."

"He has every right to feel aggrieved. We all have."

"I'll see what I can do."

★★★

As promised, Tania and Sam arrived at the family home just before ten o'clock and tried to behave as though nothing had happened. Patricia was in the kitchen having some tea and toast. Her eyes were red with crying and lack of sleep but Sam pretended not to notice.

"We had Jasmine round last night for a house-warming, along with Lawrence and Maggie," he told her with mock cheerfulness, "so Stevie is with Judy and Ed. We're just about to pick him up. Would you like to come with us and then you could come back to our place for lunch?"

Patricia looked startled.

"Stevie has missed you this week," Tania pleaded. "I'm sorry we haven't brought him round."

"Where's Dad?" enquired Sam, feigning surprise that he wasn't in.

"I'm not sure," his mother answered, giving nothing away. "He just said he had a few errands to run, bills to pay, that sort of thing."

"Well, come on then. I told Judy we'd be there before half past ten."

Within ten minutes they were on their way, leaving the coast clear for Kenneth to return home and pack a bag.

★★★

Jasmine picked up her phone and stared at it. Her dad had every right to know that man's address. She understood completely that he would want to see him face to face and give him a right rollicking. Fingers crossed, her mum and dad would manage to work things out and not let this destroy their marriage, their family life. She selected 'messages' and scrolled through her contacts. DM. She had to be diplomatic. She wrote a few words and deleted them. Three times. Then eventually:

Hello Mr McKendrick. I know that my friend Grant has now spoken to his father. He would love to send you a card to thank you for the part you played in bringing them together. Could you please send me your address as he has mislaid it. And thank you for respecting my mother and father's marriage. JC

Jasmine didn't often tell lies or do deceitful things. But this was a desperate situation. She touched 'send' and it was too late to change her mind. The message had gone. With her heart in her mouth she waited anxiously to see whether he would respond. And then he did. Within half an hour Jasmine had the information she had requested and had forwarded it to her brother.

★★★

Patricia had been so surprised to receive the invitation to lunch, and to spend time with her grandson, that she had accepted without really thinking it through. Stevie's baby antics certainly took her mind off her troubles for part of the time but she was worried sick about Kenneth and where he might have spent the night. She could not imagine what would happen next in her love life. She didn't want to give up the magical relationship she had built up with Dougie but she had to save her marriage. On the way home she began to worry that Kenneth might have returned and would cause a scene in front of their son so she didn't invite them in but just got out of the car and waved them goodbye. She had no idea that Sam already knew the whole sorry tale. Once inside it became obvious to her that her husband had indeed been home but had already left again. Many of his clothes and possessions were missing. He hadn't even left her a note. She sat down and cried, cursing herself for having gone out. Why did Sam and Tania have to pick today of all days to lift their ban on allowing her contact with Stevie? And then the truth dawned on her and she wept until her eyes were swollen and her heart was truly broken.

Chapter 12

Grant and Imogen stood outside the restaurant that Cameron had chosen for his father's birthday party.

"This is so weird," Grant professed. "I feel totally exhilarated and scared stiff at the same time."

He took a deep breath and opened the door, standing aside to let Imogen through first. The atmosphere was buzzing inside with some people already seated and half-way through their meals whilst others waited in the bar area, chatting animatedly amongst themselves, glasses of wine in their hands. Grant went over to the reception area.

"Can you direct me to the Ferguson birthday party, please," he asked.

"Ah, that's upstairs in our private function suite," replied a young lady with a clipboard. "Just take the stairs over there to the right. You can't miss it."

Definitely in the right place then. They headed towards the staircase and started to climb the steps, getting more and more nervous as they neared the top. There was a door on the left with a notice saying, 'Happy 80th birthday, Angus Ferguson'. Grant was grateful for that because it suddenly occurred to him that he hadn't actually known his grandfather's name. He took a deep breath and opened the door.

Several people were standing in a group at the far end of the room, chatting and having a drink. Between them and the door was a large round table, covered in a pristine white table cloth and beautifully laid with place settings for about a dozen people. Four sets of blue and yellow balloons bearing the number 80, two vases of yellow roses and some jolly music playing unobtrusively in the background created a festive yet dignified atmosphere. Grant and Imogen stepped inside. Immediately the talking ceased and Cameron Ferguson walked over to them. They recognised him at once.

"Grant! Imogen! I'm so glad you could join us." He embraced them both warmly. "Come over and meet everyone." A few moments of confusion followed, during which they met so many people that they both felt sure they would not remember who was who. But they were all very welcoming, so different from the last time they had been over here. They were introduced to Lauren and the two boys, James and Henry, the birthday boy himself, Angus, Lauren's brother, Ian and his wife, Flora, along with their children, Archie and Zara and, surprisingly, Cameron's brother, Scott. "There's just one more guest to arrive," Cameron then announced. "I invited Dougie since it was he who helped to bring us together. Without him I would never have known you even existed."

As he spoke the door opened again and Douglas McKendrick stepped into the room. Further introductions ensued and then they all sat down at the beautifully laid table.

"Grant, will you do me the honour of sitting next to me," Cameron invited, "and Imogen, there's a place for you on his left." Imogen breathed a sigh of relief. For a moment she had thought they were going to be separated. Angus sat on Cameron's right with Lauren and her two boys on the other side. The seat beside Imogen, on her left, was as yet unoccupied. She didn't really mind who sat there as long as she had her fiancé at her elbow. But then it turned out to be Douglas McKendrick.

"It's lovely to see you again, Imogen," he smiled, as he eased himself into the vacant chair. "You won't need to send me that card now."

She gave him a puzzled look.

"I sent Jasmine my address anyway. Maybe she didn't know I'd be seeing the two of you today."

He leaned across and shook Grant by the hand. "Thanks for contacting your dad," he said affably. "He's over the moon." Grant hadn't heard his comment to Imogen. He smiled back.

"I'm glad you pushed me into it," he confessed.

He was a charming and very handsome man. Imogen could easily see how Patricia might have been attracted to him. But to put her marriage at stake by actually sleeping with him! She felt sorry for Sam. She would always have a soft spot for Sam. But what was that about Jasmine? Was the girl colluding with Douglas and Patricia in hiding the affair from Kenneth?

Everyone was now seated and soup was being served. Imogen turned back to Dougie and asked him what he had meant about a card.

"Jasmine texted me," he disclosed. "She said Grant wanted to send me a card but he had mislaid my address. Maybe he didn't mention it to you."

"So you know Jasmine quite well?"

"No, I've never met her. The text just came out of the blue."

"But you've met Sam?"

Douglas at least had the decency to look abashed, if not remorseful. "I'm not sure what you've heard," he said in a low voice, "but yes, I've met Sam and his girlfriend, Tania. Patty and I have been good friends for years. We met through my wife, Lucinda."

Grant became aware of what was being discussed and felt uncomfortable. He gave Imogen a nudge, urging her to be careful. It wasn't the time or place for a showdown. Imogen, however, couldn't resist one more question. She turned towards Grant.

"Did you tell Jasmine that you wanted to send a card to Douglas? And that you needed his address?"

"No. Sure I know his address. We've been in his house."

"But you did mention sending a card?"

He shook his head. "When was this conversation supposed to have taken place?"

"This morning," Douglas answered, looking worried. "Never mind," he added hurriedly, "it's obviously some sort of misunderstanding. Let's enjoy this lovely meal."

Throughout the rest of the meal Grant managed to relax and enjoy the company of his new-found family. His father and grandfather made him feel very welcome and he began to open up to them about the details of his own life, his childhood, his family in Belfast. They were sad to hear that he had already been married and that his young bride had died so tragically but delighted that he had found happiness again with Imogen. Cameron asked after Catherine without any hesitation or embarrassment, but with genuine interest. Grant discovered that his father worked in the tourist industry and his grandfather had been the manager of a large clothing company, specialising in Scottish tartans and knitwear.

"I'm surprised that you're not all dressed in kilts," Grant commented. "I sort of expected that you might be."

"We normally would wear our kilts for an occasion like this," Cameron divulged, "but we were anxious that it might make you feel out of place, as if you didn't belong. So we all decided to go for shirts and trousers."

"That was very considerate. Thank you."

Scott was seated at the other end of the table. Grant was glad about that. He needed to speak to Cameron in private before he would know how to address the man. James and Henry talked amongst themselves and with their cousins; they hadn't bothered much with the newcomers after the initial greeting. Grant seized his chance in between dessert and coffee, when people started to move about and mingle. He edged Cameron into a corner and spoke to him quietly.

"Those things you told me about in the letter," he probed, "I need to know whether Scott and the boys know the truth or not, especially with him being here in the room."

Cameron nodded. "Scott may have his suspicions but we've never owned up to anything. As far as he's concerned, the boys are his nephews and he's quite happy."

"And what about the boys themselves?"

Imogen took the chance to slip out to the toilet while Grant and his dad were talking about private matters. He could fill her in later.

"We haven't told them either. Not yet. But we will. They deserve to know who their real father is, just as you did."

"So, as far as they are concerned we are brothers, not cousins."

"Definitely. We've brought the two lads up. We'll always consider them to be our sons."

"I haven't had the chance to talk to them yet," Grant told him. "How do they feel about me?"

"I'm not sure. They're a bit mixed up. But they'll come round."

"You're very trusting of me, telling me such intimate secrets that they don't know themselves. I mean, you hardly know me."

Cameron looked him straight in the eye. "You're my own flesh and blood, Grant. You'll know how special that feels when you have a child of your own some day. I don't mean that I love James and Henry any less. It's hard to explain. It's just a different kind of special. I just wanted you to know."

"Well let me return the favour," Grant confided. "Imogen is already expecting a baby. It's due next May. And, on top of that, we're getting married next Friday. That's two secrets I haven't told anyone else."

Cameron gave him a radiant smile. "Congratulations, Son, on both counts," he said. "Now come and meet the others."

They stayed for another hour or so, mingling with the other guests and enjoying an after dinner drink with large helpings of birthday cake. Angus gave a short speech, in which he mentioned how wonderful it had been to discover that he had another grandson and to finally get to meet him. Phone numbers and email addresses were exchanged along with social media contacts and photos were taken of various groupings. Grant and Imogen left the party feeling very much a part of the family and promising to keep in touch. They got a taxi back to their hotel.

On the way Imogen brought the conversation back to Douglas McKendrick. She revealed that she had overheard him talking on his mobile when she came out of the ladies' toilets. He had been standing outside the gents' with his back to her so he hadn't noticed her passing by.

"What did you hear?" asked Grant, interested in spite of the happy evening they had spent.

"He was talking to someone called Mia and telling her to be careful, not to let any strangers into the house.

He mentioned Jasmine and something about her tricking him into giving her his address."

"I don't like the sound of that," Grant agreed, "but it isn't really our business to interfere, I suppose. Sam and Jasmine obviously know him in a different context from us. In our case he's a family friend. In their case he's the enemy."

"But it does involve us if she used our names to trick him."

"That's true. Anyway, let's forget about it for tonight. The party went better than I could have expected. I like Cameron."

The taxi drew up outside their hotel. "Me too. But I'm whacked! Let's go to bed."

★★★

Douglas McKendrick was worried. Patty was neither answering her phone nor was she responding to messages. He had called her on his own phone and had also used Mia's but he had not been able to raise her all day. Was it because of what her son had said, that threat about not letting her see her grandson? Surely she wouldn't just ignore him after all they have shared. If she was going to end things she would at least tell him straight. And why did her daughter, Jasmine, want his address? He arrived home from the party and, taking a surreptitious glance around the garden, stepped inside and firmly shut the door. Mia immediately emerged from the sitting-room.

"You frightened me a bit with that phone-call," she said frenetically. "I asked Uncle Alex to stay with me until you got home."

Douglas followed her back into the room and greeted his brother with a grateful smile. "Thanks, Bro," he acknowledged. "It's probably nothing but I'm glad you were able to put her mind at ease."

"You're playing with fire," Alex chided. "I've warned you a hundred times to end that relationship." Both Alex and Mia were fully aware of the long-standing affair and of Patty's marital status. They had accepted it with reluctance but both still had reservations.

"We love each other," Douglas replied simply, and Alex sighed resignedly.

Mia said goodnight and went upstairs. She loved nothing more than to read a few chapters of a good novel before going to sleep. Indeed she was secretly writing one of her own. Maybe someday she would get it published and into the public domain but for now it remained a private hobby. As usual she looked out through the curtains for a few moments and admired the lovely back garden, softly illuminated by the moon and the stars which looked particularly bright tonight. At thirty-six, she was well aware that people thought she should be looking for a home of her own, but Mia and her dad were very close, especially since Lucinda's untimely death at the age of just fifty, ten years ago. Mia didn't have a steady boyfriend. She was happy to stay put. After all, this lovely house would be all hers one day.

Downstairs Douglas and Alex enjoyed a nightcap and a chat about the family business where they both worked. Retirement was looming and they were each relishing plans for trips abroad and generally a more restful pace of life. Alex took his leave at about eleven-thirty and Douglas went to bed, his thoughts returning to the party he had attended. It had been nice to be invited, especially since he had been the only non-family member there. He had always respected Cameron Ferguson and he liked his son. He felt proud to be the person who had helped to reunite them. It was just a pity that the process had involved Patty's family. Patty's best friend was Grant Cartwright's mother, Cathy. That made things a bit awkward for all of them.

★★★

Kenneth had only come to suss out the area. It was too late at night to make his move; he would come back in daylight when he'd had time to think. But it was definitely payback time. No-one was going to seduce his wife and get away with it. But suddenly he saw the front door opening. Stealthily, Kenneth took a step sideways, allowing himself to merge into the bushes. The bastard wasn't in bed yet! He was walking down the driveway towards him.

All of a sudden he was just feet away. For a split second common sense and decency deserted him and a blinding rage took over. Kenneth stepped out from his hiding place and accosted his adversary.

"I don't take kindly to people messing with my wife, McKendrick," he snarled into the man's face and straightaway gave him one almighty punch to the jaw. Taken completely off guard his victim staggered backwards, lost his balance, and fell onto the hard driveway, his head banging directly onto the sharp, jagged stones that bordered it. Immediately bright red blood started to ooze from a huge gash just behind his ear. His whole body shuddered momentarily and then lay perfectly motionless, his lifeless eyes staring into the moonlight.

He can't be dead!! It isn't possible!! It was only one punch! Gripped by panic and fear, Kenneth didn't wait to find out. He bolted to the end of the driveway and looked furtively around in all directions. A couple walking a dog. He slipped back into the bushes until they were out of sight, then took another look. No-one about. The nearby houses were in darkness. Good. In a state of shock Kenneth walked all the way back to the hotel where he had parked his hire car, retrieved the few belongings he had left in his room and drove off. He had no idea where he was going.

Chapter 13

Jasmine spent the weekend sorting out her new home, putting everything in its rightful place and shopping for a few extra homely items to make it her own. The pink and beige striped cushions looked fantastic on the burgundy sofa and the creamy scatter rugs co-ordinated perfectly with the chintz curtains that Imogen had left behind. Upset as she was about the state of her parents' marital harmony or lack of it, Jasmine determined to put it from her mind and let them get on with sorting things out in their own way. She didn't want any further involvement. Wandering into the front bedroom she sighed with contentment. The new duvet she had chosen with its mass of bright cheerful colours was gorgeous; she would sleep happily in here and dream of wonderful romantic encounters. Which all ended the same way. She glanced at her new calendar with its paintings by some of the great impressionist artists.

It's the second of October. I'll entice him into that bed before Christmas.

The thought both thrilled her and terrified her. She had never slept with a man, had never felt the urge to explore a man's body or to be touched intimately by anyone she met. At twenty-four she was beginning to worry that there was something wrong with her. It wasn't that she questioned her sexuality in any sense of gender. She wasn't attracted to females either. But everything had changed during this past week since he had entered her life. She couldn't stop thinking about him. She had fallen for him, hook, line and sinker.

Continuing to stroll through her new-found utopia, Jasmine entered what apparently used to be Jillian's room and was now her painting studio. She had advised Imogen that she wouldn't need the double bed that had been there when she first viewed the apartment and Grant had arranged for it to be removed to the spare room in their own house. Imogen and Jillian had already settled on some kind of agreement with regard to things they owned jointly so that Jasmine only had to deal with Imogen. She had now purchased a small folding bed, just in case she had someone staying over but that didn't take up much room and was pushed firmly against the wall. This gave her plenty of space for two easels and several canvases and drawing books as well as a cabinet for her paints, brushes and other paraphernalia and a small sofa. It was heaven.

The kitchen and bathroom were unchanged from Imogen's period of residence in the building except that Jasmine's rugs and towels were powder blue and lilac instead of yellow and orange. With everything else being white or chrome with just a few grey tiles dotted here and there, there had been no restriction on the colours she could choose.

Jasmine heard the doorbell ring as she left the bathroom on her tour of inspection. It was Maggie.

"I told you I'd call," Maggie trilled, giving her a friendly hug. "I'm dying to see your studio."

"Is Lawrence with you?"

"No, he's popped in to see his parents. Now that Tania and Sam have moved out, it's a bit less hectic there."

Jasmine was delighted to have her new friend pay such an early visit. She took her through straightaway to view her pride and joy, the studio in the back room, and Maggie was more than impressed. "You are so lucky," she enthused. "I love it." Jasmine showed her some of her work and Maggie promised to send her some images of her own. They enjoyed a cup of coffee together.

On the way out Maggie indicated that she was heading upstairs to see Jillian. "This is very convenient for me," she chortled, "having two of my friends living in the same building."

Jasmine grinned. "It is pretty handy," she agreed.

Maggie seemed to be weighing something up in her mind. "I've asked Mum to add you to the guest list for my wedding," she then disclosed.

"Really? Wow! Thank you. That's really kind of you, especially when we've only just met."

"Sure we're almost family," Maggie told her. "My future sister-in-law will also be your sister-in-law when Tania and Sam get round to tying the knot."

"Well thank you. I'd love to come. When is the wedding?"

"We've just secured a booking thanks to a late cancellation. With my dad dying not so long ago we had put things on hold but now we just want to be married as soon as possible. We've set the date for 19th November. It's a Saturday so hopefully most people will be free."

"Thanks Maggie. I'm really chuffed to be included."

She was half way up the stairs to Jillian's apartment when Maggie turned round again and asked Jasmine whether she was in a steady relationship. "I wouldn't want to leave your boyfriend out if that were the case," she said jocularly, "but Mum will go mad if I keep adding names that she doesn't recognise. We don't want a crowd of strangers. It's going to be a fairly small and intimate gathering."

Jasmine took a deep breath. "No, I'm not in a relationship," she told her friend, "but I have my sights firmly set on someone. I hope that I will be soon."

"Fair enough," laughed Maggie, "I need confirmation within the next couple of weeks."

"OK, good to have a specific target," Jasmine laughed. "I had been thinking about Christmas! I'll have to get cracking."

"Talk to you soon."

And Maggie disappeared out of view.

Jasmine felt elated. She liked Maggie. Everything was going swimmingly for her since she moved in here. And now she had a further incentive to make a move on the man of her dreams. Maggie's wedding was only six weeks away. How much more would she enjoy it as part of a couple, rather than just going alone.

★★★

Sunday was almost over. Two full days and not a word from her husband. Patty wondered for the hundredth time where he had gone. Tomorrow would be his birthday. Gosh, how she had messed things up. They should have been sightseeing, taking in the architecture of Barcelona, enjoying the tapas bars, relaxing in a fancy restaurant overlooking the beach. She checked her phone again. Nothing. Only endless texts and messages from Douglas. She ignored those, just couldn't cope with them yet. Much as she loved him too, her husband of twenty-eight years was missing. He had to come first. But where was he?

Patricia had enjoyed seeing Sam and Tania yesterday. They had reinstated contact with Stevie, lovely little Stevie, her darling grandson. But it had been a trick. They hadn't been in touch since. And where was Jasmine? Too busy enjoying her own space, revelling in the freedom of her new flat, socialising with her new friends. Molly hadn't even phoned today. It had been the longest day of her life.

***

Way up in the Scottish Highlands, in a small guesthouse by a pretty lough, Kenneth lay on the bed watching a local Scottish news programme. A body had been found on the outskirts of Edinburgh. A local man, the newsreader announced, found in the garden of his brother and business partner, Douglas McKendrick. Foul play had been ruled out. It appeared that the unfortunate man had tripped over some obstacle on his way down the driveway,

109

following a visit to his brother. He only lived a few yards away but never made it home because he caught his head on a sharp, angular stone, bursting a blood vessel to his brain. He would have been dead within minutes. The family were distraught because he had apparently lain there all night before being discovered by his niece when she took her dog for a walk on Sunday morning. Kenneth could scarcely believe what he was hearing.

I got the wrong guy! But I've gotten away with it. They definitely said that foul play wasn't suspected. Just an accident. And yes, there were lots of obstacles lying about that driveway. There were loose stones, a trowel, a small rake, terracotta pots. A visitor to the house could have tripped over any of those in the darkness. No-one will ever know it was me. As long as I stay away from home until that bruise on my hand has disappeared.

Chapter 14

Jasmine decided to stop pussy-footing around. She had to be more forthcoming, make things happen herself, not just wait for good luck to strike in her direction. A house-warming party! Not a big affair, something intimate like Sam and Tania had done. She would have them back of course, along with Maggie and Lawrence. Imogen and Grant. Gillian and Bradley from upstairs. Rebecca and Alastair. Robyn? Jasmine had never actually known her except as a cute little baby. It would be just like the old days. As long as the conversation steered well clear of their parents. She didn't want to talk about what was going on there. Her mother's behaviour had made her feel a bit ashamed and it was now evident that her father was not at home. She didn't blame him for walking out but where was he and when was he coming home? Maybe he really had paid that man a visit but Jasmine didn't even want to think about it. And Grant's parents were tied up with the same people; there were too many connections for comfort. So she would have a blanket ban on discussing anything to do with parents. Then they could have a proper party atmosphere and a bit of fun.

Robyn decided not to come. Jasmine was glad because she had only sent the invitation via Grant as a matter of courtesy. It turned out that Robyn and her boyfriend, Jack, already had plans for Friday night which included tickets for a show. But Jasmine was surprised when Grant and Imogen also declined her invitation, saying that they were going away for yet another weekend. She had immediately assumed that they wanted to spend more time with Grant's Scottish father but they had assured her that their plans had nothing to do with him. However, they had been somewhat secretive and Jasmine ended up deciding that Imogen and Sam were maybe not yet particularly comfortable in one another's company or that Grant wasn't happy with them spending time together. It couldn't have been further from the truth but how could Jasmine have known that her childhood friend and the previous occupant of her lovely apartment were getting married that very day! In the end Rebecca also decided to stay away.

So it was just the eight of them. Perfect. Jasmine would have her work colleagues over another time. Maybe. Although she got on well with people at work, she didn't often socialise with anyone in particular. She wouldn't be offending anyone. Her guests started to arrive.

"Hi Maggie." She gave her new best friend a hug and then addressed her boyfriend. "Good to see you again, Lawrence. There are drinks in the kitchen. Come and help yourselves."

The doorbell rang again, almost immediately. "Hi Tania, your brother's already here. Drinks are in the kitchen." Jasmine smirked at her own brother who was at Tania's heels. "Remember what I said. No parent talk," she instructed.

"Suits me," Sam grunted. "They can work things out for themselves from now on."

A taxi was heard pulling up at the door. Jasmine flew out to greet Alastair who was on his way upstairs, as usual. "Hey, the party's down here," she called out to him jocularly. "Come on in. Jillian and Bradley should be here any minute."

Alastair retraced his steps and allowed himself to be shepherded inside where he was introduced to the others. Sam was astounded to see him looking so fit and healthy and had to remind himself that sixteen years had passed since they last met.

And finally Jillian and Bradley came through the door. Jasmine made sure that everyone had a drink, deposited coats in the bedroom and then started to mingle and chat, her heart fluttering excitedly as she passed from one to another.

"So where is this guy you're lusting after?" Maggie quizzed, when they found themselves alone in the kitchen for a few moments. "I was hoping I might meet him tonight."

"You already have," Jasmine replied, licking her lips. "He's right here in my flat this very minute."

"Not Bradley? You can't have him, Jasmine. Jillian is one of my best friends. They're engaged for goodness sake."

"All's fair in love and war."

Maggie gave her friend a horrified stare before realising that she was pulling her leg.

"Who then?"

"Alastair, of course!"

"Alastair?"

"I have dreamt about him since the first moment I set eyes on him two weeks ago. Don't you think he's gorgeous?"

Maggie hesitated before speaking. "Jasmine, maybe you don't know about Alastair. I never met him before but Jillian has mentioned him to me. He's got some kind of brain damage. There are lots of things he can't do."

"And I suppose you can do everything. And Lawrence is some kind of Superman."

"Jasmine, I'm only trying to help."

"By perpetuating the stigma that has plagued him all his life!"

"Being friendly with someone is one thing; starting a serious relationship with him is quite another matter."

"So I should be nice to people with disabilities but keep them at arm's length!"

"You're making me sound awful now. I just thought that maybe you weren't aware of his difficulties. You could be storing up trouble for yourself."

Bradley came in to refresh his drink and the sudden silence immediately alerted him to the fact that they had either been talking about him or having a row. "Should my ears be burning?" he asked looking from one to the other.

Jasmine just left the room. Maggie was annoyed with herself. "Just a difference of opinion about something," she told Bradley. "I'd better go after her."

She found Jasmine in her studio. Her eyes were wet with unshed tears and her hands were trembling. Maggie put an arm around her.

"I already knew about Alastair," Jasmine stuttered. "I expected abusive comments and reservations from narrow-minded and bigoted people but not from you. I thought you would understand."

"I do. I'm so sorry. I spoke impulsively, thoughtlessly. I just assumed that you didn't know."

"He told me quite a lot about himself the day I moved in here. I know he has problems and I know he worries about the future but all he needs is someone who cares, someone who really likes him, someone who loves him."

"Just be careful, Jasmine. You've only known him for two weeks."

"I'm sure I can be that person. I just feel it in my bones. I go weak at the knees just at the sight of him."

"Then I think it would be absolutely wonderful if you hook up with him."
"Really?"

"Let's get back to the others. Just say I was looking at your artwork."

They left the room with Maggie loudly enthusing over the canvas that was currently on one of the easels. "How did you get those apples to look so realistic? Lawrence, come and look at this painting."

Bradley gave the two girls a wry grin as everyone else squeezed into the studio to admire the painting. "Everything OK?" he enquired kindly.

"Absolutely," they both chorused. "We'll just go and turn the oven on. I'm sure you're all ready for something to eat."

As they prepared the snacks in the kitchen, Maggie and Jasmine chatted about other things but both of them were privately trying to come up with a scheme whereby Alastair would remain behind for a while when the others left. Eventually Maggie uttered her thoughts aloud. "We've all had a few drinks so I think I'll get Eddie to collect us all when he comes for Tania and Sam."

"Eddie?" Jasmine was momentarily confused.

"Lawrence and Tania's dad. He and Judy are looking after the baby but not overnight. He said he'd collect Tania and Sam from here and then leave them home, with the baby."

"Will he have room for all of you?"

"Lawrence and I will squeeze in." She looked at Jasmine with a cunning grin. "But there won't be room for Alastair."

"He came by taxi. He probably has one booked for going home too. He uses them quite a lot because he's not allowed to drive."

"Just make sure he doesn't go upstairs with Bradley and Jillian. Once they've gone, it's up to you. If you get my drift."

Jasmine gave her friend a hug. "Right, everybody, food's ready," she called into the lounge. "Come and help yourselves."

They all flooded into the kitchen and complimented Jasmine on the delicious snacks. Sam poured them all another drink. "You've landed on your feet here, Sis", he then said, taking a good look around. "This is lovely. It's so modern compared to our place."

Jasmine laughed. "You had first refusal on it," she reminded him.

"But I couldn't have asked Tania to live here. It has Imogen's stamp on it all over. In a way I'm quite glad she wasn't able to come tonight."

"Imogen's stamp?"

"Probably just my imagination but yes, I can sort of feel her presence. It's a bit weird thinking that she sat on these chairs, cooked in that oven, chose some of these furnishings."

"Hey, you'd think she'd died, talking like that!"

Sam smiled. "All I'm saying is that you're welcome to it and Tania and I are better off where we are."

Everything went nicely to plan. After Eddie called about eleven o'clock and collected his family members, Jillian and Bradley prepared to go back up to their own flat. As expected they invited Alastair to join them while he waited for his taxi but Jasmine quickly jumped in, offering to show him some more of her paintings. Alastair had expressed great interest in them during the evening, revealing that he did a bit of painting himself. Bradley, who had spent the best part of his life looking out for Alastair, was initially taken aback when his friend accepted Jasmine's offer and chose to stay but, on reflection, he was delighted to see the independent streak that was becoming more and more evident in recent weeks. After all Alastair was a young man of thirty-one now, not the vulnerable brain-damaged child Bradley had befriended all those years ago. It had taken a long, long time but it was becoming clear that his brain was at last recovering some of the functions it had lost, slowly but surely.

"OK, see you soon," Bradley said.

"Great party, Jasmine," added Jillian. "It's a pity Imogen and Grant missed it."

"Thanks for coming."

The door closed and Jasmine was alone at last with the man who had caused her heart to flutter over the past fortnight. She was almost sure he would be able to hear the thumping palpitations as they turned to face one another.

"Don't phone for your taxi just yet," she suggested.

"I wasn't going to."

Their eyes met, smiling. "You feel it too, don't you?"

Alastair nodded. "I've never kissed anyone," he admitted in a whisper.

Jasmine took his hand and led him over to the sofa. They sat down.

"I've never kissed anyone that mattered," Jasmine told him.

"Have you ever …?"

The incomplete question hung in the air for a moment.

"Never," Jasmine confided. "I've been waiting for you." Then she laughed. "Did that sound a bit cheesy?" she asked.

"You're a lot younger than me."

"Seven years. That's nothing."

Alastair cupped his hands around her face and gently kissed her lips. "You taste nice," he said in a low, sexy voice. Jasmine's desire for him intensified tenfold as she kissed him back and suddenly they were wrapped in each other's arms sharing their first sensation of ardent, passionate love.

A phone started to ring in the bedroom. "My phone's in here," Jasmine said, reluctantly ending the embrace. "It must be yours. Your coat is in there."

"I'd better check it," Alastair agreed.

Jasmine led the way and showed him where his jacket was, placed provocatively on the bed. He took his phone from the pocket. It had stopped ringing but a message had just come through. He read it and showed it to Jasmine.

Don't bother with a taxi. I'll pick you up. Or have you decided to stay at Bradley's place for the night? Mum x

They faced each other across the bedroom, both breathing heavily with anticipation.

"Technically it wouldn't be a lie," Jasmine ventured. "This is Bradley's place. Sort of. It's the same building."

"Just what I was thinking," Alastair concurred, his eyes dancing. "But are you sure?"

"Do you really need to ask?"

Alastair selected the 'reply' function.

Yes, I'll stay over. C u 2moro

He put the phone back in his pocket and picked up the jacket. Setting it on the chair in the corner, he sat down on the bed, easing Jasmine down beside him and they kissed again with even more fervour than before.

"Just give me a few minutes," Jasmine then muttered. Feeling both nervous and elated she went to the bathroom and freshened up, then heard Alastair doing the same whilst she locked up and turned off the lights. She sat down on the sofa in the darkness. Alastair came out of the bathroom and joined her.

"You're beautiful," he said, gently stroking her hair. "We don't have to do anything if you don't want to. I'll understand."

Her response was to slip something into his hand. "You might need this," she whispered, embarrassed. "I don't even know why I had it. It's been in my toiletry bag for a couple of years."

Alastair looked down at the condom in his hand. He nodded. "Let's go to bed," he prompted.

Back in the bedroom, they both undressed in the dark and slid in between the cool, cotton sheets. When Jasmine shivered, an involuntary reaction to her unaccustomed nakedness, Alastair wrapped his arms around her. "I'll soon warm you up," he breathed. And he wasn't wrong. They spent the next hour, arms and legs entwined, hands all over each other and lips exploring places they had never been before. It was all they had dreamed of and more. In the early hours Jasmine finally fell asleep knowing that her happiness was complete. Alastair kissed her softly even as she slept. He felt ecstatic. He had grown up at last.

Chapter 15

Eleven sad days had passed since the sudden parting of his dear brother but Douglas McKendrick could still scarcely believe that he had gone. The funeral service and cremation had been very tastefully managed with mourners encouraged to remember and celebrate the positive aspects of Alex's life rather than dwell on his demise but the whole process had brought Lucinda's untimely death to the fore again for both Douglas and Mia. Alex had lived just across the road so they were at least close to his wife, Barbara, and had helped her with all the arrangements. Their only daughter lived in London and had just returned to her family there after spending a week with her mother. It was now Wednesday evening and Mia was in the kitchen washing up after dinner. Douglas was working at his computer. There was a rap at the back door.

"Auntie Barbara, hi." Mia unlocked the door and let her in. Barbara was as white as a sheet and trembling from head to toe. Mia was immediately alarmed. Her aunt had obviously suffered the worst trauma of any of them over the past week or so but she had been coping relatively well, outwardly anyway, if not in private.

"Where's your father?" she asked Mia. "I need to speak to you both."

"He's upstairs. Come into the lounge and I'll make a pot of tea. You look as though you could do with a cup."

"I've drunk enough tea this week to last a lifetime," Barbara retorted rather sharply. "Just get your father down here please."

Mia ran up and alerted Douglas to the distressed state of his sister-in-law. He came down right away.

"I need the two of you to explain something," Barbara began. "I'm not an expert in technology but I do know that things sometimes get lost in the ether, so to speak. For example, you can send a text message to someone but they don't receive it."

Douglas agreed that such things sometimes happen and that the message can eventually arrive with the recipient, even some considerable time later or, on occasions, just gets lost altogether and never arrives. "But it hasn't happened to me very often," he concluded. Both he and Mia were looking quite mystified as to where this was leading.

Barbara took a phone from her pocket. "This suddenly beeped this afternoon while I was dozing in front of the fire. I got the fright of my life."

"Why?"

"The message was from Alex." Barbara burst into tears as she recalled seeing her dead husband's name coming up on her screen. "I charged up his own phone and turned it on and there it was, the same message, sent on the day he died, at 10.27 pm."

Both her brother-in-law and her niece gasped in horror. What a dreadful thing to have happened.

"But it's what was in the message that has upset me even more," she wailed, obviously quite distraught. "You've been hiding something from me. Alex has spoken to me from beyond the grave."

Douglas and Mia just stared at her, uncomprehending. Barbara handed Douglas the phone. He read the message.

Staying for a few drinks with Dougie. He's just in from a party. I didn't want to leave Mia alone because she was scared. Will explain later. Don't wait up. Love you. Alex

Douglas handed the phone to Mia so that she could also read the text. It had indeed been sent on the day Alex died, at 10.27 pm.

"What did he mean?" Barbara asked them now. "What were you scared of, Mia?"

Douglas and Mia shared an awkward glance.

"It's nothing for you to worry about, Barbara," Douglas told her. "The police were quite adamant that it was a simple accident. Alex tripped over something and banged his head very hard against those angular border stones. They said the gash and bruising to his face were so severe he would have died almost instantly. Don't torment yourself about it."

"But what if it wasn't an accident?"

"Barbara, it was. He was carrying cash and credit cards as well as this phone. And wearing his expensive watch.

Nothing was stolen. The police took no time at all to rule out a mugging."

"So what was this about you being scared?" She aimed her question directly at Mia.

Douglas decided that he had better come clean about his affair.

"Barbara," he began, "I'm not proud of this; I've been seeing a married woman. Her son found out about it and warned me to stay clear. The day that Alex died I had a message from his sister, also asking me to leave well alone. But she also tricked me into giving her my address. I was out at a party for an old friend and I texted Mia, warning her to be careful, just in case."

"So you were expecting trouble?"

"I don't know. Maybe."

"Alex stayed here to protect your daughter and ended up taking the flak! He was murdered instead of you!"

Douglas tried to calm the situation. "No-one was murdered, Barbara. I was worried about the son turning up and hassling me and I did warn Mia not to let any strangers in until I got back but it all came to nothing."

"How do you know?" Barbara was nearly hysterical now. "When Alex was found dead on your driveway, did you not suspect this lad?"

"No, no, no. Believe me, Barbara. Patty is a lovely person from a respectable family. They don't go around murdering people. And anyway, don't you think that anyone wanting to finish me off would have double checked that they had the right person and not just clobber the first guy who happens to emerge from the house?"

"You're despicable, Dougie. Lucinda would have been so ashamed of you. An affair with a married woman! And the worst thing is, Alex has already been cremated! There's no chance for a further post mortem to see if those bruises could have been caused by a thump rather than the fall. I'm going to the police with this anyway. You should have mentioned it at the time."

"That is your prerogative, Barbara, but I assure you I would have done so myself if I had suspected any foul play. But I don't. I agree with the police. It was an accident."

"Fine! Well, we'll see about that."

Barbara retrieved her phone and stomped off across the road to her own house.

★★★

Patricia was still ignoring Dougie's calls and messages so she knew nothing about the tragedy that had befallen his family. Much as her heart ached for him, she could not bring herself to perpetuate the affair that had cost her so dearly because Kenneth had still not come home, had not even contacted her. And apart from the morning after his departure, when Sam had tricked her out of the house for a couple of hours so that Kenneth could gather up some belongings, she had not seen the rest of her family either. Only Molly remained unaware of what had happened as she continued to send cheery messages from across the world. Even her best friend was lost to her. Cathy

Cartwright was now Catherine Greenlees and she had made it quite clear that she did not approve of Patty's lifestyle, which Patty thought was a bit rich coming from someone who was no saint herself, given that her three offspring had all been fathered by different people. The last time Patty had seen her was almost five weeks ago when she had delivered a letter addressed to Cathy's son, Grant, which had come from Grant's biological father, via Dougie. Cathy had promised to pass it on, although there appeared to be some confusion as to whether she had done so. Anyway, it didn't matter. All that mattered was that she was alone in the world and feeling very sorry for herself.

She tried Kenneth's number again and again but he never answered. Leaving a message wasn't an option; she had to talk to him, hear his voice, and yet she had no idea what she was going to say to him. A simple apology would not suffice. Even a declaration that she would never betray him again was not likely to hold water. How could she make him understand that she had never stopped loving him? She poured a glass of water and swallowed yet another painkiller.

When Jasmine arrived, Patricia was fast asleep on the sofa and the house was eerily quiet. Tears came to Jasmine's eyes as she recalled the happy family life she had experienced growing up within those four walls. How could her mother have so carelessly thrown that away? Patricia's mobile was on the arm of the sofa. Jasmine picked it up and turned it on. She noticed the calls, dozens of them, made to her father's number and realised that he hadn't answered any of them. And suddenly it vibrated in her hand. A text message had just come through from DM. Jasmine opened it.

Patty please stop ignoring me. I need to know why your daughter wanted my address. It's important. D

Jasmine read it again.

Well, at least she's been ignoring him. That's good. But this message is about me!! He must have twigged that Grant didn't ask me for the address at all but why is it so important?

Suddenly aware of her mother stirring, Jasmine quickly deleted the text and replaced the phone where she had found it.

Patricia sat up and rubbed her eyes. "Jasmine, it's you! Oh, I'm so happy to see you."

"I don't want a feud developing between us, Mum. I'm worried about you."

Patricia stood up and hugged her daughter. "I've been so stupid," she avowed. "I've allowed an infatuation to get totally out of hand until I hardly realised what I was doing. It had become a sort of adventure for me. I never wanted to hurt your dad."

"You've hurt all of us," Jasmine declared, honestly.

Patricia gulped. "I know. If only your dad would give me another chance."

"Where is he, Mum?"

"I've no idea."

"Did he take his passport?"

"Yes."

"Well, you were supposed to be in Spain for his birthday. Maybe he went anyway."

"I've wondered about that myself."

"Have you tried to contact him?"

"All the time! He doesn't answer."

"Give it a few more days, Mum. He can't stay away forever. But you'll have a lot of making up to do."

"I do love him, Jasmine. That's why it hurts so much. You'll fall in love some day and you'll understand."

"Maybe I have already."

Patricia registered the radiance glowing from her daughter's dancing eyes and wished that things were different so that she could rejoice with her properly.

"That's wonderful," she said. "Who is it? Am I allowed to know?"

"Not yet. I'm not ready to tell anyone but I do love him, Mum, and I am so happy."

"I'll just have to be patient then. Thank you for calling round. I was so upset, thinking you had all deserted me. I know it's entirely my own fault but I will try to make amends. I promise."

Jasmine gave her mum another big hug and was on her way out when Patricia suddenly asked her how she had found out about Dougie in the first place. "Apparently it was you who alerted Sam and then he …"

Jasmine stared at her and saw red. Was her mum trying to blame her for the whole situation? Patricia realised that she had put her foot in it and stopped mid-sentence, but it was too late.

"So much for our big reconciliation, Mum!" She spat the words out, scornfully. "I've done my best to smooth things over but you have really blown it this time. What does it matter how I knew? What does matter is that you were fucking some other man instead of my dad. And yes, I am in love with someone now and I can tell you this – I will never cheat on him!"

She was out the front door like a shot.

Chapter 16

Kenneth came home that weekend. He just drove into his normal spot in the driveway, opened the door and stepped inside as though nothing had happened. He sat down in his customary armchair and folded his arms. Hearing the door close, Patricia looked out of the upstairs window and saw his car. Her heart started thumping. Tentatively she set down the towels she had been organising in the hot press and went down to greet him.

"Casey," she said simply. "Where have you been?"

"Spain," he told her. "I had a birthday to celebrate."

"You didn't answer your phone. I've been really worried."

"Can you blame me?"

"No. I'm so sorry. I've ended it, I promise."

"It's a bit late for that, Patricia."

"I'll do anything to make it up to you," she pleaded. "Think of the children. They'd be devastated if we break up."

"This is my home and I'm staying here," Kenneth retorted. "You can do whatever you like."

"Does that include staying here with you?"

"As long as we have separate rooms, I don't see why not. We can put on an outward show of togetherness for the neighbours. But I'm finished with you as a proper wife. You have betrayed my trust."

"Can I at least try to win it back?"

He gave her a withering glance and left the room.

Patricia sighed. At least he hadn't ordered her to leave. Surely, in time, she could bring him round. What did he mean by outward show of togetherness? Would she still cook his dinner, wash his clothes? Would they still sit down together for meals?

One step at a time. He's home, that's the main thing. What on earth has he been doing in Spain all this time? He doesn't have much of a tan.

★★★

Barbara did indeed go to the police with her husband's phone, insisting that he may have been the victim of foul play aimed at his brother and expressing her belief that the post mortem had not been adequately thorough. They paid Douglas and Mia a visit.

"We are still convinced that this was a sheer accident," the young police officer told them, "but we are surprised that you didn't mention anything at the time if you had, in fact, been expecting trouble that night. Can you explain your reasons to us now?"

"It's been blown out of all proportion," Douglas proclaimed. "This was a private matter between me and a family I am acquainted with in Belfast. I thought that there might be a bit of unpleasantness but nothing more than that, certainly not anything criminal."

The policeman consulted his notebook. "And you phoned your daughter after a conversation with a Mr Cartwright during the party you attended earlier that evening?"

"Yes, that's right. He is friendly with the same family. He lives in Belfast himself."

"Well, everything seems to be in order. Thank you for your co-operation. I'm sure you realise that we have to check these things out. Your sister-in-law is entitled to a full investigation. It's a difficult time for her."

"Of course," Douglas agreed. "You wouldn't be doing your job if you neglected to act on her information. It's just a bit embarrassing for me."

They shook hands and the matter appeared to be closed.

Chapter 17

The newly-weds chose Imogen's birthday on 20th October to announce to their family and friends that they had tied the knot two weeks ago and, to add to their happiness, that they were expecting a baby in May. Her parents were not surprised at the low-key event, knowing that Imogen never had been one for pomp and ceremony. Her brother, Vincent, reminded her that he would be a parent before her, his girlfriend, Jane, being due in February, and then remarked that he was delighted the two cousins would be able to grow up together as friends of the same age. Catherine and Mark were over the moon at the prospect of a grandchild in the family but Rebecca and Robyn were a bit miffed at missing out on a proper wedding reception. Alastair congratulated his cousin and mysteriously hinted that he now had a girlfriend too. And of course Gertrude privately decided that she would not let such an occasion go unmarked. She would organise one of her famous parties forthwith.

Jillian and Bradley were next to be told. "You're married before me?" Jillian screeched in a mixture of surprise and jealousy. "And a baby too!" But she couldn't stay cross with her friend for long and the two of them ran downstairs to spread the word to Jasmine whilst Grant and Bradley had a celebratory drink. Jasmine was amazed that they had managed to keep it so quiet.

"Sorry we missed your party," Imogen told her, "but the wedding was that very same day. How did it go?"

"Best day of my life," Jasmine proclaimed with a happy sigh and dreamy expression.

"Not Alastair?" Imogen gasped, immediately putting two and two together.

Jasmine smiled and nodded. "How did you know?"

"He hinted just now that he had a girlfriend."

"Alastair? You and Alastair?" Jillian was flabbergasted. "You never said, you dark horse! I thought it was your painting he was interested in."

"That and other things," she answered coyly.

"So what time did he go home?"

"That's for me to know and for you to guess."

"Wow! Can we tell Grant and Bradley?" Before waiting for an answer her two friends ran back upstairs to do just that.

"Bring Grant in when you come back down so I can congratulate the two of you properly," Jasmine called to Imogen. "Can I tell Sam?"

"Yes, no problem. You'd be doing me a favour. I'd rather he knew before I see him again."

As they spoke, Jasmine noticed a car pulling up outside. Two policemen got out and walked towards the building.

"We're looking for Miss Jasmine Campbell," one of them said quite pleasantly.

"Oh God, what have I done, parked on a double yellow or something?" Jasmine gabbled. "You'd better come in."

She led them into her sitting room and tried to calm herself. "Seriously, what is this about?" she asked.

One of the officers introduced himself and his colleague and then got straight to the point. "We are acting on behalf of the police force in Scotland," he explained. "They have asked us to make some enquiries in relation to a recent incident in Edinburgh."

"What sort of incident?" Jasmine queried, as the text she had deleted at her mother's house jumped into her mind.

"A man died in questionable circumstances," the policeman revealed, which really freaked her out.

"Died?" she repeated. "What can this possibly have to do with me?"

"Hopefully nothing," the officer told her, "but we have to check it out. You recently sent a text message to a Mr Douglas McKendrick, asking him for his address. We need to know why you wanted it."

"He's dead?" Jasmine exclaimed, her face draining of colour.

"No, the dead man is someone else, but there is a connection. I'm asking you again why you wanted this man's address."

Jasmine started to tremble with fear. "I told him why. A friend of mine wanted to send him a thank you card."

"Would that be a Mr Grant Cartwright?"

"Yes." It was a mere whisper.

"We have it on good authority that Mr Cartwright did not make that request, that he already knew Mr McKendrick's address and had, in fact, been in his house. Indeed Mr McKendrick and Mr Cartwright were socialising together on the very day that this man died."

"I made it up," Jasmine admitted. She was now shaking like a leaf.

"So, can you tell me the real reason why you wanted Mr McKendrick's address?"

"My brother asked me for it," she blurted out.

"Would that be Mr Sam Campbell?"

Once again her answer was a mere whisper. "Yes." These guys had certainly done their homework.

Jasmine bit her lip. What on earth was this all about? "Please tell me who died," she begged. "I don't know what it can possibly have to do with us."

"How did you and your brother know Mr McKendrick?" the police officer asked without answering her question.

"I didn't know him. And Sam only met him once. He was …, he was …, he was in a relationship with our mother. We tried to warn him off."

"So you were both angry with him?"

There was a loud knocking at the door. "That will be my friends from upstairs," Jasmine managed to say. "They're celebrating a marriage. I asked them to call."

"You had better say hello," one of the officers approved.

Jasmine opened the door and indicated to her friends that she had company.

"Is that a police car?" Jillian observed, looking out at the car park.

"Are you in any trouble?" Grant asked. "Can I help?"

Jasmine burst into tears and Grant immediately took over, sending Imogen back upstairs with the others. He marched into the room and introduced himself. "If you don't mind, I would like to sit in on the rest of this interview," he said with an authoritative air. "What has Jasmine done to deserve this harassment?"

"Did you say your name was Grant Cartwright?" one of the policemen said with a smirk on his face.

"Yes, that is correct," said Grant.

"Well then, to start with, she has tried to implicate you in a case which involves the death of a gentleman in Scotland."

"I did not!" Jasmine shouted vehemently. "I told you I made that bit up."

"But you were in Scotland on Saturday the first of October, Sir?"

"I was. That was the date of my grandfather's birthday party."

"Can I ask where you were after half past ten that night?"

"In my hotel."

"Can anyone verify that?"

Grant looked from the policeman to Jasmine and back to the policeman who was waiting for an answer. "I can't believe you asked me that. What on earth is going on?"

"Let's go back to the beginning," the police officer said. He reiterated what had already taken place before Grant's arrival. Then he addressed Jasmine again.

"So you gave Mr McKendrick's address to your brother. What happened next?"

"What do you mean, what happened?"

"What did your brother do with the information? Did he travel to Scotland?"

"No, definitely not."

"Why did he want the address?"

There was nothing else for it; she had to tell the truth. "He passed it on to our father," she mumbled.

"And did *he* travel to Scotland?"

Jasmine still didn't know who had died. But it wasn't Douglas McKendrick. She had opened a text message from him a few days ago. She looked imploringly at Grant for support but he was as confused as she was.

"I'm not sure where my father is," she said in total honesty. "He and my mother are going through a bad patch and they are currently living apart."

The officer then repeated his question to Grant. Could anyone verify his whereabouts on the evening in question? Grant was horrified.

"My only connection to this man is that he put me in touch with some of my family who had been estranged to me. I was indebted to him for that although I have to admit I felt awkward, knowing that he was in an extra-marital relationship with my friend's mother."

"That friend being Sam Campbell?"

"Yes, Sam, and also Jasmine here."

"And who told you of that relationship?"

"It was Sam. He mentioned it one day while we were playing golf, about a month ago."

The two policemen stood up and thanked them both for their information. "We will need to speak to your brother and your father," the more senior of the two told Jasmine. Then he smiled. "To be honest," he admitted, "the police over there think it was just an accident. We're just double-checking all the facts before closing the case."

★★★

Bradley watched the police car driving off. Then he, along with Jillian and Imogen went back downstairs to find out what was going on. They found Jasmine in floods of tears and Grant trying his best to console her but without much success.

"Should I ring Sam and warn him?" she spluttered. "I remember him saying that dad did threaten to kill the man."

"But that's just a turn of phrase," Grant comforted her. "He didn't mean it literally. People say things like that all the time. And anyway, they said that it's not him, it's someone else who has died."

The horrified looks from their friends brought about an explanation from Grant about what had just happened.

"If you warn Sam that they're coming, they might think that you've something to hide," cautioned Imogen.

"Maybe we have but we don't know it yet."

"You're panicking, Jasmine. Just let the guys do their job. It'll turn out to be nothing to do with any of us."

The drama had somewhat spoilt the celebratory mood for Imogen and Grant and they set off to see other friends, a little subdued. Bradley and Jillian stayed with

Jasmine for a while until she felt calmer. She was on the verge of phoning her brother, both to warn him about the police and to tell him about Imogen's marriage, when her own mobile started to ring. It was her father.

"Hello Sweetheart," he began, "I just want to let you know that I'm back home."

"Dad! At last! Where have you been?"

"I went to Spain," he told her. "I needed to do some thinking."

"Spain! Oh thank God." She turned to her friends. "He was in Spain," she gushed.

"Well, there you are," Jillian smiled. "Problem solved. We'll leave you to chat to him." She and Bradley went back home.

Kenneth sounded a bit bewildered. "Why all the excitement?" he probed. "You surely didn't think I would stay away for ever. Your mother and I have some issues to work through but it's nothing to do with you or Sam or Molly. I would never desert you."

Jasmine was feeling elated and started to babble. "I know that, Dad. It's just that I was worrying in case you'd gone to Edinburgh. The police have just been here, questioning me, and now they're heading to Sam's."

"The police?"

"Yes, they said they were making enquiries about a death over in Scotland. They think it was an accident but they have to make sure. It was awful!"

"Why were they questioning you?" He sounded really angry.

"It's got something to do with Douglas McKendrick."

"Well, if someone has killed him, I can't say I'll be sorry," bluffed Kenneth.

"No, it wasn't him. I don't know who it was. But it doesn't matter now. As long as you can prove you were in Spain, they'll know you didn't do it."

"You mean they suspect me? Of killing someone? You can't be serious."

"I don't know. I think they might."

There was silence for a moment. Jasmine thought they had been disconnected. She was just about to put the phone down when she heard his voice again. It sounded a bit shaky. "Don't let it worry you, Sweetheart. I'll look into it. And by the way, Spain was lovely even though I was on my own. But I'm home now and I'll see you soon."

"OK, bye Dad. It's good to hear your voice. I hope you and Mum aren't going to split up."

"We'll see. Bye."

★★★

Kenneth threw his phone down on the bed and racked his brain. Thank God he had phoned Jasmine in the nick of time. No-one must find out that he visited Scotland before travelling to Spain. And thank God he had sold his Rolex to that guy in the pawn shop. He didn't get anywhere near its proper value but he did get enough to make ends meet so that he hadn't used his credit card or his phone or anything else that would give away his location. Except for his airline ticket. He would have to bluff his way out of that one.

It's just a case of making my holiday in Spain so obvious that they don't even think of checking when I bought my ticket or how I paid for it. I knew it was too good to be true – that news bulletin that dismissed it as an accident. They must have changed their minds. But why? What evidence could they have found? Circumstantial only, I would think. They won't be able to prove a thing. As long as I stay calm, stick to my story. I wonder what Sam is telling them! Probably best to own up to what I said to him. Everyone says things like that in the heat of the moment. I just need plenty of Spanish souvenirs. And Patricia on my side!

Ten minutes later he went downstairs in search of his wife.

"There you are," he said amicably, finding her tending to her house plants. "Can we talk?"

Patricia looked up in surprise. This was a welcome change after three days of icy coolness.

"I'd like us to get back on track," he told her, "if you really mean it about not seeing that man ever again."

"Really? You're ready to forgive me." Patricia breathed a huge sigh of relief.

"Let's give it a try, at least," he proposed.

They shared a tentative embrace and then sat down together to watch a film on television. It was almost two hours before Kenneth heard the expected sound of the doorbell. "It's almost nine o'clock," he remarked coolly. "Who would be visiting at this time of the evening?" He opened the door and pretended to express surprise. It was two young police officers.

"Would you be Mr Kenneth Campbell?" one of them asked.

"I am indeed. How can I help you?"

"We'd like to come in and ask you a few questions," he said.

Kenneth led them into the lounge and turned off the television. "This is my wife, Patricia," he said. "Now, how can we help you? Have there been burglaries in the area again?"

"Nothing like that," the more senior officer declared. Then he hesitated. "I have to say I'm surprised to find you in. We had been led to believe that you and your wife were currently living apart."

"Gosh," Kenneth bluffed, "is nothing private these days? We did have a bit of a spat but everything's fine again. We're giving it another go. So, not a burglary then?"

"You sound very upbeat for someone who was threatening to kill a certain gentleman just two weeks ago."

"I beg your pardon?"

"We have just spoken to your son, Sam. According to him you were heading over to Scotland to confront a Mr Douglas McKendrick."

Kenneth laughed. "I may have said that in the heat of the moment."

"But there *has* been a killing in Edinburgh," the policeman now revealed.

Patricia gasped and went pale. "Dougie is dead?" she cried in horror.

"No, Mrs Campbell. The deceased man is not Douglas McKendrick, but his brother, Alex."

"What happened to him?"

"That is what we are trying to ascertain." He looked directly at Kenneth. "We believe you have been away from home, Sir. Can you please tell us where you went?"

"Spain," Kenneth said without flinching.

"Can you prove that?"

"Yes, of course. But you can't really suspect me of killing someone."

"I'm sorry. Evidence does point to the man having had an unfortunate accident but we have to check every lead. Just show us some proof that you were in Spain and we'll be on our way."

Kenneth left the room and came back with some papers. "I'm only home a couple of days," he explained, "and my boarding pass was still in my coat pocket." He handed the document to one of the policemen who immediately confirmed that it was valid proof he had been booked on that flight but not necessarily evidence that he had actually travelled. Kenneth remained calm and immediately produced a receipt for two bottles of gin purchased at the airport.

"What about the outward flight?" the officer then asked him. "Would you still have that one too?"

Kenneth said that no, he must have thrown it in the bin at his hotel.

"Some other proof of your arrival date then?"

He scratched his head as though trying to think and then, with an Oscar-winning performance, he remembered something and took out his wallet. "Ah, here's the leaflet that accompanied the key card for my room. It has the dates of my stay on it."

He handed over the small envelope, fervently hoping that the alteration to the date he had made following Jasmine's call would not be detected. It had been easy enough to change the number eleven into the number one by simply drawing a box round the date and making sure the line went straight through the first digit. His luck seemed to be in.

"That seems to be in order, Mr Campbell. Did you enjoy your stay?"

"Beautiful place," Kenneth gushed. "Take a look at these." And he started to display a series of digital images on his phone, including the odd selfie here and there, absolute evidence that he had just come home from Barcelona with its unmistakeable Gaudi architecture. "I'll enjoy it even more next time when Patricia comes with me." He patted her on the knee.

"Good to know you've resolved your differences," the young officer said, smiling, as he got up to leave.

"Something about nothing," Kenneth agreed. "A minor indiscretion, isn't that right, Darling. That's awful about the man's brother though."

"Yes, a shocking accident. Well, we'll say goodnight. Thank you for your co-operation."

Kenneth breathed a silent sigh of relief. Now he had to make sure that Patricia didn't find out about Jasmine warning him in advance; she might wonder why he hadn't mentioned it and become suspicious.

"I think we could both do with a cup of tea," he suggested to her as he came back into the room and Patricia was only too pleased to go and make one. It was a sign that things were slowly returning to normal. Whilst she was in the kitchen, Kenneth pretended to speak to Jasmine on the phone, telling her in a loud voice that he was home from his trip, and then really did ring Sam, letting him know that he was back and that he had just had a visit from the police. When Sam tried to apologise for dropping him in it, Kenneth assured him that he had done nothing wrong in telling the truth and quietly asked him to give his sister an update. Patricia came back in with the tea.

"I just phoned Jasmine and Sam to bring them up to speed," he announced casually. "They are both glad I'm home and hoping that we can work things out. What about Molly? Do I need to tell her anything?" Patricia shook her head.

"Molly never knew that anything was amiss," she said.

"Good. Now let's have that tea."

Chapter 18

On Friday evening Jasmine collected Alastair from the garden centre where he worked and they went home together to her flat. She had spent most of the week on a training course because the dental practice was being expanded and updated with a lot of new technology being brought in. She was glad it was the weekend and didn't want to see another computer screen for at least a month. It had also been a roller-coaster of a week emotionally with her parents seemingly back together, after her mother's affair coming to light, her father's disappearance, which had turned out to be a solitary sojourn in Spain, and insinuated allegations from the police about her father, brother or friend being involved in a suspicious killing in Scotland. She sat down on the sofa and exhaled with a huge and very loud sigh.

"You need a glass of wine," Alastair said, walking towards the kitchen to pour her one. "It'll help you unwind."

"Thanks," she muttered dreamily. "That would be lovely." She had picked up the day's post from the hallway on her way in and took a look through it while she waited for her wine to appear. Useless fliers and other junk mail as usual, but in amongst it all, a brown envelope addressed to her. She opened it and slid out the official looking letter.

"I hope that's not something to upset you," Alastair said kindly, setting her glass on the table.

"On the contrary," she exclaimed, "it's confirmation that the police have sent a report to their colleagues in Scotland, informing them that they have no reason whatsoever to suspect anyone from over here of being involved in the death of Mr Alex McKendrick and that consequently the case has been closed. It says that copies of this letter have also been sent to Kenneth Campbell, Sam Campbell and Grant Cartwright and that Douglas McKendrick, Mia McKendrick and Barbara McKendrick have all been informed."

"Hurray," Alastair cheered. "They had more or less told you that anyway but it's good to have it in writing." As Jasmine picked up her glass and took a sip of the refreshing Pinot Grigio, he sat down beside her and smiled. Then he took the glass from her hand, set it back on the table beside his own and took her in his arms. "I look forward to the weekend so much now," he breathed. "I love spending time with you." As he kissed her tenderly on the lips all the tension of the week started to ease away. She kissed him back and held him close, her heart almost bursting with happiness.

"Can you stay over tonight?" she whispered, licking her lips seductively. They hadn't slept together since that first encounter three weeks ago.

"Just try and stop me," he replied, nuzzling into her neck. "I've come properly prepared this time."

Jasmine closed her eyes and swooned. She could hardly wait until bedtime but somehow managed to convince herself that the agony of waiting would make it all the better. "Let's finish our wine," she said, "and I'll make us something to eat. Why don't you paint me that picture you've promised?"

Alastair had dabbled a bit with oils and water colours but, since gaining access to Jasmine's studio, he was developing this into a real hobby and proving that he had impressive artistic talent. He had promised to paint her something bright and colourful for her bedroom wall. For the next couple of hours they cooked and kissed, painted and kissed, ate dinner and kissed. Jasmine was in seventh heaven.

About eight o'clock they heard the doorbell ring. It was Maggie and Lawrence who explained that they were personally delivering some of their wedding invitations. Jasmine invited them in for a drink.

"Just a quick one, then," Maggie said, accepting the hospitality. "We want to see Jillian and Bradley too and then fit in a couple of other friends as well."

Alastair took Lawrence in to see his painting. Jasmine opened the envelope her friend had handed her and drew out the printed card. Maggie watched as her initial smile suddenly faded and her finger involuntarily touched her lips in a doubtful manner. It was clear that there was something wrong. She gave her a questioning look.

"Sorry," Jasmine faltered. "It's a beautiful card, Maggie." She hesitated, looking again at the names inscribed on it: Miss Jasmine Campbell and Mr Alastair Cartwright. "It's just that Alastair's name is wrong."

Maggie looked at the card over her friend's shoulder. "I knew I'd spell something wrongly," she joked, "after me doing a magazine article all about spelling! Sorry, I know there are various ways of spelling Alastair; I thought I'd got the right one. I'll do you another one."

"No, Alastair is fine," Jasmine told her. "It's Cartwright. That's not his name."

Maggie looked confused. "Oh, sorry, I just presumed. I mean, he's Grant's cousin. I thought they were all Cartwrights. The fact that they all live with their mothers and there are no dads."

"That's true for Grant, Rebecca and Robyn," Jasmine agreed, "although Robyn is apparently now calling herself Cartwright-Greenlees since their mother got married this summer. Grant has recently met his real dad but he's sticking to Cartwright, the name he has had all his life. However, it's different for Alastair. He did have a dad and his mother was happily married to him. He died."

"Gosh, I didn't know that. Thank goodness he hasn't seen it yet. Give it back to me and I'll do you another one. What *is* his surname?"

"Henning," said Jasmine. "Alastair Henning. His father was an American and the rest of his Henning relations are over in New York so it's just Alastair and his mum keeping the name alive on this side of the pond."

"Henning?" Maggie echoed nervously. "His father was American? But he died? I had no idea. How long ago did this happen?"

"Alastair was just a little boy, about five years old at the time. It was a hit and run accident. His father was killed and he was left with a bad leg and brain damage, as you know. Sure you tried to warn me against starting a relationship with him. I thought you knew his history."

Alastair and Lawrence emerged from the studio where they had been viewing the work in progress. Maggie grabbed her fiancé's arm. "Time we were away," she ordered with an urgency that surprised him. "I'll get that fixed for you, Jasmine."

They were out through the door in a flash and headed straight for their car.

"I thought they were going up to see Jillian and Bradley," Jasmine said, confused.

"Never mind," Alastair riposted. "Let's lock up and turn off the lights before anyone else disturbs us."

Within ten minutes the young lovers were in bed, hungry for each other yet still relatively inexperienced in sexual matters. They held each other close and kissed.

"I love you, Jasmine," Alastair breathed, "I love everything about you." Tenderly he touched her face, her neck, her breasts, her nipples, her tummy, his fingers gliding ever so gently over her smooth, creamy skin.

"Oh Alastair, I love you too," she whispered, breathlessly, willing him to continue the journey downwards, downwards and beyond. And he did. And it was so, so, blissful and so perfect and so fulfilling until she cried out because it was unbearable and yet she still wanted more. And then her own hands began to explore, to manipulate, to titillate and she felt his body respond to her touch. At last, when they joined together as one, the overwhelming joy they experienced surpassed everything they had dared to anticipate. They fell asleep in one another's arms, blissfully happy and never wanting to be apart, ever again.

★★★

Maggie sat in the car outside her mother's house. She was agitated and tearful. "It's too late to uninvite them to the wedding," she wailed, "but I had no idea who he was. My dad killed his dad and ruined his childhood. He has brain damage. He had to attend a special school because of his learning difficulties. He's still not allowed to drive."

Lawrence tried his best to comfort her. "You suffered too, Mags. Your childhood wasn't plain sailing. None of it was your fault."

"What do I tell Mum? She's starting to look happy again, happier than I've seen her in years, and this is going to set her back to square one."

"Do you need to tell her anything?"

Maggie thought about that for a moment. "I could just write another invitation myself but what about the place cards and the guest lists for the tables? She'll see his name on the day and that'll be even worse."

"It's just a name. Are you sure she would make the connection?"

"I did, straightaway. It's engrained in my mind. She'll be the same."

"Then let's get it over with." They got out of the car and went inside.

Greta was sitting at the kitchen table, half-way through a Sudoku puzzle. She looked up in delight at the unexpected visitors but Maggie's eyes were still red and her face still a bit blotchy so her expression soon turned to one of concern. "Is something wrong?" she asked gently, setting down her pencil.

"That letter you told me about," Maggie faltered, "is there any way they could trace who sent it? You said you did it anonymously."

Greta looked startled. "Are you still tormenting yourself about that?" she asked with a heavy sigh.

"I'll tell you why in a minute. Are you sure you didn't identify yourself or give any obvious clues?"

"I signed it 'Marguerite'."

Maggie gave a wry smile. That was a pet name the family sometimes used for her mum on account of the fact that she had been born in France and still had quite an affinity with the country. She said nothing for a moment.

"Why does it matter?" Greta persisted.

"A member of the Henning family has been invited to the wedding."

Greta gasped. "That's not possible," she countered. "The invitations are all out. I wrote them myself."

"It's Jasmine's boyfriend, Alastair. I thought his name was Cartwright but it's not. It's Henning."

"An unfortunate coincidence," Greta concurred, "but I'm sure there are other families with the same name. This man was an American."

"That's right. He was Alastair's father. And Alastair himself was badly injured in the same accident. He still bears the scars today. He suffered brain damage."

Maggie started to cry again and Lawrence put a soothing arm around her. Greta looked stricken. She knew that a son had also been involved but had not been aware of the seriousness of his injuries. "Do they know it was your father?" she whispered.

"No."

"Thank God."

"I can't uninvite them."

"Of course not."

"I said I'd bring them another invitation."

"I'll write it for you now."

As Greta wrote the name on the card, the tears also came to her own eyes. It was only about six weeks since she had learnt the truth herself, the truth about how her husband had mown down Mr Henning and injured his son. He had driven on and had never been caught, only owning up to her on his death-bed. Both she and Maggie had been plagued by his erratic and destructive behaviour in the intervening years as he had struggled unsuccessfully with his shame and guilt.

Greta handed Maggie the new card. "Just apologise for the mistake and play it cool," she advised. "If you say nothing and I say nothing, no-one will ever know."

"And you won't mind him being there?"

"Why should we mind? The lad has done nothing to be ashamed of, quite the contrary. I learnt how to have a brass neck a long time ago."

★★★

Jasmine's flat was in darkness. "Just leave it in the post-box," suggested Lawrence. "You can give her a ring tomorrow." Then he added, "Those two have the right idea. Time we were in bed too. It's been a stressful couple of hours."

They shared a warm embrace and headed home.

Chapter 19

Although Patricia knew that Dougie had a brother living nearby, she had never actually met him. However, she knew that they were close and she felt sad for him, knowing that Alex had died. But she didn't dare make contact, not now that Kenneth was in a forgiving frame of mind. She wasn't sure what had brought about the transformation but she wasn't going to analyse it too carefully. After four nights of non-communication and separate rooms they were once again living properly as man and wife and the affair that had threatened to ruin their marriage was hardly mentioned. When the letter had arrived on Friday morning, informing them that there would be no charges against any of the family in relation to the unexplained death, they had both promised to put the whole sad episode behind them. Kenneth was working extra hours to make up for the time he had lost with his unscheduled holiday and Patricia was coping by keeping herself busy.

Arriving home on Monday at her customary hour around tea-time, and knowing that Kenneth wouldn't be in until about eight o'clock, Patricia decided to do some extra laundry that had been building up. She went upstairs and emptied the linen basket onto the bedroom floor and then proceeded to sort the garments into white or pale-coloured items, black or very dark clothing, and red things, which she always did separately, ever since she had inadvertently dyed some of Kenneth's underwear a rather nice shade of pink. She viewed the three piles and decided to start with the dark wash as it appeared to be the largest. Downstairs she loaded the items into the machine, one at a time, opening buttons, closing zips and checking pockets. Nothing was as annoying as a stray tissue getting into a dark wash. It was next to impossible to remove the tiny white fragments from the accompanying shirts and trousers. The last item to go in was a pair of casual trousers which she hadn't seen Kenneth wearing for some time. She put her hand into the pocket and pulled out a few scraps of paper. At least they weren't tissues. But then she took a closer look. They were receipts.

Patricia sat down and stared at the evidence in her hands. The first receipt was for petrol, paid for in cash, from a garage in central Scotland. It was dated the fourth of October. The second one, bearing the same date, was for a meal purchased at a road-side café about fifty miles further north. Kenneth had told the police that he travelled to Spain on the first day of the month, the same day that he had disappeared from home. Patricia started to sweat profusely. The implications of her find were so obvious. She opened a drawer where she kept personal belongings in the form of family photos, notebooks, recipe cards and the like and placed the two receipts in the centre of an old diary, then checked her watch and saw that she still had an hour before Kenneth was due home. She went to his study and turned on his computer. She knew his password. They had never had occasion before to mistrust one another. Within a few minutes Patricia had all the proof she needed. Kenneth had purchased an airline ticket to travel from Scotland to Spain on the eleventh of October. No wonder she hadn't noticed much of a tan. He'd only been there for four days. Turning the computer off and leaving everything exactly as she had found it, Patricia left the room and went back downstairs.

★★★

Gertrude had been afraid to broach the subject with Catherine but she decided now that she could put it off no longer. Grant and Imogen had been married for over three weeks and, with it being Hallowe'en night, the sound of fireworks and the excited voices of neighbourhood children in fancy dress were putting her in the mood for a party.

"I want to celebrate Grant's wedding," she told her daughter. "How would you feel about me inviting Mr Ferguson?"

Catherine had almost expected the request so she wasn't too surprised. However, she did try to stall any decision by pointing out that her son and daughter-in-law had deliberately married in secret because they didn't want any fuss.

"I realise that," Gertrude agreed, "and I respect their right to avoid all the formality involved, especially after what happened the last time." She was of course referring to Grant's first wedding to Zoe, who had been terminally ill at the time. "But we still need to mark the occasion and, now that he's formed a bond with his father, I think he should be there."

"You're quite right. I won't stand in your way." Gertrude had been ready for an argument. She stared at Catherine, open-mouthed. "Mark and I will help you to organise it. I can't put off seeing the man forever. He's part of Grant's life now."

"Good for you," Gertrude managed at last with a grin. "That is such a sensible attitude."

The two women sat down together to discuss the proposed event, where and when they would have it, who else would be invited, and whether they would keep it secret from the happy couple or include them in the arrangements. In the end they agreed to keep it a small family affair so that it wouldn't turn into the wedding reception they had decided against in the first place. Gertrude phoned around a few local venues and managed to book a room for a Saturday afternoon, two weeks away. She was told that it could accommodate up to thirty-five people. Then Catherine phoned Grant and told him to keep the date free; she and Mark were taking him and his bride out for lunch.

Chapter 20

The list was chopped and changed several times until both Gertrude and Catherine were happy with it. Thirty-three people would fit into that room nicely; they had been together to check it out. There was a good balanced age-range, divided fairly equally gender-wise. Hopefully it was a group that would gel successfully and create a party atmosphere. Gertrude ran her eye over it one more time.

Gertrude herself, the groom's grandmother;

Catherine and Mark, Grant's mother and step-father;

Grant and Imogen, the newly-weds;

Rebecca and Robyn, Grant's sisters, and Robyn's boyfriend, **Jack**;

Thomasina, Catherine's sister and Grant's aunt;

Alastair, Grant's cousin, and his girlfriend, **Jasmine**;

Daphne and Adrian, Grant's in-laws from his marriage to Zoe;

Erica, Zoe's sister;

Bradley, honorary family member, and his fiancée, **Jillian**;

Joanna and Keith, Imogen's parents;

Joanna's mum and dad;

Vincent, Imogen's half-brother, and his girlfriend, **Jane**;

Holly, one of Imogen's best friends (along with Jillian);

Dorothy and Robert, Jillian and Vincent's parents;

Cameron Ferguson and his wife, **Lauren**;

Angus Ferguson, Grant's new-found grandfather;

James and Henry, Grant's new-found half-brothers;

Patty Campbell and her husband, **Kenneth**;

Douglas McKendrick

They had deliberated over those last three names for some time, but yes, they definitely deserved to be invited. Catherine's friend, Patty, had been instrumental in helping to bring Grant and Cameron together, and Douglas McKendrick had been the link. Hopefully everyone would be able to come. It had been purposefully timed early in the day so that the Scottish contingent would be able to get a flight home and not have the expense of staying over.

And now the day of the party had arrived. Grant and Imogen had been told that lunch would be at two o'clock. Everyone else had been asked to arrive half an hour earlier so that even latecomers would be in situ well before the guests of honour made an appearance. Gertrude, Catherine and Mark manned the door to greet their friends as they came in and point them in the direction of the drinks table. As usual, Gertrude, her looks belying her seventy-four years, was resplendent in a rich, red and gold outfit, set off by her customary, jangly beads and bracelets. Everyone else had been asked to dress casually.

First to arrive were Joanna and Keith, accompanied by Dorothy and Robert, all best friends again after twenty-five years of the two couples avoiding one another. They were accompanied by Imogen's maternal grandparents.

"You've beaten us to it," Keith said amicably, shaking Mark by the hand. "This is a lovely idea."

"We're delighted you could come," Mark replied, but before there was time for any prolonged conversation the door opened again and in came three more guests, people the four friends didn't recognise. Catherine immediately made the introductions. It was Zoe's family. Joanna and Daphne shared an awkward glance and then gave each other an emotional embrace that said more than a thousand words. They walked off together towards the drinks table, followed by their husbands and Joanna's elderly but remarkably agile parents. Gertrude chatted to Erica for a few minutes whilst Dorothy turned again to Catherine.

"It was really kind of you to invite us," she said smiling.

"You're very welcome," Catherine replied. "Sure your son is Imogen's brother and your daughter is engaged to our Bradley. You're part of the family now on two counts."

Thomasina arrived next along with Alastair and Jasmine, with Bradley, Jillian and Holly at their heels, and they were followed swiftly by Rebecca, Robyn and

Jack. Rebecca and Erica remembered meeting each other at Catherine and Mark's wedding back in the summer and were glad to renew the acquaintance, especially since nearly everyone else was part of a couple. They all moved forward into the room where there was now quite an excited buzz of conversation and laughter. Gertrude looked around and counted. "Ten more to arrive," she remarked. She looked at her watch. It was only twenty past one. Things were going nicely.

It was five minutes before the door opened again and two couples arrived at once. Vincent and Jane were warmly greeted by Gertrude who recalled that the pair hadn't turned up the last time they were supposed to meet. Vincent had been involved in a serious incident at work that day, an incident that had claimed the lives of his two colleagues. "It's lovely to see you looking so strong and healthy," she told him, "and you too, Jane." She gently patted Jane's baby bump and congratulated them on the pregnancy. At the same time Catherine and Mark were welcoming Patty and Kenneth. Catherine had always known her friend as Patty.

"I was so happy to be invited to this," Patty gushed. "Nearly everyone else here is family."

"If it wasn't for you, I wouldn't have been able to help Grant find his father," Catherine pointed out. "Our friendship goes back a long way." She noticed Kenneth's face clouding over. "But enough about that," she added quickly. "Maybe we will be family some day."

Patty nodded. "Your nephew and our daughter. Don't they make a lovely couple! I could hardly believe the way Alastair has come on when Jasmine brought him in recently. I remember him as a little boy with a limp and limited speech."

"Thomasina is over the moon about it," Catherine agreed. "She has spent her life worrying about him. There she is over there in the cream and purple top."

Patricia and Kenneth headed over to reintroduce themselves.

"Maybe I should have warned her about Douglas McKendrick coming," Catherine muttered under her breath. "I'm not sure how the land lies there at the moment."

Mark giggled. "I hope we're not in for fireworks," he said in jest.

With twenty minutes to spare, the Scottish guests all arrived en masse.

★★★

Kenneth was still chatting to Thomasina when Patricia glanced over at the small crowd entering the room and saw him. Her lover. Here in the same room as her. Here in the same room as her husband who had tried to kill him. Here in the same room as her husband who had in fact murdered his brother six weeks ago and had got away with it. She went weak at the knees. Douglas hadn't spotted her yet. "I'll just do some mingling," she managed to say. "Lovely to meet you again, Thomasina."

As she wandered over towards the new arrivals, she was aware of some friendly banter going on between Cathy and the man who was obviously Grant's father. She could see the resemblance. There was also an older man and two lads with a fair-haired woman who was clearly their mother. They were all joining in the fun, as were Mark and Gertrude. It was all very good-natured. And there was Dougie. He suddenly caught a glimpse of her out of the corner of his eye and beamed with pleasure. He came straight over to her.

"What an unexpected delight," he declared affectionately. "I had no idea that you'd be here. I was going to try to get in touch later. You've been avoiding me."

"Shh," hissed Patty, nervously. "Kenneth is here too."

Douglas took the hint and lowered his voice. "I've missed you," he told her. "Did your son spill the beans? I suppose you should be quite proud of his skills. He'd make a good detective."

Patty was momentarily baffled by this remark. "What do you mean?" she asked him.

"Following you on the plane that night. Catching us in a compromising situation. The way he threatened to keep his son from you. I've been desperate to know how it all panned out but you haven't answered my calls." He paused for a moment and then added, "I'm so sorry for all that business with the police. It was Barbara. She insisted on all leads being checked out. But it probably led to Sam telling his dad about me. Would I be right?"

"Can we talk about this later?" Patty whispered. "I have to get back to Kenneth before he realises who you are."

She walked away. Luckily, Jasmine had engaged her father in a conversation with Bradley and Jillian, reminding him that they were her neighbours from the flat upstairs. He was busy chatting and didn't notice his wife's clandestine encounter with one of the Scottish 'relatives'. But Patricia was still anxious. Those tell-tale receipts were still inside that old diary. She couldn't decide what to do about the situation, if anything.

★★★

"Something's going on," remarked Imogen, as they approached the steps leading up to the hotel foyer and reception. "That's my dad's car."

"I noticed Aunt Thomasina's too, close to where we parked," Grant admitted. "So it's maybe not just Mum and Mark." They climbed the steps and there was Mark, patiently waiting for them at reception. "Good timing," he remarked approvingly as he checked his watch and saw that it was two o'clock on the dot. "We're down this corridor." The main restaurant was to the left but Mark turned right and headed off without explanation. The young newly-weds exchanged a puzzled glance and followed him.

The first two people Grant saw when Mark led them into the function room were Catherine and Cameron, standing together and smiling a welcome. Opposite them stood Joanna, Keith and Lauren. They could not believe their eyes.

"I hope you're not angry," Mark said triumphantly, enjoying the role he had been asked to play.

"Angry!" exclaimed Grant. "This is the most wonderful surprise."

166

Imogen allowed all six of them to give her a hug and then she looked around to see who else was in the room. All Grant's family, and her own, her best friends and one or two people she didn't recognise.

"You don't mind, Darling?" Joanna asked tentatively, because her daughter still hadn't spoken.

"Thank you," she breathed in reply, shaking her head. "This is perfect."

"I know you didn't want a wedding reception."

"We didn't want a formal wedding with all the arguments and fuss. But there's nothing wrong with a party!" She gave her mum another hug.

As Grant also now registered who else was present, his gaze landed on Daphne and a lump came to his throat. How nice of her to come. Taking Imogen by the hand, he went straight over to her and introduced them. Daphne embraced them both and whispered her congratulations, Erica too. Adrian shook his hand. Grant then hugged his grandfather and welcomed his young half-brothers whilst Imogen chided Jillian and Holly for their stealthiness in concealing the arrangements. But she was joking; she couldn't have been happier. Catherine and Cameron were still standing by the door, laughing and sharing amusing anecdotes with their spouses without a trace of awkwardness. Grant had never dreamt that he would ever experience such a scene.

They all sat down and lunch was served.

★★★

167

Patricia and Kenneth were seated at a round table with Daphne and Adrian, Vincent and Jane, and Erica and Rebecca. They all introduced themselves to each other and joined in with some general conversation about the weather, the food, the newly-wed couple, Jane's baby bump and various other topics. But gradually, Patricia withdrew into herself and started thinking.

This is surreal, sitting here making small talk and pretending that everything is normal. I never expected to see Dougie again. Much as I love him and miss him dreadfully, I know that I was in the wrong, carrying on an affair with him behind Casey's back. I've been with Casey for twenty-eight years. We have three children together and now wee Stevie as well. I can't blame Sam for making me choose. I can't blame Jasmine for swearing at me. So I did choose. I chose my family and let Dougie go. I sat there and let Casey hoodwink the police even though I had my suspicions. And then I found the evidence and I did nothing. I'm a bad person through and through.

I still have those receipts. I could still expose him. But what would Sam and Jasmine think of me? It could ruin their lives. Would they ever forgive me?

Do I still love Casey? Does he love me? Why did he suddenly change his mind and take me back just a few days after saying we were finished? To shut me up! He knew I would find out.

"Are you all right, Auntie Patty?" It was Rebecca jolting her from her thoughts and looking concerned. "You've gone very quiet."

"Sorry, Dear," she replied. "I do feel a bit queasy. I think I'll go out into the fresh air for a minute. It's very warm in here." Kenneth offered to go with her. "No, I'll be fine, thanks," she reassured him. She pushed her chair back and left the table.

Dougie spotted her leaving and followed her almost immediately. "Come with me," he instructed authoritatively, taking her by the hand, and her heart lurched at his familiar touch. He led her past the reception area and up the stairs, taking a key card from his pocket. She followed blindly until he opened a door and took her into a bedroom. And then she was in his arms as he kissed her hotly, even more passionately than ever before and she kissed him back with an intensity of desire that thrilled him. Then, throwing themselves down on the bed, they wasted no time in breathlessly satisfying that desire.

"I booked the room for the night so that I could go searching for you," he said at last, fondling her breast. "I never dreamt you'd actually be here."

"We have to get back," she cried. "They'll miss us and put two and two together. But I'll come back. I'll find some excuse."

"I'll be waiting for you, however long it takes."

Patty went to the bathroom to tidy herself up and then returned to the function suite where dessert was now being served.

"I was just about to come looking for you," Kenneth remarked. "Are you feeling better?" She assured everyone that the queasiness had passed and sat down with a smile on her face. It was another five minutes before she noticed Dougie coming back in and taking his seat beside Angus, Lauren and the boys. Others had also been going in and out to the toilet so nobody would have noticed any anomaly but Patty now knew one thing for sure.

I cannot go on like this. I need him in my life. Whatever happens to the family, I have to make a clean break from Casey. I refuse to spend the rest of my life chained to a murderer.

As she ate her profiteroles covered in warm, delicious chocolate sauce, she turned again to her husband and spoke in a low voice. "You're probably bored stiff," she said cunningly. "You don't really know any of these people and I know you have some reservations about Cathy. But thank you for coming with me and showing a united front. Why don't you meet up with some of your own friends later on?"

"I might just do that," Kenneth agreed.

"I didn't get much of a chance to talk to Grant and Imogen yet so I'd like to hang around for a while after the meal. I'm sure Jasmine would leave me home if you want to head on."

"Good idea." Kenneth was only too happy to make an early escape. He left twenty minutes later, still unaware that his nemesis was in the building.

Chapter 21

The guests began to disperse after four o'clock. One by one they congratulated Grant and his new wife, thanked Catherine and Gertrude and headed out to their cars or taxis. Patty gave Catherine a hug. "I'm glad our friendship is back on track," she said with genuine feeling.

"Me too," Catherine told her. "See you soon."

Cameron and his family had already left for the airport. There was no sign of Douglas. Patty slipped out when none of the remaining company was looking and made her way back to the room her lover had booked. She tapped on the door and he opened it right away. She stepped inside.

"How long can you stay?" he asked her, his eyes full of love.

"Maybe forever."

They made love again, getting into the bed properly this time and taking it more gently, more slowly, their naked bodies revelling in the joy of fulfilment. Afterwards they talked about the pain of separation and the trauma that they had suffered since their last weekend together when they had been intercepted by Sam and Tania.

"I was so sorry to hear about your brother," Patty soothed. "Tell me exactly what happened." Maybe, just maybe there was still a chance that she was mistaken and that Kenneth wasn't involved at all.

"It was the day of Cameron's party," he recalled. "He was celebrating his father's eightieth birthday and his reunion with his son. It was a bit like today. I had been invited along because I had helped them find one another. I ended up sitting beside Imogen."

"What has that got to do with what happened later?" Patty asked him.

"Well, earlier that day I had received a text message from your daughter, Jasmine. She asked me for my address and pretended that she wanted it for Grant. It became clear to me during the meal that she had not been telling the truth so presumably she wanted it for her brother, Sam."

"Sam?"

"He did threaten us that weekend."

"How did Jasmine even have your number?"

"I don't know."

"I don't like the sound of this."

"Well, I have to admit I was a bit concerned. I phoned home and told Mia to be careful, not to answer the door to any strangers."

"So what happened next?"

"I arrived home to find that Alex had called to see me. When he found that I wasn't at home, Mia had told him about my phone call and had said she felt a bit scared so he had stayed with her until I got there. He remained at our place for another half an hour or so, discussing the business with me. Mia had gone to bed before he left."

"And then?"

"He had a bad fall on the way down the driveway, hit his head really hard against some sharp stones. He was dead when we discovered him lying there the next morning. It was horrendous, especially for Mia, who saw him first."

Patty considered the evidence. "So it was an unfortunate accident," she murmured.

Douglas decided to be honest. "We did suspect your son at first. He *had* threatened us and he *had* tricked me, through his sister, into giving him my address."

"My son, not my husband?"

"I didn't think your husband knew anything about us. But I realise now that he did, didn't he? Sam must have told him."

Patty sighed. "Sam didn't need to tell him anything. Casey listened to a voicemail on my phone, wondering who Mia was. It was you, using her line."

Her lover looked embarrassed. "So that's how he found out. I'm so sorry."

Dougie went on to explain how the police had discounted foul play until Barbara had later discovered the delayed text message and had become suspicious. "It *was* a bit spooky," he confessed, "and the police said they had to investigate. I'm really sorry for bringing your family into that. Everyone had a cast-iron alibi."

"Yes, even Casey."

Dougie gave her a strange look. "That's why you broke off contact with me. He had found out."

"Yes."

"And it wasn't your son who spilt the beans at all. It was me. I told him myself!"

"Yes."

"So where do we go from here?"

"I'm going to leave him, Dougie. I want to be with you."

***

Kenneth heard the door opening and closing, the key turning in the lock. She didn't come up straight away but went to the kitchen and faffed around for some time. Eventually he heard her mounting the stairs.

"Where have you been until this time?" he asked with some exasperation. "It's two o'clock in the morning."

Patricia didn't answer him. She just turned on the light and handed him two pieces of paper. His face went pale.

"Where did you get these?" he demanded.

"They were in a pocket, in your black trousers. I was putting them in the wash."

Kenneth exhaled loudly and covered his face with his hands. He thought he had been so clever. Time stood still for a few minutes. Then he spoke again, this time in a pathetic whimper. "I only hit him once. I didn't mean to kill him."

"I thought as much," accepted his wife, "but you didn't even get the right person!"

"What are you going to do?"

Patricia took a deep breath. "I saw Dougie today," she admitted. "I had no idea that he would be there, I promise

174

you that. But being in the same room as both of you at the same time made me see things from a new angle."

"Go on."

"Our marriage has been dead for some time, Kenneth."

"And whose fault is that?"

"Partly mine, partly yours."

"No, Patricia. A hundred percent yours."

"I don't want to argue with you about that. But I've come to a decision."

"Which is?"

"You give me my freedom and I'll allow you to have yours."

He squinted at her expecting an explanation.

"I'm leaving you, Kenneth. You let me go amicably with half of what we own and without turning the family against me, and I'll make sure you don't end up facing a murder or manslaughter charge."

"You'll keep this evidence to yourself? You haven't already told anyone?"

"I promise. As long as you keep your side of the bargain."

"But I've broken the law. I took someone's life! You'll be an accessory."

"Take it or leave it."

Kenneth nodded his head resignedly. Patricia turned on her heels and left the room.

Part Two

Chapter 22

Grant,

I accept that I have to acknowledge your existence but I'm warning you that I will not let my boys be side-lined. If you try to take anything that is rightfully theirs, I'm telling you now that I will not stand by and watch in silence. Just let things be.

Scott Ferguson

The email had appeared out of the blue, literally, since Grant and Imogen were sitting under a clear, cerulean sky in the Algarve, enjoying a late honeymoon. With Imogen being six months pregnant by now, they were taking it easy, going for gentle strolls rather than long walks and driving about in their hire car, taking in the beautiful sights and sounds of nature. The countryside was awash with an abundance of magnificent yellow cascades of blooms from the acacia trees towering over masses of bright yellow Bermuda buttercups and dotted here and there with crown daisies, blood-red poppies, clumps of purple heather and patches of wild broom and French lavender, all swaying in the soft, warm breeze. Its beauty was breath-taking. They had stopped at a coastal snack bar for a light tapas lunch of savoury *salgados* and a selection of Portuguese cheeses washed down with a glass of local *vinho verde* for Grant, fresh *sumo laranja* for Imogen, and were admiring the clumps of yellow sea aster and bright pink sand stock, growing up through the surrounding path as the waves of the Atlantic lapped onto the picturesque, almost deserted beach below. After all, it was only mid-March. They had seen photographs of the same beach, taken during the main summer season, when the sand was dotted with colourful parasols and stripy towels, the water's edge with bathers in skimpy bikinis and shorts covered in bold flowery patterns. Imogen took a bite of her *patanisca bacalhau* and savoured the taste of the warm, salty cod, whilst Grant tried one of the *rissois camarão*. "Mmm, very tasty," he pronounced. He always had been very partial to prawns and other seafood. The *batatinhas assadas* complemented both little fish cakes perfectly. Having just keyed in the password for the local Wi-Fi, both of their phones had jumped into life, alerting them to messages from home.

"Jillian and Bradley say 'hello'," Imogen told her husband as she read the friendly text from her best friend, also now a married woman. Grant didn't answer, clearly absorbed in something on his own mobile. Assuming that it was somebody from work, needing advice from the boss, Imogen carried on reading her own messages. Vincent had sent her a new photo of little Anna who had been born just two weeks ago. She was gorgeous. And she was wearing the cute two-piece suit that she and Grant had given to Jane when they visited her in the hospital just after the birth. Imogen noticed that Grant was still distracted; she would show him the picture later. But she was a bit annoyed that his assistant manager or whoever was disturbing him during their honeymoon. Surely the woman could cope without him for ten days. She sent a quick reply to Jillian and to Vincent, including a photo of their beautiful surroundings, and then popped another little potato into her mouth. She looked longingly at Grant's wine glass, tempted to take a sip, but held back in case she would not be able to resist drinking too much. Better to stick to her juice. It was really quite convenient, her being pregnant. It meant that she could do the driving and let Grant enjoy the local wines and beers. At last Grant looked up from his phone and let out a big sigh. Imogen gave him a questioning look. "Is it Brenda?" she quizzed. "I sometimes wonder why you ever employed her."

Grant shook his head. "No, no," he told her. "Nothing to do with work."

"What then?"

Grant had read the short message three times now, totally baffled. He held the phone out to his wife so that she could read it for herself. She also was stunned and simply stared at it, uncomprehending.

"I had a feeling that Scott had it in for me," muttered Grant. "He's the one member of the family who hasn't been very welcoming. I know we've only met him once but he hardly spoke to me and I detected a coldness."

"I thought he wasn't supposed to know that the boys were actually his," put in Imogen.

"That's what Cameron said. But I suppose the man isn't stupid."

"Well he can't have it both ways, let someone else claim them and bring them up and then suddenly decide that he's their dad after all. What does he mean anyway?"

"Search me!"

"They do seem to be quite well off. Has Cameron mentioned anything to you about money or gifts? Has it something to do with some kind of legacy?"

"He sent me that cheque that I burnt and then paid our hotel bill when we went over. Other than that, no. We've stayed well clear of financial matters following that fiasco when we first met him. Do you remember? He brought his solicitor along."

"But he has been very apologetic about that."

"I know. And I'm pretty sure he was being genuine. Cameron's not the problem. It's my Uncle Scott."

"You don't trust him?"

Grant sighed noisily. "Well, look at what we know about him. He slept with his brother's wife after deceiving her into thinking he was her husband. Maybe she *was* taken in but *he* knew what he was doing. They've all passed it off as some kind of joke and blamed it on too much drink. But I don't see anything funny or acceptable about it. The man raped her in reality. And you wonder whether I trust him?"

"I agree. I'd call it rape. I always thought that but I didn't want to upset you by saying anything."

Grant gave her a funny look.

"They're your family. It's not for me to interfere. And anyway, who am I to judge? When you think about how Vincent came into the world."

Grant nodded his head. "True," he murmured. "And me for that matter." Then he squeezed her hand and told her, "We're married now. Your family is mine and my family is yours. So don't hold anything back. Your opinion matters to me. In everything."

"What are you going to do about the email?" Imogen asked him.

"I don't know."

"I hope there's nothing wrong. I mean, why now?"

"That's what's worrying me. Maybe Cameron isn't well or something if he's talking about dividing out his stuff. I hope that isn't the case when I'm only getting to know him."

Imogen looked thoughtful. "He's probably just sorting out his will which is a sensible thing for anyone to do," she tried to reassure him. "He'll want to share things three ways instead of two, now that he knows about you. It's just like my parents including Vincent. I'm hardly going to take exception to that. I think it's great having a brother I didn't know about until recently."

Grant smiled. "Not everyone would be as magnanimous as you," he told her.

"You can hardly ask Cameron about it. You might come across as appearing to be a bit mercenary."

"I just want to know that he's OK. Maybe Douglas McKendrick would know something."

Douglas had become a good friend and it was easier now that things were out in the open regarding his

183

relationship with Sam's mother. Patricia had left her family behind some weeks before Christmas and had moved over to Scotland to live with her lover. Grant and Imogen had both been amazed when Kenneth had accepted it and had even used his influence to ensure that neither Sam nor Jasmine judged their mother harshly. He had taken the lion's share of the blame himself, explaining to the pair that their marriage had been failing for some time and convincing them that he had not devoted enough time or energy to making any real attempt to save it. He had taken Patricia for granted and was not surprised that she had turned to someone else for solace and love. During another round of golf, Sam had opened up to Grant about the situation, indicating that his initial anger had turned to confusion and was now verging on a reluctant acceptance. Yet, he told his friend, his father's account of things didn't seem to fit comfortably with his mood on that first morning when Kenneth had called at his new flat after spending the whole night in his car. He had been ready to do battle then. Still, he had obviously done a lot of thinking during his solitary Spanish trip and had come to view the situation differently.

Imogen read her husband's mind. "I think it's very sad," she said. "When Sam and I were together his parents appeared to be perfectly happy. I never got to know them very well but they were both very pleasant to me. I remember them joking and laughing together all the time."

"I was just thinking the same," Grant admitted. "They were both at that millennium party at my grandparents' place. You would never have guessed that they would end up splitting and living apart. Some people just don't try hard enough at making things work. I mean, they have three children together."

"It'll never happen to us," Imogen stated firmly with a determined look on her face.

"Too right," her husband agreed, smiling.

"So you think you might contact Douglas?" Imogen said, getting back to the strange email.

"Maybe. Indirectly. He might let something slip."

"Good idea."

Grant thought about it for a few minutes. He couldn't really enjoy the stunning view or the tasty tapas lunch with this hanging over him. He keyed in a message to Douglas.

Hi Dougie. Imogen and I are having a lovely time in the Algarve. Just want to thank you again for urging me to get in touch with my dad that time. I'm so glad that I took your advice. Hope everything is well with you.

"Does that sound really trite?" Grant asked Imogen, showing her what he had written. "He's been through the mill since then, what with his brother's accident and everything."

Imogen assured him that it was fine and he clicked on the 'send' option. A reply came through almost immediately.

Hello you two. Good to know you are enjoying yourselves. Just by coincidence, I was talking to your grandfather

185

yesterday. I was helping Barbara to sort out her affairs and we met him at the solicitor's.

"Bingo!" exclaimed Grant. "Now how can I get him to elaborate?"

"Just keep the conversation going," Imogen suggested. "He might end up telling us more." Grant keyed in another reply.

Angus is a brilliant man for eighty. It's great that he can still get about on his own and has his wits fully about him. I hope I'm still as independent at that age.

Douglas sent another answer.

That's very true but he wasn't actually on his own on this occasion. Your Uncle Scott was with him. I wasn't sure whether he's come home for a holiday or whether he's moved back for good. Anyway, you two enjoy the rest of your honeymoon. I look forward to seeing you both on your next visit over here. Patty says hello and sends her love to Sam and Jasmine and wee Stevie. You will probably see them all before we do. I know they're your friends and I'm sorry for any embarrassment we've caused you but I want you to know that we are very happy together.

Grant popped another salty snack into his mouth and took a sip of his wine, breathing in the warm spring air. He watched as a couple about their own age appeared and started playing with their dog on the beach whilst another family with two toddlers began to make preparations for a picnic. He smiled at Imogen. "I'm not going to let it annoy me," he pronounced. "Scott's email is quite aggressive, verging on rude, but I hardly know the man. I'm just going to ignore it. If Cameron has anything to tell me, I'm sure he'll do it when the time is right. Now, where do you fancy going this afternoon?"

Happily, Imogen unfolded the map and they studied the unfamiliar place names, planning out a drive through the hills of the Alentejo. The waiter approached their table to see whether they wanted anything else.

"*A conta por favor*," Grant told him with a smile. "*Obrigado.*"

They paid for their meal and set off for another adventure.

★★★

Back home in Belfast Jasmine was arriving at the garden centre to pick Alastair up at the end of his shift. Being a few minutes early, she decided to have a look around the gift shop while she waited. It would be Tania's birthday in a couple of days' time and she had spotted some lovely scarfs the last day she was in. She headed over to the small clothing department and perused the colourful selection, finally choosing a blue one with a peacock pattern and a pink one covered in a summery floral motif. There was quite a long queue at the cash desk and the reason for this became evident when she overheard two other customers complaining.

"I'm all for giving people like that a job," one of them was saying, "but you'd at least think they could have another till operating as well. I'm going to be late for my bus."

"I know," the second voice hissed in reply. "They could always use him out in the garden area. He could be watering plants or something. It's ridiculous having him as a cashier. He obviously hasn't a clue."

Jasmine glanced up and saw her boyfriend checking in a basket of homemade biscuits, jams and marmalades. It didn't happen very often but sometimes, when they were short-staffed, Alastair was asked to take on tasks outside his usual remit. Jasmine felt her blood beginning to boil at the nasty comments.

"People like that!" she said scathingly to the first woman, who was holding a toddler by the hand. "You should think next time before you speak. What sort of example is that to set to a child?" Both women looked startled but at least a little shamefaced.

"Good for you, Miss," called an elderly man further up the queue as he turned round to confront the pair and flashed a smile at Jasmine. "I was disgusted with those remarks too. That young lad has been working here for years. He's a genius with plants. He's certainly taught me a thing or two. So what, if he's a bit slow on the till. You should be ashamed of yourselves." Jasmine beamed with pleasure and the two women muttered an apology.

"It's just that we're running late," the one with the child tried to excuse herself. "Actually, I think I'll come back another time." She set her intended purchases down on the nearest shelf and hurried from the shop, despite the noisy protestations from the toddler who would now miss out on the bag of jelly babies. The older lady stood her ground, clutching two beautiful plants, a healthy looking camellia laden with pink buds and a bushy, fragrant lavender.

"Alastair probably grew those from tiny seedlings," Jasmine told her.

"Alastair?"

"The guy on the till."

"Oh, so you know him personally." Her face flushed red. "I shouldn't have been so judgmental."

"He's my boyfriend."

"Look, I'm sorry. I accept that I was out of order. You were quite right to speak up." Her eyes were now darting nervously around the store.

Jasmine accepted the apology. "It's just that I hate to witness people heckling him," she explained. "He's had to put up with a lot of emotional abuse over the years. It's not his fault that he had learning difficulties growing up."

The lady with the plants nodded her head. "Is it a genetic condition he has?"

"No, he was born perfectly normal. It's the result of an accident he had when he was a little boy." She smiled again at the elderly gentleman who was now leaving with his trowel and packets of seeds, then turned back to her new friend. "There you go now. It hasn't been such a long wait after all." It was only then that Alastair caught Jasmine's eye in the queue. He looked at his watch and smiled.

"I've been chatting to your lovely girlfriend," the plant lady told him. "She said that you're the gardener who tends these shrubs. You've done a super job with them. They look really healthy and sturdy." Jasmine patted her on the arm to show that she appreciated her change of attitude but behind them, in the line of waiting customers, she could already detect further jibes and sobriquets. Luckily Alastair was concentrating so hard on not making a mistake that he did not appear to notice. It turned out that he had been covering for a colleague who had been taken ill. No sooner had he processed Jasmine's scarf purchase than his line manager turned up to let him go. They walked out to the car together.

"I get a bit flustered when I'm on the till," Alastair admitted, "but most people are very understanding. It just got very busy there at the end."

"Hey, you don't need to make any excuses to me. You were doing a great job."

"But I'm not deaf. I can hear what people are saying. I've just got used to blocking it out."

"Well, I think you're amazing," Jasmine replied with a lump in her throat.

"I never thought I'd have a girlfriend like you," Alastair confided. "Thanks for sticking up for me."

"So you heard all that!"

"It happens all the time."

Jasmine felt her pulse quickening. It infuriated her that there were still so many insensitive individuals around but she took a deep breath and started up the engine. Time to forget about it for now. They only had an hour to get ready. "My dad confirmed that table for tonight," she reminded Alastair. They were going out for a meal with Jasmine's dad, Kenneth, and Alastair's mum, Thomasina, a sign that both parents had accepted that they were in a serious relationship. It would be the first meeting between the two other than a brief encounter at Grant and Imogen's wedding party. Alastair had already left a change of clothing at Jasmine's flat so they went there to freshen up. Forty minutes later they were stepping into their taxi.

The two young people arrived at the restaurant first and were shown to a table by the window and handed menus. They each ordered a gin and tonic and sat down side by side, leaving the two seats opposite them for their respective parents. "This is cosy," Jasmine remarked happily, glancing around her and taking in the open kitchen, the trendy wine-rack along one wall and the tastefully laid tables, half of which were already occupied. "We'll be able to see them coming from here." Their drinks arrived and they both took a sip. Jasmine sighed with contentment. "It's good to see Dad getting on with his life," she declared. "I can't get over how well he has accepted everything with Mum moving away. I really miss her but she seems to be happy with that man."

Alastair laughed. "That man! You still refuse to call him by name."

"OK, Douglas then. She seems to be happy with Douglas."

"Here he comes now."

Kenneth was walking past the window. He spotted his daughter and gave her a friendly wave, then came in through the door and headed over to the table. He gave Jasmine a hug and shook Alastair by the hand. "So, how was your day?" he asked brightly as he hung up his coat on a hook behind the table.

"Busy," said Alastair.

"Not bad," Jasmine declared. "But what about you, Dad? I worry about you on your own."

"Hey, it's my job to worry about you," Kenneth replied. "You're still my little girl." He indicated to the waiter that he would also have a gin and tonic, which arrived promptly.

"You know what I mean," Jasmine persisted. "I'm still angry with Mum for what she has done to you. And I still can't understand why you didn't fight harder to keep her. Do you think she'll ever come back? Would you take her back if she did?"

"Those are awkward questions, Love. Let's leave it for tonight and enjoy our meal. But, for the record, I would do anything for your mother. She's still my wife and I still love her. I don't want to hear anyone badmouthing her." Kenneth immediately changed the subject and started chatting to Alastair about the garden centre and asking him why he had been so busy. Jasmine listened as her boyfriend related a few amusing tales about his day at work but, in reality, her thoughts were on her father's strange response to her questions. If he stills loves Patricia so much, why has he just let her go into the arms of another man, complete with financial security and no recriminations? It didn't make any sense but she didn't have time to analyse her thoughts any further because she suddenly spotted Thomasina at the window.

"Here's your mum," Jasmine announced, interrupting the conversation. Alastair stood up to greet her.

"Hi Mum, you remember Jasmine's dad, Kenneth."

"It's lovely to meet you properly, Kenneth. I'm Thomasina. Or Tamsin, if you prefer. It's less of a mouthful."

"I think it's a lovely name," Kenneth answered. "Reminds me of Thomas Hardy."

"Ah, yes, *The Return of the Native*. I think that's where my parents got it from. Are you a fan too?"

"I am indeed."

Jasmine and Alastair exchanged a smile. At least that was one topic of common interest to keep some conversation flowing. Thomasina gave Jasmine a hug and sat down opposite her son and next to Kenneth. They all picked up their menus and started to consider the various options. Kenneth ordered a drink for Tamsin and a refill for himself.

"It all sounds delicious," Jasmine commented, "and smells even better."

"I like the look of that goat's cheese fritter," Thomasina replied, eyeing the dish that had just been set down on a neighbouring table. "I think I'll go for that."

"The steaks are amazing in here," put in Kenneth, downing his second gin. "Patricia and I used to come here the odd time."

"I'm going to have the wild mushroom linguini," Alastair decided.

Soon they had all chosen a starter and a main course. The waiter took their order and collected the menus back in. They opted to share a bottle of red wine and some sparkling water.

"Don't they make a lovely pair," Kenneth remarked, waving a finger across from his daughter to her boyfriend.

"I am really happy for Alastair," Thomasina replied. "I think Jasmine is a lovely girl. My mother and my sister love her too."

"That's Patricia's friend, Cathy. Your sister."

"Yes, that's right."

"Small world."

"I'm sorry the way things have turned out for you. You must be having a difficult time adjusting. It's still very early days."

"Life hasn't treated you very kindly either."

"No, I've been a widow for over twenty-six years."

"And you never met anyone else?"

"I didn't have time. In the beginning it was all about Alastair. He had special needs. Learning difficulties. And so many hospital appointments and operations."

"It's hard to believe now. He's grown into such a lovely young man. You should be very proud."

"He's still not a hundred percent in some ways. You don't worry about Jasmine becoming too close to him?"

"Absolutely not. I have never seen her so happy."

Jasmine and Alastair were only vaguely aware that their parents were talking about them. They were, for the moment, absorbed in their own thoughts and feelings for one another and sharing private murmurings of love, their hands clasped firmly beneath the table.

"Soup?" enquired a friendly waitress, balancing two bowls with accompanying homemade wheaten bread.

"Yes, that's for me, thanks," said Jasmine.

"And over here," echoed Kenneth.

"Salted and chilli squid?"

"Mmm, that's mine," Alastair pronounced.

"And the goat's cheese fritter for yourself, then?" She placed the dish down in front of Thomasina.

"Thank you, yes. That looks scrummy."

Every dish was cooked to perfection and full of colour and flavour. All the tables were fully occupied by now and there was a lively buzz of conversation filling the atmosphere along with some unobtrusive Ed Sheeran music in the background. Jasmine felt very relaxed. Kenneth poured everyone a glass of wine. "Your mother doesn't know what she's missing," he stated, taking a large gulp of his own.

Thomasina gave him a sympathetic smile. "I hope it's just a temporary blip," she said kindly. "It's clear that you miss her very much."

"I do. We were together for twenty-eight glorious years. But more than anything I want her to be happy, so if that means that she stays away for good, so be it."

"Raymond and I only had six years before he died. Tomorrow will actually be my wedding anniversary. Thirty-three years since we tied the knot." It was barely a whisper but she managed to remain dry-eyed as she said it. Jasmine reached across and squeezed her hand. Kenneth refilled his glass.

"A car accident wasn't it?"

"Not so much an accident. An unlawful killing. Hit and run."

"Shocking. Absolutely shocking. I'll just go and order another bottle." Kenneth went over to the bar.

"Your dad is drinking a lot," observed Alastair. "He's more upset about your mum leaving than he likes to admit."

"I know." Jasmine excused herself and went to the ladies' restroom. But as she passed the bar she overheard her father speaking to a friend, who had asked him how he was coping on his own. Jasmine was confused by his reply.

"I'm better off without the bitch. Turns out she was cheating on me for years. Her fancy man is welcome to her."

"I hope you have a good lawyer in that case," the friend replied. "You don't want her getting away with any of your assets."

"The spiteful cow has already got half of everything and damn cunning she was about it."

Jasmine hurried past before he would spot her. She used the facilities and returned to the table to find that the main courses had been delivered and her father had already made a start on the second bottle of wine. He was beginning to slur his words. At this rate he was going to embarrass her in front of Alastair's mum.

"So it should have been thirty-three years and you only got six," he was now saying. "That's a sad story."

Thomasina blinked at him, surprised that he had returned to the topic.

"And some bastard just knocked him down and left him to die. Was it at least instantaneous? He didn't suffer?"

"Dad!" Jasmine was enraged.

Tears came to Thomasina's eyes. "That's something I'll never know," she sobbed. "It's been the worst aspect of the whole thing. The sleepless nights I've had, wondering whether he could have been saved if help had arrived in time."

"No, no, you don't have to worry about that. He was already dead."

They all stared at him. How could he possibly know that? Kenneth took another huge gulp from his wine glass. Jasmine moved the bottle out of his reach. "Phone for a taxi," she muttered to Alastair under her breath. "I've got to get him out of here." Then she looked imploringly at Thomasina. "I'm so sorry," she breathed. "I don't know what's got into him. I hope you won't hold it against me."

Meanwhile Kenneth was realising what he had said. "That's what you have to believe," he stammered. "Don't torture yourself about it. He died on the spot and there was nothing anyone could do to bring him back."

How could any of them have known that, in his drunken fug, he was seeing a totally different person, dead to the world, his bulging eyes staring blankly into the heavens?

The taxi arrived and Jasmine bungled him in, giving the driver both the fare and the address. Kenneth managed a slurred apology and promised to go straight to bed, assuring his daughter that he did not need any assistance. He was just a bit tipsy.

"Understatement of the year," Jasmine muttered, feeling very embarrassed as she rejoined her boyfriend and his mother, who both laughed it off and told her not to worry. The man was obviously under a lot of stress. But she did worry. Until he called to let her know that he was safely at home and in bed.

"Well, that's enough drama for tonight," Alastair remarked. "Why don't we order some desserts?" Just as he spoke, one of the staff members came over to inform them that Mr Campbell had phoned in his credit card details to pay the bill and had insisted that they would all stay on to enjoy desserts and coffee, explaining that he had left early since he was feeling unwell. Jasmine breathed a sigh of relief. He can't have been that drunk. But his behaviour had been very strange.

About twenty minutes later, when their sweet choices had been ordered and eaten, Jasmine was aware of some movement past their table as several people left the restaurant at once and a few late-comers arrived. And suddenly she heard someone address her by name.

"Jasmine! Alastair!" It was their friend, Maggie. "I never noticed you over here."

"Hi Maggie." Jasmine responded, pleased that the commotion caused by her dad had clearly gone undetected by other customers. "We're just about to have coffee if you want to join us."

"OK, that would be lovely. I'm with my mum. She's just gone to the toilet. Oh, here she comes now."

"No problem. You can squeeze in here beside us. The more the merrier." Maggie eased herself onto the bench next to her friend and Greta took the spare seat beside Thomasina. Jasmine was on the verge of making the necessary introductions when Maggie suddenly spoke first, extending her right arm across the table to shake hands with Thomasina.

"It's lovely to meet you, Mrs Campbell," she gushed. "Jasmine and I have become great friends. We share a love of painting. And I know your son, Sam, as well. Tania is my sister-in-law."

Jasmine laughed. "You've got it wrong, Maggie. This isn't my mum. It's Alastair's mum, Thomasina Henning. Thomasina, this is my friend, Maggie Hopkins and her mother. It's Greta, isn't that right? I met you at the wedding."

"Alastair's mother!" Maggie exclaimed, aghast. "Oh, I didn't realise." Greta looked as though she had seen a ghost.

"Is Lawrence not with you tonight?"

Neither of them answered but he obviously wasn't. There was no sign of him.

"Sorry, I don't think we have time for coffee after all," Maggie bluffed, her face flushing bright red. "I just remembered there's somewhere else we need to be." She stood up, looking flustered, but Greta sat on as they all noticed her eyes filling up with tears. She started to shake like a leaf.

"Come on, Mum. Let's go," Maggie urged, reaching for her mother's arm and averting her gaze from everyone else. Greta just shook her head.

"What's going on?" asked Alastair.

"I think my mum wants to talk to yours," Maggie said hesitantly, looking for some sign that she was correct. Greta managed a nod, her heart lurching and the tears now streaming down her face. Instinctively Jasmine, Alastair and Maggie all moved away, leaving the two older women alone at the table. Greta grabbed Thomasina's hand and clasped it tightly in both of hers.

"I wrote you a letter," she confessed in a broken voice, as Thomasina's head began to spin. "I'm Marguerite."

Chapter 23

"So how was your night out with Dad?" Sam asked his sister, looking at his watch. What was she doing here so early on a Sunday morning? He wasn't even dressed yet.

"We were asked to leave," Jasmine replied, her face expressionless.

Sam scowled in disbelief. "What do you mean?" he demanded.

"We were asked to leave," she repeated with a sigh. "Kicked out of the restaurant. And that was *after* we had already sent Dad home in a taxi, drunk out of his mind. I will never be able to show my face there again."

"Dad was drunk?"

"I think he's having a breakdown."

Tania strolled into the room in her yellow dressing-gown, Stevie in her arms, wearing nothing but a nappy. "You've caught us napping," she joked, not having heard Jasmine's remarks. "Coffee?"

Jasmine looked her straight in the eye. "Do you know who your brother is married to?"

Tania gave her a curious look. "Last time I checked she was your best friend. Whatever has happened?"

201

"She's only the daughter of the thug who ruined my boyfriend's life, the bastard who killed his father." Jasmine burst into tears. Tania just stared at her open-mouthed.

Sam looked confused. "Where does Dad come into this?"

"He doesn't. It just all happened the same night, one disaster after another. It was horrendous."

Stevie seemed to detect the tension in the room and started to cry. Jasmine wiped the tears from her cheeks and glanced from her brother, clad in creased black boxer shorts and a grey tee shirt, to his fiancée and the naked baby. "I'm sorry," she sniffed. "I shouldn't have come round so early."

"Just give us a few minutes," Tania soothed as they both scuttled back to the bedroom to get dressed. "Why don't you make yourself a coffee?"

Sam returned in a couple of minutes and urged his sister to start from the beginning and tell him what had happened. She filled him in on the night's events.

"So he was quite upbeat at the start of the meal?"

"Absolutely. And perfectly charming to Alastair's mum."

"But he was drinking too much?"

"In the end I had to move the wine to the other end of the table. But it was too late."

"And he spoke positively about Mum?"

"At the table, yes. But then I heard him slating her to one of his friends at the bar. He called her a spiteful cow!"

"He's just trying to save face. Put it down to a bit of bravado."

Jasmine shuddered at the memory. "It was when he started quizzing Thomasina about what had happened to her husband and assuring her that the man wouldn't have suffered. Things he knew nothing about! It was so embarrassing. I couldn't get him to shut up."

"You did the right thing, sending him home."

"The restaurant staff were very understanding at that stage. We all pretended he had been feeling ill and they appeared to accept that."

"So why did they ask you to leave?"

Tania came back in, dressed now in jeans and a sweater, and strapped Stevie into his bouncing cradle with a breakfast drink. He smiled at them all, kicking his chubby little legs in delight as he sucked at the bottle. Jasmine continued her story.

"When Maggie invited me to her wedding last November, I remember there was a mix-up about Alastair's name. She had put Cartwright on the invitation and she acted very strangely when I told her it was actually Henning. She practically ran from my apartment. But then she delivered a new card and it was never mentioned again."

Jasmine stopped to draw breath.

"Well, it turns out that, once she knew his name, she was able to put two and two together and work out that Alastair and his father were the people her dad ploughed into back in 1990."

"You can hardly blame her, Jaz," reasoned Sam. "It was her father's mistake, not hers."

"What happened last night?" quizzed Tania.

"Maggie was there having a meal with her mum. We only spotted them at the end, when we were ordering coffees, and I invited them to join us. Maggie mistook Thomasina for our mum at first so they agreed and sat down but when Greta realised who was actually sitting beside her she really freaked out and spilt the beans. The weeping and wailing from the two of them was awful. Meanwhile Maggie was owning up to me and poor Alastair was stuck in the middle. I know she isn't to blame. But I can't get past the association. Or the fact that she has known for four months and just pushed it under the carpet. I got really angry with her and yelled a few home truths in her direction. It's no wonder they asked us all to leave. People were trying to enjoy a nice relaxing meal."

"Where is Alastair now?"

"He went home with his mum. So much for the romantic night we had planned. The mood was broken."

"Have you spoken to Dad this morning?"

Jasmine shook her head. "I was hoping you might come with me. His behaviour was very irrational. I don't think he's coping at all."

"Of course I will," smiled Sam reassuringly.

"I wonder whether Lawrence knows about Maggie's secret," Tania muttered. "A murderer in the family. They've certainly kept that quiet."

"Apparently she didn't know anything about it herself until recently. The guy owned up to Greta on his deathbed. That's the story she gave me anyway. I was just so mortified for Alastair. He's been living with the consequences of it all most of his life."

Tania gave her a hug. "He's got you," she said. "He'll be OK."

Sam and Jasmine drove to the family home in silence, each absorbed in their own private thoughts. Molly was due home any day now. What on earth were they going to tell her? They didn't even understand it themselves. Kenneth was in the kitchen, dressed and clean-shaven. That was a bonus.

"You embarrassed me last night," Jasmine accused, not mincing her words and coming straight to the point.

Kenneth accepted the rebuke. "Sorry, Love. I did hit the bottle a bit."

"I heard you talking to your friend. You were dissing Mum. And it was just a few minutes after telling me you loved her and would do anything for her."

"I'm under a lot of stress. Don't take it to heart."

"Well which is it? Do you still love her or do you think she is a 'spiteful cow'?"

"Did I say that?"

"You know you did."

Kenneth ran a hand through his hair. Even at fifty-five, he still had quite a lot of it, although it was rapidly turning grey. Sam came to his defence.

"It's OK, Dad. Nothing wrong with a bit of bravado, saving face in front of your friends. But you need to cut down on the drinking."

"I couldn't understand why you were obsessing about Alastair's mum and the accident," put in Jasmine. "It happened so long ago."

"I don't know. It just caught my imagination. It was the drink. I'm so sorry, Love."

"So what's the party-line for Molly? Did you ditch our mum or let her go amicably? She knows nothing about this yet."

"Amicably. Yes, all sorted amicably. She has nothing to worry about."

Sam took the bull by the horns. "That's not what you were saying, Dad, the time you begged me for that bastard's address and told me he would soon be a dead man."

Kenneth flinched. "Don't be stupid," he scoffed angrily. "Have you never made an idle threat? I was in shock."

Jasmine frowned at her brother. What was he implying? That their dad had sent a hitman to Scotland while he himself travelled to Spain? Was he mad? How would Kenneth even know people like that and, if he did, how ridiculous would it be to believe that a person in that line of 'work' wouldn't double check that he had the right target? She changed the subject.

"You missed the real drama last night, Dad."

Kenneth looked interested. "What was that?"

"We found out who killed Alastair's dad."

Kenneth looked very uncomfortable. "How could the truth have come out now, so long after the event?" he enquired, raising an eyebrow and scowling.

"It was Greta Redpath's husband. Greta's daughter, Maggie, is one of my best friends. *Was* one of my best friends."

"And how did this come to light?"

Whilst Jasmine explained what had happened in the restaurant, Sam glanced around at the neat and tidy kitchen and breathed in the fresh lemony fragrance. His father was managing remarkably well on his own. In some ways. He brought the conversation back to their own family.

"Why are you letting Mum call all the shots, when she is the guilty party?"

"What do you mean? How can she be the guilty one?"

"Well, she's the one who had the affair! Waken up, Dad."

Kenneth gave himself a shake. "Sorry, you're getting me all confused, talking about two different things," he backtracked. "Yes, of course she caused the break-up but I'm trying to save you all as much distress as possible. You don't need to worry about me. I'll be fine."

"You're allowing her to trample all over you."

"Don't talk about your mother like that. Show some respect."

"Like you did at the bar last night!"

Jasmine stormed out of the house. Something wasn't adding up here. It was time to pay her mother a visit.

Sam lingered for a few extra minutes. "Is there something you're hiding from us, Dad?" he asked gently. "You can trust me. Tell me anything. I'm on your side."

Kenneth rolled his eyes and parted his lips but no words came out. Then he hugged his son tightly and patted his back several times. "Nothing to tell, Son," he whispered. "Nothing to tell." Their eyes met briefly and they both knew it was a lie. But Sam turned on his heels and followed his sister outside, keeping his sense of foreboding to himself.

★★★

Gertrude answered the door to Bradley and Jillian. "Come in, come in. And thanks for coming so promptly. Grant and Imogen are in Portugal," she reminded them, "and we've been in touch with them of course, but we wanted to tell you something ourselves before it becomes common knowledge."

They both gave her a questioning look, still wondering why they had been summoned to the house.

"There's been a development. You were both here when I read out that letter we received via the police."

Jillian gulped, hoping that her face wouldn't give her away. She alone had picked up on the connection with Maggie right away but had never told a soul, not even Bradley.

"Marguerite has made herself known. Thomasina had a visit from the police this morning. The woman's real name is Margaret Redpath, sometimes shortened to Greta. I believe you know her, Jillian." There was no hint of rebuke in the remark; she was just stating a fact. Jillian nodded. "Thomasina actually met her last night and the truth emerged in conversation. Apparently the woman contacted the police today so that they could put the record straight so now the case really is closed."

"Will there be any consequences?" asked Bradley.

"Legally, no. The man is already dead and left no assets worth talking about. But at least we have a name. Redpath, Dennis Redpath."

"Is Alastair OK?" It was Bradley's first thought. He had been looking out for his friend for so long. Indeed Alastair had recently been Best Man at his wedding to Jillian.

"It's awkward," admitted Gertrude. "His girlfriend, Jasmine, and Mrs Redpath's daughter, Maggie, are very good friends. But then you know that. She's your friend too."

"It's so nice of you to tell us personally," Bradley said, giving his surrogate grandmother a hug.

"I wouldn't have it any other way," she smiled. "You're part of the family."

Jillian was afraid to speak. But then Gertrude put her at ease. "Neither Margaret nor Maggie knew anything about this themselves, like it said in the letter. Neither of them has done anything wrong. Hopefully we can all get past the fallout and remain friends."

"I hope it doesn't come between Alastair and Jasmine," Jillian said hesitantly.

"It won't. Those two are made for one another. Now, come and have a coffee. I want to show you some pictures I took at the wedding. Your dress was gorgeous, Jillian. Have you not got your official album yet? I can't understand why these things take so long. And what about your new niece? I hope you have a picture or two on your phone. I can't wait to see her. It won't be long now until Imogen has her baby. Just think about it. I'll be a great-grandmother. Milk and sugar? I can never remember."

Jillian and Bradley followed her into the kitchen, both smiling. Granny Gertrude was always a ray of sunshine even on the darkest of days.

Chapter 24

OK. So you've chosen to ignore me which isn't very polite. Don't say you haven't been warned when your cosy little world comes crashing down. You will always be an outsider. Scott

Grant handed the phone to Imogen. "I think maybe I do need to contact Cameron after all," he said.

Imogen read the message for herself and nodded. "Do it now before you take cold feet. The guy seems to be looking for trouble."

Grant forwarded the two emails and added a comment:

Hi Cameron. I don't understand these messages from your brother. Thought maybe I should alert you to some friction in the family?? Grant

A reply came through almost immediately.

Thanks for showing me this. I need to speak to Dad and then I'll get back to you.

They were enjoying their last day in the Algarve before flying home and had stopped at a beachfront restaurant in Albufeira. A young waitress arrived to take their order.

"*Frango com piri-piri, por favor, e batatas fritas,*" Imogen said with a smile, "*e uma aqua mineral com gaz.*"

"*Sim. E por você, o senhor?*"

"*Cataplana peixes frescas e um copo de vinho tinto, por favor.*"

The waitress complimented them on their Portuguese and took the order into the kitchen.

"Jillian said there is snow forecast for tomorrow," Imogen laughed. "Isn't it hard to believe when we're sitting here in the sunshine, wearing tee shirts?"

"I don't think it'll come to much. Did she say anything about the whole fiasco with Alastair and Maggie?"

"She hasn't seen Maggie. But apparently Alastair is fine. He stayed over with Jasmine last night." She paused and then added, "I'm really glad that the mystery has been solved at last."

"I'm sure you are." Grant gave her a wry smile. "Have you told your parents?"

"No," Imogen admitted. "I'm too embarrassed to mention it. Hopefully the news will filter through from Dorothy or Vincent. I don't ever want to talk to them about it or think about the things I discovered in Mum's diaries. Ever. Chapter closed."

"I'll get Mum to tell them on the QT. Save any awkwardness."

"Thanks."

They nibbled on some bread and olives and watched people strolling past and taking photographs of the beach. And then Grant's phone started to ring. He checked the caller display and saw Cameron's name.

"Hi, Dad," Grant said, accepting the call and moving away from the table into a quieter area outside, where he sat down on a bench.

"Oh, you just made my day," Cameron said, sounding very upbeat.

"By sending you those emails?"

"No. By what you just said. You called me 'Dad'."

Grant laughed. "So I did. Slip of the tongue."

"Aww, don't go spoiling it now."

"OK, Dad."

"I hope you're having a lovely holiday. How is Imogen?"

"Great, thanks. I hope you didn't mind me sending you that stuff. I ignored the first one a week ago but when the second one came in today I felt annoyed."

"I'm not surprised," Cameron told him. "Scott has always been very competitive but now he has turned nasty. Those messages to you were a disgrace."

"Is he still in Canada?"

"No, he suddenly arrived home. He claims that he wants to be closer to Dad now that he's getting on a bit. Says that eighty was a big milestone. But he has an ulterior motive."

"He's worked out that the boys are actually his?"

"Yes, but you have nothing to worry about. He has shot himself in the foot. In fact it's bloody funny."

Cameron started to laugh. Grant glanced back at the table and noticed that their meals had just arrived. "Can I phone you back?" he asked amicably. "We're just in the middle of lunch here. It's our last day."

"That's fine, Son. It'll give me the chance to check a few facts. But be prepared for a laugh. Talk to you soon."

Imogen gave him a questioning look as he retook his place at the table. The cataplana looked really appetising and was filling the air with the most heavenly aromas. It consisted of pieces of fish cooked in a type of stew made up of onions, garlic, herbs, tomatoes and peppers. The spicy chicken dish was also delicious. They both tucked in hungrily.

"I told him I'd phone back after lunch," Grant explained. "But he says we shouldn't worry. In fact he seemed to find the whole thing amusing."

"Amusing?"

"Yes, although he did say the messages were a disgrace. Let's just enjoy our lunch. We'll find out what it's all about later on."

Grant was just savouring his last tasty mouthful when he heard a message coming through on his phone. Imogen popped a chip into her mouth and looked across the table at him. "Anything important?" she asked.

"It's Cameron again." He opened the message.

Sorry. I couldn't wait to tell you this. But give me a ring anyway and we can have a good laugh together. We have a tradition in the family which concerns quite a valuable heirloom in the form of some antique jewellery. It is passed down to the eldest descendant on the death of the current owner, who is presently my father, Angus. With us being twins, it was agreed years ago that we would forfeit the opportunity and move it on to the next generation. Scott was determined that it wouldn't go to you so he persuaded my father to change the rules in favour of the youngest living descendant at the time of his death instead of the eldest. That way it would go to Henry, which isn't very fair to James, but that is beside the point. It seems that Scott has known all along that he was actually the father of both boys.

Anyway, he took Dad to see our solicitor and made the arrangements. So there it is, set in tablets of stone for the foreseeable future.

But what he didn't know, and I told Dad to make sure he doesn't find out, is that Imogen is pregnant! So, as long as Angus doesn't drop dead within the next few weeks, his youngest descendant will be your baby. Ha ha. I can't wait to see Scott's face when he finds out.

Enjoy the rest of your lunch. Dad.

They both read the message and appreciated the irony of it.

"I wonder how much the jewellery is actually worth," Grant surmised.

"Why does he not want Scott to find out about the baby? You don't think the man would try to harm me in any way? Or make sure his dad dies before the baby is born?"

"No! He's just milking the situation for as long as possible to get his own back. He sounds like a bit of a devious bastard, this uncle of mine, but I suppose he's only trying to look out for his own."

"But he has never accepted that they are his own!"

As soon as they had finished their meal and moved away from the restaurant, Grant took out his phone and called his father. Imogen listened as they both had another laugh at Scott's expense. Then she saw Grant nodding in response to something she couldn't hear. "I agree with you," Grant said after a moment. "The sooner, the better. They have the right to know." He listened again, still nodding his head, and then remarked, "Of course, that's true. And I hope he does." Imogen wandered down onto the beach to let him finish his conversation in peace. She kicked off her sandals and paddled in the water, allowing the waves to splash around her ankles. Although the air was warm for March, the water still felt very cold. One or two hardy individuals were in swimming a little further along and she shivered at the very idea of it. But they were laughing and squealing with delight, obviously enjoying the experience. Presently she saw Grant approaching and, as ever, her heart filled with love at the sight of him.

"Cameron and Lauren are going to have a heart-to-heart with the boys tonight and tell them the truth," Grant divulged.

"Good."

"And he said we shouldn't get our hopes up just yet regarding that jewellery. Angus could live for years. Eighty isn't old nowadays and he's in pretty good health. There could be more babies in the family before he goes."

"That's true," Imogen agreed, "although James is only sixteen."

"What about Scott himself? He might decide to have another child just to spite us."

"At fifty-one?"

"Plenty of fathers are that age and older."

"Not if they've any sense. And sure he doesn't even have a partner."

"That hasn't stopped him before."

Imogen remained doubtful. "Is he really going to give up his bachelor lifestyle for the sake of a piece of jewellery?"

"Several pieces of jewellery. Last valued at 100K!"

"No!"

"Yes, apparently so."

As they wrapped their arms around each other, giggling and frolicking on the wet sand, a larger wave suddenly rolled in and crashed over them, soaking them both to the waist. They laughed even louder and then shared a passionate kiss as they got drenched again.

"I love you, Mr Cartwright," Imogen gushed.

"And I love you, Mrs Cartwright-Ferguson."

"Decision made?" They had recently been discussing names with both themselves and the imminent arrival in mind.

"Yep."

"So what happened to Fergus Cartwright or Carter Ferguson?"

"Well, it might be a girl."

"True. Does she still inherit the jewellery?"

"Yes, gender doesn't come into it."

"Cartwright-Ferguson it is then. I like it."

Imogen screamed and then giggled as the next wave sent some spray splashing right over their heads.

Chapter 25

Jasmine sat on the sofa in her treasured studio and stared at the blank canvas on her easel. She didn't have the heart to begin a picture, or even to think of a subject, because the memory of that disastrous evening in the restaurant, three weeks ago, was refusing to fade. She worried about her father. She was furious with her mother. She missed Maggie. And she blamed herself.

None of this would have happened if I hadn't listened in to that phone call six months ago. Or if I had chosen to ignore it. Mum and Dad wouldn't have split up. Mum would still be having the odd weekend away, but was it doing us any harm? Compared to this! I wouldn't have been out for that meal with Dad so we wouldn't have met Maggie and her mother. I would never have known about her connection with Alastair and the accident. Why did I have to get involved?

But then she looked at it from a different angle.

Mum mentioned Grant Cartwright's name in that telephone conversation with Douglas McKendrick. All that business about a letter he should have received. And I told Sam. That's what they were talking about in the supermarket that time. When Grant told him about this flat. Which is how

I ended up living here. Otherwise I might never have met Alastair.

She began to cheer up. She couldn't imagine life now without her adorable and captivating boyfriend and was definitely head over heels in love with every bone in his body. Finding out the name of the person responsible for his injuries, and realising that the culprit was connected to a family they knew, had been in some ways traumatic for both Alastair and his mother, but in other ways cathartic. At long last they had the closure they had always craved. But whilst none of them laid any blame at Maggie's door, Jasmine had not yet found the inner strength she needed to make contact and Maggie hadn't been in touch with her either. Their friendship was in limbo, maybe even extinct.

Jasmine picked up a picture which was sitting on the floor, propped up against the wall. It was a seascape that her friend had given her in exchange for a portrait she had painted, working from a photograph of Lawrence. As she admired the clever brushstrokes making up the fabric of the fishing boats and the range of blue and green hues used to depict the realistic-looking waves, her mobile started to ring in her handbag. By the time she located it in the bedroom, the ringing had stopped but a text message was buzzing through. She saw DM in the caller display and opened it right away.

I don't want to alarm you Jasmine but your mother has taken ill and is in hospital. Give me a ring. Douglas

She called him immediately.

219

"What's happened? Why is Mum in hospital?"

"I don't know what's wrong. She collapsed earlier this morning."

"I'm coming over to see her. Have you told the rest of the family too?"

"No. I thought you would be the easiest to approach. Perhaps you could inform them for me."

"Yes, of course." *Was that some kind of compliment? It didn't really matter.* "Is she conscious?"

Douglas told her that Patty was drifting in and out of consciousness and that the doctors were doing various tests. He sounded worried.

"I'll be there as soon as possible," Jasmine promised. "Text me the details of where she is. Please. And thank you for calling me."

Douglas assured her that he would keep her abreast of any developments and sent the requested information. Jasmine phoned her brother.

"So you're going to head over today?" Sam was trying to get his head round the unexpected development. "How are you placed for work?"

"I'm due a few days off before Easter. I'll just take them now. It'll be fine. I wanted to visit Mum anyway. There's something very strange about her break-up with Dad. I think they're keeping something from us."

"Well, let me know how she is. I suppose I should tell him."

"Maybe wait until we know more," Jasmine cautioned. "We don't want him coming face to face with McKendrick in a hospital ward."

"I think Scotland is the last place on earth that he'll want to visit," Sam replied. "I'll say nothing until I hear from you."

"What about Molly?"

"Same goes for her. She doesn't even know about the split yet! If she extends this holiday any longer she won't recognise us as the family she left behind."

"At least she has the spirit of adventure. I envy her that. We must seem awfully dull in comparison."

"But will she be able to cope when she comes back to earth with a bump and has to start studying? And she'll need a part-time job. She'll have to start paying her way. She can't go on sponging off Mum and Dad."

Jasmine was in total agreement with her brother on that score but felt they were digressing from the problem in hand. She ended the conversation and set about booking herself a plane ticket to Edinburgh and organising a few days' leave. Then she phoned Alastair to explain what was happening. Within a couple of hours she had a bag packed and was heading for the airport.

★★★

Patricia gradually became aware of a buzz of conversation around her, the beeping of machines, a strong smell of antiseptic. She tried to open her eyes. They felt so tired, so heavy, so glazed over. But after a few minutes the hospital ward began to come into focus. Three beds opposite her, one on either side of her, all occupied by patients who were sitting up, chatting to visitors. A tube attached to a cannula in her left hand leading to a bag of liquid which was slowly dripping into her veins. Then the blurred vision disappeared again as her eyes failed in their struggle to remain open. Numbly she racked her brain, trying to make sense of it all.

What am I doing in hospital? What's wrong with me? Why isn't Kenneth here? Everyone else has visitors.

Aware suddenly of a movement by her side, Patricia forced her eyes open again and saw that there was a nurse checking her drip. She cleared her throat with a little cough to attract her attention.

"Ah, you're awake," said the nurse. "How are you feeling?"

It was the Scottish accent that immediately brought Patricia back down to earth, reminding her where she lived nowadays. Tears formed in her eyes as the full extent of the realisation dawned on her.

Of course Kenneth isn't here. He's miles away across the sea in Belfast, thinking that I don't love him anymore. But I do. More than ever. I've made such a mess of things.

She tried to focus her eyes on the nurse who was now leaning over her and smiling. "Where am I?" she asked tentatively. "What's happened to me? I can't remember."

"I'll just go and let the doctor know you're awake," the nurse replied. "That's some sleep you've had."

Patricia closed her eyes again and allowed her thoughts to drift into the realms she had hitherto avoided.

I want my old life back. I want to be with Casey. In my own house. Where I can see the children regularly. I don't belong here. Mia resents me. We used to get on so well. She didn't seem to mind me having an affair with her dad. Until I moved in. Now she obviously feels threatened. She's become so cold and hostile. Even her dog has turned against me and growls at me when we're alone together. Mia was mistress of the house for so long. She had her own way of doing things. If I were in her shoes I would feel resentful. How long is it since her mother died? Over ten years. Dougie had led her to believe that she would inherit the house, lock, stock and barrel. But what if he marries me? He has hinted at it. Where would that leave Mia? And where would it leave me? And then there's Barbara! I feel so uncomfortable around Dougie's sister-in-law. She only lives across the road and she's been so welcoming to me, inviting me over for coffee, showing me albums of photos taken over the years. So many pictures of that handsome, smiling face. Her husband. The man that Casey killed.

The tears came now, thick and fast. Patricia allowed them to flow. She still had no idea why she was in hospital. The visitors were starting to drift away from the other beds around her and she was dimly aware of a bell ringing in the background. The nurse came back and pulled a blue curtain around her bed.

"Doctor's on her way," she said kindly, noticing the tears and thrusting a wad of tissues into her hand. Then she checked her blood pressure and temperature and filled in the chart which was hanging over the end of the bed. Patricia spotted that she had beautiful brown eyes. She reminded her of Molly, the daughter she hadn't seen for almost a year. She wondered briefly whether the others had told Molly what was going on. She hadn't. She had somehow managed to palm her off when she asked difficult questions, had kept the conversation focused on Molly's travels and adventures, the places she'd seen, the people she'd met, giving her only the most trivial of information about herself. Now she asked herself why.

She's going to find out eventually. She'll be furious that we've kept this from her. And I don't even know how to explain it now. The biggest mistake of my life.

Dr Melrose arrived and introduced herself. She checked the observations on the chart and asked Patricia how she was feeling, why she was crying.

"I was just thinking about my family," Patricia bluffed, "and wondering how I came to be here."

"You passed out at home this morning. Your husband has been here most of the day. He's just gone downstairs for something to eat. I've asked the nurse to tell him that you're awake."

"My husband?" For a split second Patricia's heart was filled with warmth and hope.

"Mr McKendrick," the doctor replied, consulting her notes.

"Of course," Patricia sighed, deflated.

"Is there someone else we should have contacted?"

Sadly Patricia shook her head. "No, no it's fine. I live with Mr McKendrick."

"Ah, but he's not your husband. Sorry."

"So what's wrong with me?" Patricia asked, changing the subject.

"It would appear to be a medication issue," Dr Melrose told her. "I need to know exactly what you took this morning, especially anything you haven't had before and anything was wasn't prescribed by your GP.

Did you maybe take a double dose of something? There are traces of various substances in your bloodstream." When Patricia didn't answer at once the doctor added, "Is everything all right in your life at the moment? You looked disappointed when you realised that it wasn't your husband who was here. Are you still in touch with him? Is your life happy?"

Patricia dried her tears and stared at the doctor, horrified. "You think I did this on purpose! You think I tried to top myself!"

"I didn't say that." The doctor spoke calmly. "I just need to know what you've taken and why."

"I know you didn't say it. But you're thinking it. Well, let me tell you the truth. No, everything is not all right in my life. But it's my own fault. My husband did not leave me; I left him. And I regret it. It's not that I don't love Dougie as well but I miss my home and my family. More than you can imagine. However, I did not and would not try to harm myself or do myself in. I have so much to live for. Three children. And a grandson. I love them all dearly."

"I have to consider all options, Patricia. I'm sorry. You just looked so sad."

"I am a bit sad. But I'm not suicidal. You have to take my word for it."

"Not even a cry for help?"

"No, never!"

"OK, I believe you," she smiled. "Now start by telling me what drugs you take on a regular basis."

Before she could answer Douglas arrived, racing over to the bed with a wide smile on his flushed face.

"I've been sitting here for hours," he quipped jocularly, "and then you go and waken up as soon as I leave the room!" As he kissed her tenderly on the cheek, Patricia gave the doctor a look of caution, hoping to convey the fact that the things they had just discussed should remain private. The doctor gave her a nod in return.

Following some discussion and a couple of phone calls it turned out that Patricia had indeed taken the wrong medicine that morning. She had absent-mindedly swallowed what was in the little cup that Mia had put out for her father on the breakfast table and, not realising that his daughter had organised his pills for him, Douglas had simply taken a second dose from the bottles in the kitchen cupboard so the mistake had not been spotted. Instead of her own medication for mild headaches, Patricia had in fact taken drugs that Douglas used daily to treat a potentially serious heart condition. In addition to this the sleeping tablet that she now remembered taking in the early hours had probably exacerbated the effect on her body. It was little wonder that she had collapsed but fortunately, according to Dr Melrose, there should not be any long-term consequences. They would keep her in overnight for observation but she would probably be discharged in the morning.

Douglas breathed a sigh of relief. "I shouldn't have worried your family," he said, as the doctor moved away.

"You told them about this?" Patricia quizzed.

"I spoke to Jasmine."

Patricia just nodded her head.

"I hope you don't mind but I was feeling very anxious. It could have been something really serious."

"Hey, you don't need to justify yourself. Of course I don't mind. You did the right thing."

"She's probably on her way over here as we speak."

Patricia took a deep breath, revelling in the anticipation of seeing her elder daughter. Would she really come rushing to her bedside? Where would she stay? Not with Dougie, surely. That would be so awkward. And more ammunition for Mia. What time of day was it anyway? Her eyes were so heavy, her mind so confused. She took a glance at Douglas and felt guilty when she saw the concern and the tiredness etched on his face. Stress wasn't good for him; he never dwelt on the fact that he had a heart condition but the shared knowledge had always been there in the background. "You go on home," she said gently. "I'll be fine now. I'm sorry you've wasted all those hours."

"Well, if you don't mind, I maybe will call it a day."

"You need to rest. You must be exhausted. I'm in good hands here."

"I love you, Patty. I don't know what I would have done if you hadn't come through this. I was so worried."

"Go home," she answered firmly, dismissing him with a smile.

He gave her a kiss. "OK, see you tomorrow. I love you."

She couldn't bring herself to say it back but just followed him sadly with her eyes as he left the ward.

Despite the recriminations and regrets going through her mind she was soon fast asleep, unaware of the unspeakable anguish that awaited her in the morning.

★★★

They both received the devastating news at once, Kenneth in his lonely sitting-room in Belfast and Patricia in her hospital bed in Edinburgh, the same text message that simultaneously shattered both their worlds. Molly was missing, presumed drowned.

Part Three

Chapter 26

"Meet Victoria Esme," Imogen said proudly, as she carefully laid the baby in Jasmine's lap and smiled happily at Alastair. "She's two months old today." Jasmine stared at the child and panicked. She didn't know how to react. Her emotions were all over the place these days.

"Here, give her to me." Jillian noticed her friend's discomfort and immediately jumped to her aid with outstretched arms. Imogen and Grant had arrived for an impromptu visit, unannounced, while Jillian was entertaining her friends from downstairs.

"No, it's OK." Jasmine told her. "She's gorgeous. And it feels nice, cuddling her."

Grant had gone straight to the kitchen where he was sharing a joke with Bradley. Alastair leaned over his girlfriend and softly touched the baby's face, then gently lifted one little hand and examined the tiny fingers. He gave Jasmine a questioning glance. She shook her head. "No," she mouthed, shaking her head again. And then, without warning, she started to cry. Imogen was alarmed and quickly retrieved her daughter from her friend's lap, muttering an apology and something about it being too soon. Jasmine nodded, keeping her thoughts to herself.

I feel so guilty every time I even smile. It doesn't seem right to smile, to laugh, to feel happiness. So how have I managed to get myself pregnant? Before my sister is even cold in her grave. She would have been twenty-three last month, just a couple of weeks after this child was born. Her whole life ahead of her. A glittering career, boyfriends, marriage, babies of her own. But none of that is going to happen now. And how have I consoled myself? I'm a disgrace. I've sullied her memory. I want this baby so much but I don't deserve it.

Alastair was now sitting beside her on the sofa, his arm around her, his head resting against hers, his voice soothing in her ear. "We should tell them," he whispered. "They'll all understand. Life goes on."

"Everything all right?" quizzed Bradley, emerging from the kitchen and picking up on the atmosphere.

"Jasmine's just feeling a bit fragile," Jillian answered. "Molly's death is still very raw for her, for all of us. It's only been three or four months."

"I just feel so guilty about having any sense of happiness," Jasmine sniffed.

"Well, that's the last thing she would have wanted," Grant put in. "The best way you can honour your sister's memory is by getting on with your life and making every day count. I should know." They all expressed their agreement.

"Best thing you could do is have your own baby," Imogen trilled. "Bring a new life into the world. It's such a wonderful feeling." She gazed lovingly at little Victoria as she spoke and planted a gentle kiss on her forehead.

"Would that not seem as though we were trying to replace her," Jasmine interjected, wiping her eyes and giving Alastair's hand a squeeze.

Knowing glances were suddenly exchanged all round. It was Bradley who spoke. "Have you something to tell us all, Alastair?"

"Maybe," his friend grinned, looking at Jasmine for permission. She hesitated and then gave him a nod and a watery smile.

"I'm pregnant," she confirmed.

"Mum doesn't even know yet," Alastair then warned his cousin, "so don't you go saying anything at home."

"We'll have to tell them all soon," said Jasmine. "My parents don't know anything either. I've been afraid of their reaction. But you've made me feel so much better about it. Thanks everyone, especially you, Grant."

Grant smiled and whispered something to Bradley as the girls gushed their congratulations.

"We're not in any hurry, thanks," Bradley retorted, brushing off the remark. "We're happy enough with things as they are for the moment."

Jillian immediately concurred, guessing what Grant had said and explaining that they wanted to enjoy a few years of freedom before tying themselves down with a family. They had plans to travel and see a bit of the world.

"Don't leave it too long," quipped Imogen. "We'll both be thirty before the year is out." Jillian and Imogen were the same age and had been best friends ever since going through school together.

"No doubt Granny will be organising one of her famous parties," said Alastair.

"Wait till she hears about you!" Grant replied, laughing. He went over and shook his cousin by the hand.

Bradley followed suit but didn't stop with a handshake. He threw his arms around his friend and hugged him with genuine affection and delight. "Such wonderful news," he enthused, "and so unexpected."

Jasmine understood the veiled comment at once. None of them had expected Alastair to lead a normal life. She remembered Maggie warning her off him, telling her that he was brain-damaged, that there were things he couldn't do. And she recalled the nasty comments she had been witness to at the garden centre.

"That's all thanks to you, Brad." It was Grant, voicing aloud what they were all thinking.

No-one else spoke but they all knew what he meant. It was Bradley's friendship over the years that had normalised Alastair when others had shunned him. Grant himself had acknowledged this almost a year ago when he had finally let go of his childhood jealousy and had accepted Bradley as a real friend.

"I only meant that it was unexpected now, so soon," Bradley retorted, embarrassed, "not that it wouldn't happen eventually."

Alastair bristled. "Would you all stop talking about me as though I was some kind of freak," he blurted out indignantly, annoyed at the inference. "I didn't need Bradley or anyone else to show me how to make babies!"

Both men were taken aback and muttered an apology whilst Alastair took a deep breath and tried to regain his cool. And suddenly there was another knock at the door.

"More visitors," trilled Jillian. "I should have organised a party!" She went out to welcome the newcomers and then led them into the room.

Jasmine stiffened when she realised who had arrived as Maggie and Lawrence materialised in front of her. She hadn't seen her friend since the disastrous scene in the restaurant five months ago when Greta and Thomasina had come face to face.

"Oh, sorry," Maggie gulped, as she caught sight of Jasmine on the sofa. "I don't want to be rude but I didn't expect you to be here. We just tiptoed past your flat hoping you wouldn't spot us." She averted her gaze from Alastair, embarrassed.

"Look, Imogen's here with the baby," Jillian gushed, hoping to avoid any unpleasantness. But Maggie continued to look directly at her erstwhile friend as though she hadn't even heard. Instinctively the others all began to back away into the kitchen. Even Lawrence followed them in.

"You don't need to feel that you're treading on eggshells around us," Jasmine said with a lump in her throat. "You don't have to tiptoe past my flat."

"I'm so sorry about your sister," Maggie uttered.

"I got your card," Jasmine answered with a nod. "I kept hoping you might call."

"I didn't think I'd be welcome." She was aware of Alastair's quickening breath and forced herself to look at him at last. "I can't expect you ever to forgive me."

"There's nothing to forgive," he told her. "It was never your fault."

"I can understand why you didn't tell us," added Jasmine. "It was an awkward situation."

"But you never phoned or texted. I was afraid to approach you. He was my father. The association will always be there, in the background."

Jasmine squeezed up closer to her boyfriend and patted the sofa, indicating that Maggie should sit down with them. "I didn't know how to break the ice either," she admitted. "And then Molly died. And everything changed."

"Sam told us your mother has come back home. Do you think she'll stay?"

"Probably not. She only came home to support Dad and help with the arrangements but her life is in Scotland now with that man, McKendrick."

"Are you going to tell Maggie our news?" Alastair asked, his breathing back on an even keel.

"We're expecting a baby," Jasmine divulged with a smile.

"No!"

"Yes!"

"Well congratulations!" Maggie gave her a warm hug. "That's brilliant news." Then she added, "Can we really be friends again?"

"I hope so."

Maggie looked at Alastair for confirmation.

"Maybe our mums will even be friends some day," he mused. "I'm glad you called in here this morning. Jasmine has missed you."

The sound of laughter was now filtering through from the kitchen. "She's already a potential heiress," Imogen was saying with a giggle, "and Grant's Uncle Scott is away back to Canada in disgust."

"I'm so glad that I've got to know them all," Grant added. "To think that I rejected him at first and burnt that letter."

Jasmine smiled to herself. A lot of good things had come from that overheard phone call almost a year ago. "Come and see Victoria Esme," she said, standing up and beckoning to Maggie as Alastair led them both towards the merry throng in the kitchen.

"Ah," cried Grant with a modicum of glee, as he saw them approaching and trying to make up for his earlier comment which had enraged his cousin. "The very man. It's never too soon to start practising. Come and help me change this nappy."

Chapter 27

Patricia smiled as she waved goodbye to Tania and Stevie after a fun afternoon in the garden. In spite of the inauspicious start to their relationship, she had become very fond of Sam's fiancée and loved spending time with her grandson. *How time flies,* she thought to herself; Stevie would be two before Christmas. She began to tidy up the toys which were strewn around the grass and the remainder of the impromptu picnic they had enjoyed. Kenneth would soon be back from his round of golf with Sam. Jasmine and Alastair were coming for tea. Everything seemed so normal.

But, in reality, life was anything but normal. Molly's ghost was everywhere, plaguing her with unanswered questions, blaming her for all that had gone wrong in the family. Douglas was becoming impatient about her not giving him a date for her return to Scotland. Kenneth was in denial that he was hiding a guilty secret. Patricia poured herself a glass of wine and sat down on the wooden bench under the rowan tree to enjoy the late afternoon sunshine. She had never seen such an abundance of orangey-red berries in previous years; it was quite a magnificent display. Her gaze landed next on the cluster of terracotta pots on the patio, sporting a colourful array of petunias, antirrhinums and cosmos, then on the flowerbed full of pink and purple fuchsias and bright yellow sunflowers. So much beauty around her but so much sadness in her heart. She closed her eyes and drifted into a gentle sleep.

***

"Ask her to stay, Dad, before it's too late."

"I can't, Son. We had an agreement."

Patricia heard the muffled voices coming from the kitchen. She was still sitting on the garden bench. Checking her watch, she pretended to sleep on and listened.

"Well I don't understand your agreement. You want her here and she clearly wants to be here. You're still married."

"I don't expect you to understand."

"So you're just going to let her walk away again? Back into the arms of that bastard?"

"She loves him. She's only here because of Molly."

"I don't think so. She told Jaz that she made a mistake."

"I couldn't have coped without her. Thank God she was here, especially when Molly's body was recovered. And the funeral. We were all there for each other though I still don't know how we managed to get through it. But Jasmine's got the wrong end of the stick about your mum. This has all been for Molly. She'll be gone again soon."

"No, Dad, open your eyes. She doesn't want to go back. She spoke to Jaz *before* this all happened. Do you remember? Jaz went over to visit Mum in hospital. They were together when the news about Molly came through. The first message. The one that said she was missing."

"And she'd already told your sister that she wanted to come home?"

"Yes."

"I don't believe you. She wanted her freedom and I granted her that wish."

"And what did she give you in return?"

"What do you mean?"

A lengthy silence ensued. Patricia held her breath, waiting for Sam's answer. Surely he could not have discovered any inkling of the truth. She was still horrified by what Kenneth had done but also ashamed of the emotional blackmail she herself had deployed against him. The manner in which they had used one another was so abhorrent to her now, so regrettable. What had happened to the happy couple they used to be when they loved and respected one another? When she heard her son speaking again she had to strain her ears to pick up what he was saying.

"I don't really know what I mean. Jaz and I have just wondered why you accepted the situation so lightly and agreed to everything on her terms. After all, it was Mum's fault in the first place."

"Not entirely."

"Dad, it doesn't really matter now. The crux of the matter is this. She wants to stay here with you. Can you not forgive her and let that happen?"

Patricia now got up from her bench and headed towards the hushed voices.

"Hello, you two," she said cheerily. "I must have dropped off for a moment. I didn't realise you were back."

Sam smiled at his mother. Kenneth scowled and indicated the back door, lying wide open.

"We could have been burgled," he chastised her, but in a semi-jocular manner. "You've been asleep for at least half an hour."

"Sorry, my eyes just grew so heavy, sitting there in the sun."

"Never mind. There's no harm done." He turned to Sam. "Thanks for the game, Son. We should do it more often."

"I had a lovely afternoon with Tania and Stevie," Patricia told them.

"I know. She texted me," Sam replied.

"You young people are never without a phone in your hand," Patricia retorted. But in truth she was pleased that Tania had not just been humouring her. She really must have enjoyed spending time together.

Sam headed for his car, both parents automatically walking alongside him. Patricia gave him a wave as he drove off and then decided to take the bull by the horns. She turned towards her husband. "I wasn't actually asleep all that time," she confessed. "I heard the two of you talking."

Kenneth just looked at her and nodded, a sad expression on his face.

"What Sam told you is true," she continued, her heart in her mouth. "I did have that conversation with Jasmine in the hospital. Before we knew about Molly."

Kenneth let out a huge sigh. "If only we could turn the clock back," he muttered.

They ambled back round to the garden bench and sat down together, side by side. It was now in the shade but the air was still warm.

"I never stopped loving you," Patricia declared in a quiet, even voice. "I am so sorry for everything."

"But you still love him too?"

"No, I don't. It was an infatuation, an adventure. I was flattered and carried away with the excitement, the duplicity."

"Because you were bored with me."

"I was never bored with you, my darling. I loved our life together."

"But when it came to the crunch, you chose him."

Patricia sighed. "I was so confused that day. He appeared out of the blue at Grant Cartwright's wedding reception and he seduced me. I had no idea that he was going to be there. And I thought that you didn't really want me back, not properly, that you were just going through the motions with me to keep the police at bay."

Kenneth shuddered. "You can't still love me, knowing what I've done."

"You only did it because of me."

"I only meant to give him a fright, to ward him off."

"You've never actually told me what happened."

"Only because I can't bear to think about it. I do still love you, Patricia. I'm dreading the day that you return to him."

"Then ask me to stay." It was a mere whisper.

"Can you live with the guilt?"

Patricia grabbed his hand and held it tightly in her own. Her heart was pounding in her chest. "I'll never mention it again, Kenneth, whether I stay here or go back to Scotland. I know it was an accident and it would never have happened if I hadn't driven you to it so it is my fault as much as yours. No-one else knows or suspects anything. We can put this behind us and move on. I love you, only you."

Kenneth looked her straight in the eye and smiled. "I'd like that," he said simply. "I never stopped loving you either. I acted defensively out of jealousy and anger."

"So what do you want me to do?"

"Stay." He kissed her tenderly on the lips and enfolded her in his arms. "Please stay here where you belong and move back into our bedroom with me."

"Tonight?"

"Yes, tonight."

Patricia felt a surge of happiness wash over her like a cooling breeze on a sweltering summer's evening. She snuggled into her husband's warm embrace, feeling the old, familiar sensation of his heart beating against hers, the most wonderful feeling in the world. Unbelievably her greatest wish was being granted, her impossible dream coming true. She whispered lovingly into his ear.

"I will never be unfaithful to you again. I promise you that. Just let me talk to Dougie one last time. I owe him that, a proper explanation."

"Yes, of course," Kenneth agreed. "Do it now before Jasmine arrives."

They shared another kiss and then Patricia disappeared into the house to make the call.

★★★

Jasmine was over the moon. Her parents were back together. Douglas McKendrick was history. Grant Cartwright was happily reunited with his biological father and his baby daughter, Victoria, was apparently heiress to a fortune. And she, herself, was looking forward to motherhood with the man of her dreams, someone she might never have met had she not acted upon the information she had gleaned from that overheard phone call in this very house. The one blip on the horizon was that her sister was dead, her beautiful, fun-loving sister who had lived life to the full and who had ironically died on a beautiful, sandy beach, caught up in a sudden tidal wave while she was having an innocent evening swim, and not whilst participating in one of the potentially hazardous activities she had undertaken during the previous months. Jasmine comforted herself in the knowledge that Molly's final year had been a happy one, full of adventure. But she missed her dreadfully and the house seemed so empty without her.

Emerging from the small downstairs bathroom and walking past that same coat-stand where she had concealed herself eleven months ago, Jasmine took a deep breath in preparation for the conversation ahead. Now that her friends knew about her pregnancy she figured that it was only fair to inform her parents before they stumbled on the news from someone else. She retook her place at the table and smiled nervously at Alastair. He reached for her hand and gave it a loving squeeze.

"Are you feeling all right?" Patricia asked, a worried expression on her face. "You've been running to the toilet a lot recently. That's twice since we started this meal."

"I'm fine, thanks." Jasmine hesitated for a moment and then just blurted it out. "Apparently it's normal when you're pregnant."

She waited anxiously for the reaction from her parents and from Thomasina who had joined them for the meal. They all remained silent.

"Are you not happy for us?" Alastair faltered, somewhat crestfallen.

"I know the timing isn't ideal," added Jasmine, "but it just happened and we're going to make it work. We love one another."

Thomasina could contain herself no longer. She beamed with pleasure and let out a very contented sigh. "It's wonderful news," she pronounced. "I know I'm a guest in this house and maybe I'm overstepping the mark by speaking up first, but if you all knew what Alastair and I have been through over so many years you would appreciate what this means to me." She leapt out of her seat and enfolded Jasmine in a warm embrace. "I thought I would never see this day. He has changed so much since he met you. You have given him back his life." Then she looked directly at Kenneth. "Do you not approve?" she quizzed him.

"I can't say I'm not shocked," Kenneth replied, addressing his daughter. "We've only just got over the embarrassment of Sam getting Tania pregnant, a girl we had never even met. And now it's happened to you. You haven't been together for very long. And these things don't just happen!"

"But look how that turned out," Patricia countered, giving her husband a cautionary glance. "Stevie is the light of our world. And they're getting married."

"It's just so soon after Molly," her husband retorted, fighting away a tear.

"On the contrary, it's just what we all need," Patricia said, brushing aside the negative remark. "New blood in the family. Molly would have been over the moon."

"Life goes on," Thomasina put in, tentatively. "I had to pull myself together after Ray's life was wiped out in a flash, for no good reason, and I had to live with the knowledge, for year upon year, that the culprit had got away with it. You learn to value good news when it comes along."

The reference to her dead husband reminded Kenneth of the night he'd met Alastair's mother in the restaurant. Although he had been quite drunk at the time, he still had a clear memory of the conversation they had engaged in. He immediately felt very uncomfortable when he realised that she was remembering it too.

"Even today I still have nightmares about his last moments and wonder whether he could have been saved if they'd found him in time." Then she added a further comment that made Kenneth start to sweat profusely. "Catherine was just saying yesterday that she has a friend over in Scotland who is feeling exactly the same. Her husband died after a fall in the garden and lay all night before being discovered." Thomasina had momentarily forgotten the connection between Cameron's friend, Douglas, and Jasmine's mother. To Kenneth and Patricia's horror she continued her anecdote. "Now that Alastair's cousin, Grant, has formed a healthy relationship with his father, my sister is also renewing old acquaintances. She and Mark have become quite friendly with Cameron and his wife. They came over here recently to see their new grandchild. Victoria Esme. She is such a pretty little thing. Gosh, I'm just getting over the fact that Catherine is a grandmother and now I'm going to be one myself!"

In the absence of any congratulatory remarks from Jasmine's parents and annoyed that they had both gone so quiet, Thomasina continued to prattle on about her sister's family. "Anyway, Cameron is very friendly with this guy, Douglas McKendrick, and it was his brother who just suddenly dropped dead. He split his head wide open and was found the next morning in a pool of blood. His wife is absolutely traumatised by the thought that he might have been lying there in agony for hours while she was sleeping peacefully just across the road, unaware of what had happened. I've had years to come to terms with what happened to me but it's still all very raw as far as she is concerned. This incident took place fairly recently."

Jasmine glanced nervously at Alastair, hoping that he could somehow divert his mother and turn the conversation to a more appropriate topic. The silence in the room was deafening. Thomasina looked confused. "Sorry," she said after a moment, "I didn't mean to sound so morbid. I'm just saying that we should celebrate good news and not dwell on the bad things that have happened. Congratulations, you two." She raised her glass to make a toast. Neither Patricia nor Kenneth followed suit. Jasmine felt gutted.

The sound of the kitchen door opening and closing in the background, followed by footsteps in the hallway suddenly alerted them all to the fact that someone else had entered the house. Kenneth jumped up to investigate.

"It'll just be Sam," Patricia said in a flat tone. "I phoned him earlier on to say that he'd gone home without Stevie's bunny rabbit. He won't go to bed without it." Then she stood up and walked over to her daughter. "Just give us some time to get our heads round this," she smiled, giving her a hug. "Of course it's good news. Just a bit of a shock coming on top of everything else." She patted Alastair on the shoulder. Jasmine returned the smile with a watery one of her own. Something wasn't adding up here. Her mother had been in quite an upbeat frame of mind at the start of the meal and had initially made a positive comment about the pregnancy. Now she appeared to be tense and edgy, even frightened. Jasmine excused herself from the table for yet another visit to the bathroom.

It was indeed Sam who had arrived to collect the toy rabbit. He and Kenneth had gone into the sitting room and were now talking to one another in low voices. Jasmine stopped to listen, wondering how her dad was relaying the news about her being in the family way and how Sam would react, hopefully in a more positive manner than their parents. But he hadn't come rushing to congratulate her so she sensed that he too maybe disapproved of the timing. Thank goodness for her friends earlier in the day! She placed a hand on the door to ease it open so that she could confront her brother in person but suddenly stopped, realising that they were not discussing her condition at all, but something entirely different.

"Don't say it, Dad. As long as you don't actually put it into words, I can go on believing that it never happened."

"I knew you had worked it out."

"I've been hoping I was wrong."

"Your mother and I had hoped to put it behind us and get our lives back on track, but listening to that woman tonight has really unsettled me."

"So Mum knows about it too."

Jasmine frowned. What could they possibly be talking about that was of more importance than her big announcement? She pushed the door open and burst in.

"Well, have you told him?" she asked, addressing her father.

Kenneth looked blankly at his daughter as though she had spoken in a foreign language. Sam answered her instead.

"Yes, he's given me the rundown. Mum's home for good. Hopefully we can all forget about it now."

"I'm having a baby," Jasmine told her brother. "Dad obviously disapproves but I thought you might have been more understanding."

"I don't disapprove, Love," Kenneth then pronounced. "You just took me by surprise. I hadn't even mentioned it yet to your brother. I thought you'd want to tell him yourself."

"A baby! Good for you, Sis." Sam seemed genuinely happy for her. "Where's Alastair?" He strode out of the room in search of her boyfriend so that he could offer his congratulations.

Kenneth took Jasmine in his arms. "We've all been through so much," he whispered, "but it'll all be fine. It'll be more than fine. Your mum's right. It's just what we need when you think about it. A new baby in the family."

Jasmine felt a warm glow of contentment. For a brief moment she wondered what her father and her brother had been discussing but she didn't dwell on it. Something to do with her parents' separation. All in the past now. Water under the bridge. Time to live for the future.

Chapter 28

The holiday in Italy had been wonderful, marred only by an overwhelming sadness that would never go away. Yet the awful realisation that they would never see their daughter again was mixed with a strange sense of gratitude that the girl had been blissfully unaware of the shocking things they had both done and the dreadful way they had treated one another. Back at home now Patricia and Kenneth were settling into their new life together with a quiet contentment and their indiscretions of the past year were hardly mentioned. Douglas had arranged for the return of any jewellery and other important items that Patricia had left in Scotland, delivering them via Grant and Cathy to avoid any embarrassment. Life was back on an even keel.

Gertrude Cartwright would be seventy-five on the ninth of September and her family were throwing her a surprise party.

"Please say you'll both come," Cathy urged, talking to her friend on the phone. "Mum's always organising celebrations for other members of the family. It's time for us to honour her for a change."

"That's only a week away," Patricia replied, trying to think of a valid excuse. "I'm not sure. I'll have to check with Casey."

"There won't be anyone coming from Scotland," Catherine reassured her, fully understanding her reserve.

"No? Not even Grant's father?"

"No, we decided to keep it more local and just invite people Mum has known all her life. Cameron has only come into our lives very recently. He doesn't really know Mum very well at all."

"And Grant doesn't mind?"

"It's not his party. This is for Mum."

"Well, in that case we'd love to come."

"Brilliant. It'll be just like the old days. Your family and mine. Just one or two others."

"Thanks, Cathy. I'll look forward to it. But are you sure you wouldn't rather just limit it to family?"

Catherine laughed. "You *are* family now. You and my sister will soon be grandmothers to the same child," she reminded her.

"That's true. It came as a bit of a shock at first but I'm delighted for them now. Yes, it'll do us all the world of good to get together in a party atmosphere."

"And you're sure Kenneth will be happy to come?"

"I'll let you know. But yes, I think so. We've put all that behind us. He's perfectly happy again about us being friends. And we're both very fond of your mother. Any idea what she'd like as a gift?"

The two friends chatted on for some time and when Patricia put the idea to Kenneth later on that day, he accepted the invitation without any outward sign of reluctance. These people were part of Jasmine's family now. There was no way he was going to shun them or jeopardise her chance of happiness. There was no reason not to go.

★★★

Catherine and Mark were really looking forward to entertaining the family in their stunning new home on the outskirts of the city. By the time Gertrude was due to arrive with Thomasina, everyone else should already be in situ. Grant and Imogen were coming of course along with their daughter, Victoria Esme, now just over three months old. Rebecca, Robyn and Jack had all helped with the preparations and the girls were excited about renewing their acquaintance with the Campbell family, albeit saddened by the fact that Molly would be missing. As well as Alastair's girlfriend, Jasmine, Sam Campbell would be there, accompanied by his wife, Tania, and their little boy, Stevie. And of course Bradley Harrington had been invited along with his wife, Jillian. Patty and Kenneth would complete the intimate gathering.

Everything went according to plan and Gertrude was thrilled to find that the family had organised the event to celebrate her birthday. She loved a party but she was usually the one doing all the work. All she had to do this time was turn up and enjoy herself. And that's exactly what she did, joining the others in Catherine's large modern kitchen for drinks and nibbles. She would open her gifts later.

"Oops! Great timing, Victoria," Imogen laughed, as a rather pungent smell pervaded the air. "Come on, let's

253

get you cleaned up." Grabbing her changing bag from the chair where she had dumped it on the way in, she made her way upstairs and into the room which Catherine had made available for such eventualities. Spreading her plastic mat out on the bed, she placed the baby on it and fished out some wipes and a fresh nappy. With well-practised precision she took no time at all to have the child clean and swathed in a mist of fragrant baby powder. Planting a kiss on her forehead and holding her close for a cuddle, she then placed her gently into the cradle Grant had left in earlier in the day.

"You make a lovely mother, Imogen."

Swinging round to face the door, she encountered the smiling face of Sam Campbell. Imogen smiled back, involuntarily licking her lips and feeling her heart lurch just a little. Sam stepped into the room and gently closed the door behind him.

"What are you doing?" Imogen asked, somewhat alarmed. "Where's Tania?"

"She's downstairs with Stevie and all the others," Sam answered calmly. "I was just on my way back from the bathroom and I spotted you there with your baby. It just seems so surreal. I always thought that we would have a baby together. But look at us now. You have one with Grant. I have one with Tania."

"Open the door, Sam."

"Oh, Imogen, you don't need to be afraid of me. I wouldn't hurt a hair on your head."

"What do you want then?"

"Same as you."

Imogen gave him a questioning look.

"A kiss. Just for old times' sake. A goodbye kiss. We never did end it properly."

"Are you drunk?"

"You can't tell me that you don't feel it too. There's still something there, something special between us. There always will be."

"I love Grant," Imogen said firmly.

"I know you do. And I like the bloke. We've become good friends again."

"I thought you loved Tania."

"I do." Sam made a frustrated gesture with his hands. "You've got it all wrong, Imogen. I'm not suggesting that we do anything improper. I just want to say sorry. For the stupid fling with Holly. I just want to say sorry. And to know that you forgive me."

"I forgave you a long time ago, Sam."

"Then can we not have a goodbye kiss?"

Imogen's resolve weakened and she moved towards him, allowing him to take her into his arms. "A hug, yes, but not a kiss," she insisted. "I won't betray my husband."

"He's so lucky to have you, Imogen."

"Things have worked out for the best, for both of us."

Sam nodded. "You're right. Thank you," he breathed.

"For what?"

"For not letting me kiss you. It wouldn't be fair to Tania."

Imogen glanced at the cradle and saw that Victoria had fallen asleep. "We should get back to the party," she proposed.

"In a minute," Sam answered. "Did you know that you loved Grant right from the start?"

Imogen laughed. "Yes," she told him, "but so many things conspired against us for a while."

Sam raised his eyebrows, hoping she might elaborate.

"Well, firstly I thought he was married and cheating on his wife. Secondly I had to control my guilty conscience when I found out the truth as I tried to compete with Zoe's ghost. Then, to top it all, I got it into my head that my parents had killed one of his relatives!"

"You what?"

"It was a stupid misunderstanding that came from something I read in an old diary of my mum's. Gosh, I don't even know why I'm telling you about it but you asked me once how I suddenly discovered I had a brother. Well, that came from the diary too. It was some eye-opener."

Sam ignored the reference to Imogen's brother, Vincent, and the details about how he had come into the world but he pounced on the other piece of information. "You really thought they'd killed someone? And you kept schtoom about it?"

"Well, you can't shop your own parents, can you? No matter what they've done."

Sam opened the door and furtively looked out. No-one about. The sound of merriment still coming from the kitchen. He closed the door again.

"Can I tell you a secret?" he asked hesitantly.

"You look very serious all of a sudden," Imogen replied, not directly answering his question.

"Well, it *is* something serious. I'll go mad if I don't tell somebody. But you mustn't tell anyone else. Not even Grant. Especially not Grant."

Downstairs some of the family could be heard moving from the kitchen into the spacious and airy living-room where Gertrude would eventually open her presents, others heading out into the garden to cool down.

"You can't ask me to keep anything from Grant," Imogen entreated.

"Please. You'll understand. After what you just told me about your parents, I just know you'll understand. I need your support, Imogen. I can't keep this bottled up any longer."

★★★

"Where on earth has Imogen got to?" Jillian trilled, as she retrieved her wedding album from Gertrude who had been gushing over the artistic photos that had been taken on her big day.

"She went upstairs to change Victoria's nappy," Tania observed, bouncing Stevie on her knee.

"But that was ages ago," put in Rebecca.

"Did you get that baby monitoring system set up?" Catherine quizzed, addressing her son.

"Just sorting it now," Grant answered, as he continued to fiddle with some cables attached to a large television screen in the corner of the room.

"All this modern technology is just too much for me," laughed Patty. "Do you really mean that we'll be able to keep an eye on the children while they're sleeping upstairs and we're socialising down here?"

"Here we go now," Grant answered, as the bedroom with its yellow and lilac wallpaper jumped into view.

"What's Sam doing up there?" Tania said crossly. "I wondered where he'd got to."

There was an uneasy silence for a moment. They could all see the sleeping baby in the cradle but they were more interested in the obvious tension between the two adults in the room.

"Is there no volume control?" Catherine asked. "Surely that's the whole point of the thing, so that we can be alerted as soon as the baby starts to cry."

"Here, let me have a look," Bradley offered, jumping up to assist his friend.

By now all eyes were on the screen as it suddenly burst into life, complete with surround sound volume.

"You really expect me to keep this to myself!" It was Imogen's voice in a loud high-pitched screech.

"I had to tell somebody. I've been going mad with no-one to talk to about it."

"Grant is my husband. I refuse to have any secrets from him."

"Even if it's to protect him and those he loves?"

"You're a bastard, Sam. You had no right involving me in this."

"Turn it off," instructed Mark. "This has nothing to do with the rest of us. We shouldn't be eavesdropping on a private conversation."

Whilst they all agreed with him in principle, no-one made a move. They all remained firmly rooted to the spot, eyes focused on the large screen. And then, just as Kenneth could be seen bursting into the bedroom to warn them that they had a captive audience, the punchline was spoken.

"So your dad pretended to be in Spain but he actually travelled to Edinburgh and murdered that man. And your mum has known about it all this time!"

Downstairs in the living-room there was a corporate gasp as nine pairs of eyes turned to stare accusingly at Patricia. Mark pulled the plug from the wall, bringing an eerie silence to the room.

Catherine was the first to speak. "Tell me it isn't true," she pleaded in a whisper.

Patty just shook her head in despair, her face as white as a sheet. Footsteps could be heard on the stairs and then Kenneth and Sam appeared at the door, faces ashen and guilt-ridden.

"What have I done?" stammered the younger man.

Jasmine and Alastair came running in from the garden along with Robyn and Jack, followed closely by Thomasina who had been to the bathroom. They all picked up on the atmosphere immediately.

"What's happened?" Robyn demanded.

No-one answered.

Thomasina glanced at her sister hoping for an explanation but Catherine just rolled her eyes and dismissed her with a gesture of frustration.

Kenneth went over to Patricia and held out his hand. She grasped it tightly and stood up to join him. They could at least put on a united front and attempt to show some degree of dignity. Kenneth spoke briefly to Gertrude.

"I'm so sorry for ruining your party," he said evenly and then, addressing the rest of the room, he added,

"Just for the record, I didn't do it on purpose. It was an accident, a very tragic and regrettable accident. I'll hand myself in to the police tomorrow."

Patricia couldn't speak. She just allowed her husband to lead her in a trance towards the front door where they met Imogen who had just come down the stairs, her baby in her arms. She stood across the doorway, blocking their exit.

"Tell them, Grant," Imogen screamed into the room. "Two wrongs don't make a right but it definitely goes half-way in my book. Tell them. They all have the right to know."

And suddenly all eyes were on Grant.

"Tell us what?" quizzed Bradley with a puzzled expression on his face. He was of course speaking for everyone in the room.

Chapter 29

"We went over to Edinburgh last weekend," Grant began hesitantly, as Imogen gently shepherded Kenneth and Patricia back into the room and those who had been out of earshot during the screen drama were brought up to speed through hushed whispers from those around them. "I wanted to spend some time with my father and to introduce the rest of the family to Victoria."

No-one passed comment. What could this possibly have to do with what had just transpired? Sam looked utterly wretched believing that his carelessness had undoubtedly cost his father his freedom, possibly his mother too.

Grant's eyes darted nervously around the room. Imogen gave him a look of encouragement but she stayed firmly rooted beside Patricia, a protective arm around her quivering shoulder.

"We had a lovely time," Grant then continued, "right up until we were about to leave again for the airport. That was when my dad dropped his bombshell."

In spite of the circumstances the rest of the family were now interested.

"There has hardly been time for us to take it in yet. And he specifically asked us not to say anything."

"Things have changed," prompted Imogen.

"Yes, yes they have," Grant agreed, obviously weighing something up in his mind. A vein was now pulsing in his neck.

"So tell them. I think we can keep the police out of this. On both sides of the water."

Grant bit his lip. "Cameron is still on friendly terms with Douglas McKendrick," he offered. "In spite of everything."

Patricia and Kenneth both shuddered. They had hoped that they would get through the evening without hearing that man's name mentioned. But Sam had put paid to that. However, they didn't blame him for anything. The lad was only trying to ease his own conscience, to find a way of living with the dreadful truth that his father was a killer. How could he have known that he would be overheard?

"But he told us that he had recently discovered something about his friend, something that affects all of us here in this room. And Imogen's right. Aunty Patty and her husband should not be taking all the flak for this. There's more to it than meets the eye."

"You're talking in riddles, Grant. Spit it out and get to the point."

Grant eyeballed his step-father and nodded. Then, taking a deep breath, he decided to spill the beans once and for all. He looked straight at Patricia.

"Douglas told my father that his daughter, Mia, deliberately gave you a cocktail of drugs, hoping that it would kill you. You weren't supposed to wake up that time, when Jasmine visited you in the hospital."

You could have heard a pin drop in the room.

"And what's more, Douglas has also discovered that it was his sister-in-law, Barbara McKendrick, who put Mia up to it, who gave her the idea. Apparently the two of them had discussed ways of getting rid of you."

"So, before you go running to the police to hand yourself in," put in Imogen, "ask yourself this question. Which is worse? To try to kill someone and fail or to actually kill someone by mistake?"

"Mia wanted me dead?" Patricia could scarcely fathom the enormity of this disclosure. "And Barbara! I thought Barbara was my friend."

"This doesn't really change anything," muttered Kenneth, resigned now to his fate. "I still killed an innocent man."

"We all know you didn't mean to kill him," Catherine said gently. "What's done is done. You can't bring him back. But Grant and Imogen have got a point."

"The way I see it," interjected Gertrude with her customary sagacity, "you have just been handed a 'get out of jail free card' on a plate."

Thomasina nodded. "They're not going to want the police sniffing around, maybe discovering the truth about the drugs incident. You just lie low and let it all blow over."

"I don't want you going to prison, Daddy." It was Jasmine speaking for the first time.

"My baby needs a grandpa," Alastair chipped in.

"What were you doing shut away in that room with Imogen anyway?" Tania suddenly seethed, addressing her husband with a scowl.

"Nothing. I just went up to use the bathroom and I saw her there with the baby. We were chatting, that's all."

"Well you have a baby too. You should have been down here with him, not ensconced in a bedroom with your ex, telling her secrets you hadn't even told me."

As Sam and Tania looked daggers at one another and then burst out laughing, Patricia and Kenneth dared to breathe again. The focus was shifting away from them. Their secret was out in the open. But they were safe. They were amongst friends, the best friends in the world.

"Let's get this party back on track," said Mark, picking up one of the wrapped gifts at random and handing it to Gertrude, as Grant sidled over to his wife.

"I hope we've done the right thing," he whispered.

"You have," Jasmine told them, having just caught the hushed remark. "Thank you so much for speaking up." After a pause she added, "You know, I think I knew about Dad, somewhere deep in my sub conscience. I just hadn't let it come to the surface. But I heard him talking to Sam one day and I sort of wondered."

"It's a lot for you to take in," Imogen sympathised. Then she turned to Grant. "Are you going to tell your dad?" she asked him.

Jasmine looked horrified.

"Yes, I'll phone him tonight. It's the right thing to do."

"No, you can't."

"Jasmine, I have to tell him. He's been honest with me." Grant beckoned to her to follow him out to the kitchen so that they could talk about it without destroying any more of Gertrude's party atmosphere. Imogen and Alastair joined them. There was an uneasy calm for a few moments.

"Why did your dad tell you those things anyway," Jasmine suddenly quizzed Grant with a puzzled expression on her face. "And how did he even know about it? Why would Douglas McKendrick have owned up to him? Surely he would have wanted to protect his daughter."

"Just be glad that he did. We don't really need to know his reasons for confiding in Dad."

Jasmine turned on him angrily. "You're making this up, aren't you? There isn't a shred of truth in your story! Mum told me that she took those tablets by accident."

Alastair put a comforting arm around his girlfriend. "Just go along with it, even if it isn't true," he soothed. "If it stops your dad from handing himself in to the police, what does it matter? We all know he's not a violent man. It was an accident. Nothing we can do will make it easier for that man's family and that includes putting your dad through the courts. He'll never really forgive himself for what happened and that is punishment enough."

"How can you say that," Jasmine screamed, "after all that has happened to you in the past?"

"You don't want him to end up like Dennis Redpath," Alastair said quietly. "He needs our support."

They all stared at Alastair in amazement and no-one spoke for some minutes. Gertrude's voice could be heard in the distance, thanking someone for their gift.

"Let's get back to the party," Imogen suggested, looking at her husband with an air of uncertainty. "Are you still going to tell your dad about this?"

Grant nodded. "Probably. But don't worry," he told the others. "It won't go any further."

"How do you know?" Jasmine was sceptical.

"Because I wasn't making anything up. What I told you was perfectly true. I don't know why McKendrick confided in my dad but I'm glad that he felt he could trust me. Now I have to trust him."

He took Imogen's hand and led her back to join the rest of the family.

★★★

Jasmine and Alastair strolled hand in hand through Catherine and Mark's lovely garden, breathing in the warm September air laden with the fragrance of honeysuckle, phlox and lavender, and taking in the beauty of their surroundings but still reeling with shock following the surprise disclosures which threatened their familial harmony.

"That girl tried to kill my mother." Jasmine uttered aloud the thought that kept reverberating through her brain.

"And very nearly succeeded," added Alastair.

"What a mess! How did my mum ever become involved with people like that?"

"It is ironic that the only innocent member of the family is the one who ended up dead."

Jasmine shook her head. "I think he had a daughter," she recalled. "And, to be honest, I think Douglas himself is a decent enough guy."

"Don't torment yourself," Alastair soothed. "Just let it all blow over. There have been faults on both sides."

"Tell me more about your family in America," Jasmine nudged, changing the subject with a smile. "I can't wait to meet them all."

Alastair responded that he would love to pay a visit to his Henning relations and they ended up agreeing that they would arrange a trip soon after the birth of their baby. They sat down on a bench beside the greenhouse.

"Your parents kind of stole my thunder today," Alastair remarked rather mysteriously. "I had a couple of things I wanted to tell you."

Jasmine squinted sideways at him with an air of puzzlement. "Well, tell me now," she urged.

"The first one is about my mum. She's seeing someone. A man."

"Oh, that's wonderful news! She's been on her own for so long. Who is he? Is it serious? Have you met him?"

Alastair laughed at his girlfriend's exuberance and briefly answered her three questions. "His name is Gabriel. Yes, I think it could be. And yes, I have met him."

"Brilliant! What's he like? How did they meet?"

Alastair hesitated for just a moment and then told her, "Actually they met through me."

"Someone from the garden centre?"

"No."

"Your art classes?"

"No."

"A friend of Bradley's?"

"No."

Alastair's eyes were now dancing with mischief. "I did say I had a couple of things to tell you," he reminded her.

"Well, finish the first one! How do you know this guy, Gabriel?"

"The two things are connected."

"In what way?"

"I had a check-up at the hospital recently."

"Ah, he's a doctor."

"No."

Jasmine's excitement was now turning to frustration. "So there's a connection between Gabriel and the hospital. Just tell me. He works there but not as a doctor?"

"He doesn't work there. The hospital sort of referred me to him."

"Oh no! What's wrong with you? You've been doing so well recently." Jasmine's mood of euphoria was abruptly deflated as she prepared to hear the worst. He had been a bit secretive about that appointment and had taken to going out on his own quite a lot since then, for more than an hour at a time.

But Alastair was still smiling. And suddenly Jasmine was in his arms as he hugged her close and whispered in her ear, his warm breath tickling the sensitive skin of her neck. "Gabriel is my driving instructor. My consultant said that I've made amazing progress and there are no longer any medical grounds to stop me living a perfectly normal life. I've been given the all-clear to drive. I'm doing my test next week."

Chapter 30

"That was the garage," Jasmine called to Alastair who was outside the flat chatting to Bradley. "My car is ready at last."

"Ok," he grinned in reply. "Let me know when you're ready and I'll take you over to get it."

"Just give me five minutes."

The two men continued to discuss their respective vehicles, Bradley's pristine silver BMW and Alastair's spanking new Volkswagen Golf GTI in Tornado Red, whilst Jasmine finished her coffee, freshened up and grabbed her coat, scarf and bag. She would be glad to have her own car back following the engine repair job, which had taken almost two weeks due to the required parts being out of stock. At least the breakdown had come at an opportune time with Alastair driving now and having his own transport. It was almost two months since he passed his test.

"We're lucky that they're open on a Saturday morning," Jasmine remarked as she stepped inside and nestled into the luxuriant leather seat. "I thought I'd have to wait until Monday and it would have been difficult to find the time to organise things. Thanks for taking me over." The garage was a good half an hour away in normal conditions. With the ongoing roadworks en route it would probably take them closer to an hour.

"No problem," Alastair assured her, as they both waved goodbye to Bradley and headed out of their small carpark. "Do you want the heated seat on?"

"Oh, yes please," Jasmine gushed. "This car is so comfortable. And roomy. It's going to be brilliant for the baby."

As expected, the journey was frustratingly slow with lane closures and temporary traffic lights causing multiple delays. But Jasmine didn't let it annoy her. It may have been a cold November morning but she was toasting hot, revelling in the delicious warmth that was now pervading her body.

"Looks like we're in for a heavy shower," Alastair commented, looking at the overcast sky. The first drops of rain hit the windscreen as he spoke. It was almost sleet. "What do you want to do afterwards? Do we need to go shopping?"

"I could do that on the way home," Jasmine suggested. "I'll meet you back at the flat about lunchtime."

"Good idea. There's no point in us taking both cars to the shops. It's hard enough finding one parking space on a Saturday morning. We can do something together later on."

"I told your mum we'd call in. She wants to show me which plants will need watering while she's away with Gabriel."

Alastair smiled. "She's been really happy since she

met him. I think it's brilliant, the two of them going on holiday together."

"Absolutely," agreed Jasmine.

Arriving at the car repair centre at last, they both spotted Jasmine's blue Volvo parked at the far end of the cluttered grounds. "Give me your key and I'll move it up to the gate for you," Alastair volunteered, as he eased his own vehicle into the only space available. "They must be making a fortune here. Look how busy it is."

"Thanks," smiled Jasmine, fishing her bunch of keys from her handbag and handing them over, glad that she would not have to negotiate the narrow exit route herself. She went in to the small office to settle her bill and retrieve the spare key she had left with the mechanic, who assured her that the car was now running perfectly. Alastair jumped out of the driving seat when he saw her coming and stood in the rain as he waved her off before making a beeline for his own Golf.

"I'll pick up something nice for our lunch," Jasmine called out of the window as she activated the windscreen wipers at their fastest speed. It was now blowing nothing short of a gale.

The journey home was even slower with the weather causing havoc in addition to the roadworks and the planned detour to the shopping centre taking ages due to long queues at the tills. Jasmine finally arrived at her own front door just a few minutes before midday. She was surprised to see that Alastair hadn't made it home yet.

★★★

Back at the repair garage Alastair was frantically trying to think of a way of getting in touch with his girlfriend. After waving her off he had tried unsuccessfully to access his own vehicle only to realise, when it was too late, that he had thrown his own keys down on her passenger seat when he got in to move the car into an easy position for her to exit the grounds. For the first ten minutes or so he had lived in hope that she would notice them and would return to make the handover. But as he stood there in the pouring rain, it slowly dawned on him that it wasn't going to happen. His phone, his wallet and his coat were all firmly locked inside the gleaming red car, all clearly and frustratingly visible. With a sinking heart he realised that he didn't even know her mobile number if he were to borrow a phone. It was all too easy nowadays to just select a name from your list of contacts and to be automatically connected without memorising anything. She had said she'd go shopping. But where? And for how long? There was no point getting a taxi home to collect his spare key because he wouldn't be able to access the building. Drenched now from head to toe, Alastair glanced at his watch. It was 11.40 am.

"Everything all right, Mate?" It was one of the mechanics working on another vehicle. Alastair told him what had happened. "We close early on a Saturday," the mechanic then said with a hint of urgency. "The boss will be locking those gates at one o'clock sharp."

"So my car could be trapped in here until Monday?" Alastair replied despondently. "Will I at least be able to get into the grounds to retrieve my phone and wallet?"

"Not after one o'clock. We have pretty good security.

We have to, with all these expensive cars about the place. People rely on us to keep them safe."

"Life was a lot simpler before I became a driver," Alastair muttered to himself, trying to see the funny side of the situation without much success. Then the mechanic handed him a lifeline.

"If your girlfriend's car was being repaired here, we would have her number in the system. Go and explain what has happened to Ryan over there in the office and hopefully you'll be able to raise her in time."

"Of course! Thanks." Alastair made a beeline for the office and spoke to the young man who was able to find Jasmine's number immediately. He tried to phone her using the garage landline but to no avail.

"She turns it off when she's driving," Alastair acknowledged, feeling more frustrated than ever. "And sometimes she forgets to turn it on again for ages. If she's already in the supermarket, there's a good chance that there's no signal anyway."

"Is there anyone else I can phone for you?" Ryan asked.

"I don't know anyone's number. Do you have a book?"

"I don't think so. No-one uses a phone book anymore."

Alastair sighed, disheartened and miserable. His only chance was that Jasmine might even now spot the bunch of keys on her passenger seat and come back before the gates were shut. But he knew only too well that she would have set her bag down on that same seat and the keys were most likely hidden from view. He racked his brain for someone who might be able to intercept her movements. If only he had a number for Bradley or Jillian.

Jasmine parked her car and stared out at the rain which was still streaming down the windows. At least the door of the flat was only a few steps away but she had several bags of shopping to bring in from the boot. Picking up her handbag from the passenger seat, she prepared to battle against the elements and opened the car door. A blast of icy cold wind nearly tore it off its hinges. Jasmine grabbed her pink and green fleecy scarf and wrapped it around her neck. But what was that shiny object still sitting there, nestling snuggly behind the armrest? A bunch of keys. Those careless mechanics had left someone else's keys in her car. Well, they could come and collect them from her. She wasn't making that wearisome journey all over again. If they were in a hurry for them they would surely have called her. Jasmine popped the keys into her bag and hurried to unlock the door of the apartment. Then she made three extra trips to the car to fetch her shopping, deposited the bags in the kitchen and turned on the coffee machine. Oh, it was lovely to be home. The heating was on and she revelled in the cosy warmth that enveloped her. But where was Alastair? He should have been back by now.

Fishing out her phone from her turquoise blue Kipling bag, Jasmine discovered that it was quite dead. She had meant to charge it up overnight but had forgotten. She plugged it in. She would call the garage as soon as it was powered up and let them know about those keys. How come she hadn't noticed them earlier? Of course, that was it; she had parked indoors at the shopping centre so she hadn't needed her scarf. It hadn't been moved since she had thrown it down on the passenger seat as she got into the car at the repair garage. The thought went through her head, fleetingly, that Alastair mustn't have spotted them either when he moved the car for her. She sat down to enjoy her coffee.

★★★

It was now twenty past twelve. Alastair was almost feeling tearful. He was so cold and wet and miserable, standing there looking at his pride and joy, the newest, shiniest car in sight, yet not able to access it. Suddenly he heard someone address him by name.

"You're not Alastair Henning by any chance?"

The face looked vaguely familiar but Alastair took some prompting before he could place it. He gave a nod of uncertainty.

"Geography," encouraged the newcomer. "And history."

Alastair smiled, now recognising the teacher from his old school. "Mr Newell," he affirmed. "Sorry, it took me a minute to register."

"You're soaking, Lad. Is there something wrong? If you're waiting for someone, do you want to come and sit in my car? My lady friend is here to pick up her car but it isn't quite ready yet."

"Lady friend? Sorry, I don't mean to be rude. I just remember Mrs Newell teaching in the school as well."

"Your memory serves you well. My wife died three years ago."

Mr Newell was now opening the door for Alastair to slide into the back seat of his car.

"I'm sorry to hear that, Sir," Alastair uttered, thankful to be out of the rain at least.

"Margaret, this is one of my former pupils," Mr Newell said, addressing his companion in the passenger seat as he got back in himself and closed the door. "He's soaked to the skin waiting for someone to pick him up. I invited him to join us here in the dry."

The woman turned round to acknowledge him and they both got a bit of a shock.

"Mrs Redpath!" exclaimed Alastair.

"Alastair Henning!" breathed Margaret.

"Oh, you know one another?" The geography teacher was taken by surprise and waited for clarification.

"We do indeed." It was Alastair who provided the explanation. "Greta's daughter is a good friend of mine and of my girlfriend." He suddenly felt a glimmer of hope, a chance to solve his predicament. He turned to Margaret. "Actually," he gushed, "you could do me the greatest favour. Could you phone Maggie and get Jillian's number for me? Now. It's quite urgent."

"Yes, of course," Greta agreed, pleased that he appeared quite friendly and had not mentioned the other reason why they knew one another. "Have you left your own phone at home or something?"

"It's locked inside that red car."

In no time at all Greta had phoned Maggie and obtained Jillian's number, Greta had then phoned Jillian, handing the phone to Alastair so he could explain what had happened and Jillian was now hammering on Jasmine's door with Bradley in hot pursuit.

"What on earth is the matter?"

Jasmine had just finished tidying away her shopping and washing out her coffee mug when she heard the almighty racket outside. She opened the door to find her two friends looking flushed and excited.

"Alastair's stranded at the garage," Jillian said hurriedly. "His keys are in your car."

"Those are Alastair's keys!" cried Jasmine feeling very stupid. "I didn't recognise them. He hasn't had the car for very long."

"You mean you knew they were there all that time? He's been standing in the rain for hours, trying to get in touch with you."

"No, I only found them a few minutes ago. And my phone is dead."

"The garage closes at one o'clock," Bradley announced, taking charge. "Give me the keys and I'll take them over to him. I might just make it in time."

Jasmine, grateful that she didn't have to make the return journey herself, handed over the keys at once and Bradley rushed out to his own car.

"I feel awful now," Jasmine told Jillian, "sitting here in the heat and drinking coffee while he's out there getting drenched. So he phoned you when he couldn't contact me?"

"Just there now," Jillian confirmed. "I didn't recognise the number so he's lucky I answered it. I usually ignore calls from unfamiliar numbers."

"Me too. You hear of so many dodgy scams. Whose

phone was he using?"

"No idea. But it wasn't his own. I have him listed in my contacts so his name would have come up."

"And he only just called you now? It must be almost two hours since I left him standing in the rain. His car must be locked."

"With his phone inside!"

Jillian stayed for coffee and they both waited anxiously for some sign that Bradley had made the journey before the deadline when the gates would close for the weekend. They tried to relax and talk about other things.

"I'm so glad that Thomasina has hooked up with Gabriel," Jillian remarked. "He seems like a nice man."

"Alastair is over the moon," Jasmine concurred. "It's almost like he has a dad again. They're going on holiday together next week."

"Wow! It is serious then."

"Definitely. They're like two teenagers, madly in love."

"Does he have a family of his own?"

"No, he's been a widower for years. He never had any children. I'm just so happy for both of them."

Jillian's phone rang.

"Is that Bradley? Has he arrived?" Jasmine, almost feeling sick now with nerves, glanced at her watch. 12.55

Jillian shook her head, noticing her brother's name in the caller display.

"Hi Vinnie. It's not a good time. Can I call you back?"

No sooner had she disconnected the call than it rang again.

"Imogen. Sorry, I'm waiting for an important call. Catch you later."

Unbelievably the phone rang for a third time. Jillian glanced at the caller display and saw Maggie's name. "I'm not even going to answer it this time," she told Jasmine. "Hopefully Bradley will ring any minute now."

"Surely they'll keep the place open for him when they know he's on his way."

"Hope so."

But the silence dragged on and the deadline passed.

★★★

"I'll go and check whether your car is ready yet," Danny Newell told Margaret. "They said they'd only be ten minutes or so." Then he turned to Alastair. "You stay where you are. I'll let them know that your keys are on the way over and make sure they don't close up before they get here."

Alastair smiled. "Thanks Mr Newell," he said relieved.

"Danny," the teacher corrected him. "We're not in school anymore."

"Was he a good teacher?" Margaret asked.

"The best."

Danny headed out into the wind and went to seek out the mechanic who had been working on Greta's car. Alastair felt a little awkward, left alone with the woman whose husband had caused the death of his own father. But he suddenly realised that the awkwardness was on account of her feelings rather than his own. He had adjusted to the situation some time ago and bore her no ill will. He tried to put her at ease.

"So which do you prefer, Margaret or Greta?"

"Either. But I don't think I'll ever use Marguerite again."

"Why not? It's a lovely name. Does Danny know about..."

Greta interrupted him. "Yes, he does. But I never actually told him the names of those involved. I didn't realise that he used to teach at your old school."

"So he isn't there any longer?"

"No, he left teaching after his wife died. He's working in finance now."

"I seem to remember he had a couple of children."

"Yes, that's right. Tom has followed him into teaching and Sally is a nurse."

"Any grandchildren?"

"No, not yet. Maggie told me you have a baby on the way. Congratulations."

"Thanks. It's due in March."

It all felt a bit surreal, sitting there in soaking wet clothes, engaging in small talk with Greta Redpath. And yet Alastair had a strange sensation of calmness. He cleared his throat and swallowed nervously. And then he said what was really on his mind. "I'm glad you've found a special friend. You deserve some happiness."

Greta also gulped apprehensively, obviously a little on edge. "That is very kind and means so much to me, Alastair," she said. "I think about you and your mother a lot. I hope she is well?"

Alastair nodded. "She's great, thanks. Actually she's in a new relationship too. She's met this guy called Gabriel

Duffy. They're going on holiday together next week and she's talking about moving in with him."

"And you'd be happy with that?"

"Absolutely. He's a top bloke. I introduced them." He paused for a moment and then added, "She thinks about you and Maggie a lot too. She'll be delighted for you."

"As I am for her. I'm so glad I bumped into you today. You've grown into such a lovely young man. Your mother must be so proud of you."

Danny opened the door to tell Margaret that her car was now ready, accompanied by Bradley who had arrived at exactly one o'clock. Danny had recognised him at once.

"You're the lad who used to visit our school as part of the buddy system," he exclaimed.

"Ah, I thought I knew your face from somewhere," Bradley replied. "Yes, Alastair and I have been friends ever since. He was recently Best Man at my wedding."

"How wonderful!" Danny chortled. Then he noticed that both Alastair and Margaret were looking somewhat emotional, as they emerged from the car.

"I'll tell you later," Margaret told Danny. "But don't worry. It's all good."

Spontaneously Alastair embraced her and she hugged him back, tears now falling from her eyes. Then he turned to his friend who was holding out his bunch of keys and looking a bit mystified. "Thanks so much, Brad. I can't wait to get home and out of these wet clothes. See you there."

Chapter 31

Patricia and Kenneth were both in stitches as Jasmine and Alastair related their adventures of the morning, each from their own perspective. Alastair, now looking clean and fresh following his warm shower and change of clothes, embellished the story even more with tales of other cars relentlessly passing in and out of the garage forecourt, splashing him with huge splodges of dirty water and mud, whilst appetising aromas of frying bacon and garlic bread emanated from houses across the road as he stood in the rain, hungry and shivering against the cold. Jasmine kept apologising profusely as she regretted throwing her scarf down on top of the keys before calmly strolling around the shops and arriving home to a cosy apartment and welcoming hot drink.

"It's the fact that you didn't even try to contact me when you did find them!" teased Alastair, milking the situation to give her parents an extra laugh. He wasn't really cross with her at all. It was his own fault. He knew that.

They had called for a brief visit on their way to Thomasina's home. Alastair no longer lived there, having moved in with Jasmine as they prepared for the birth of their child.

"That was a stroke of luck meeting your old teacher," grinned Patricia. "And he was with someone who knew how to get in touch with you?"

"Margaret Redpath," Jasmine revealed with a smile.

"Gosh! What a coincidence". Patricia was goggle-eyed. "Were you not upset to see her, Alastair?"

"Not at all. I'm happy for her. Especially now that my mum is in a settled relationship too."

"She's still seeing Gabriel?"

"Yes. They're heading off to Portugal together next week."

"We're just heading over to see her now," put in Jasmine.

"Well, be sure to give her our best wishes," said Patricia, "and tell her we hope she has a lovely time."

Kenneth nodded his agreement as they both accompanied the younger couple to the door and out to their car. The postman was just passing by and handed Patricia a pile of rather soggy mail. It had at least stopped raining by now and the sun was trying to break through.

"Bye, Love," Kenneth said, giving his daughter a protective hug. "You look after yourself and that grandchild of ours."

"Don't worry about me, Dad," she answered coyly. "I might have some exciting news for you soon."

Patricia smiled to herself. Alastair had already let it slip that they were secretly engaged. She had promised to say nothing until they were ready to go public with the announcement, knowing that they were taking their time in respect of Molly's memory. As the young couple drove off, Patricia headed back into the house and Kenneth went round to the back garden to survey the damage done by the wind and heavy rain of the morning. He would have some tidying up to do.

Most of the damp mail went straight into the bin. There were flyers for local supermarkets advertising their current special offers and reminders for appointments that were already in the diary. But in amongst them was an envelope bearing an Edinburgh postmark. Surely not. Patricia considered not opening it. She didn't want any reminders of the life she had left behind. But curiosity got the better of her. With a trembling hand she eased the envelope open and slipped out the handwritten letter. She looked at the end of it first for a signature. And there it was. Dougie.

Patricia took a deep breath and swallowed hard. What could he want after all this time? She glanced out of the window and saw Kenneth at the bottom of the garden, brushing soggy leaves from the path and shovelling them into the compost bin. Getting everything back to normal. She placed the letter on top of the radiator to dry it out. Stalling tactics. It wasn't really that wet. She put the kettle on.

Five minutes and a cup of tea later Patricia retrieved the sheet of paper, now crisp and dry, and sat down to read the words of her former lover. Her heart was pounding. Kenneth was now trundling the brown bin out to the gate ready for collection on Monday morning. A feeling of disloyalty grated on her conscience. But she had to

know why Dougie had suddenly decided to get in touch.
She focused her eyes on the familiar handwriting.

My Dearest Patty,
    Please do not be alarmed. I have no
intention of causing any trouble between
you and your husband. You chose to be
with him and I have accepted that. I just
want to make you aware of a situation
that has developed over here and might well
end up hitting the newspapers and causing
you some embarrassment. It's about my
brother, Alex. It turns out that he was
quite the hypocrite when he criticised
our relationship and tried to make me feel
guilty and ashamed. He was apparently a
bit of a Lothario himself. Several people
have come forward, claiming something
from his financial estate and saying that
he had made promises to them in return
for sexual favours. That, in itself, would
be bad enough when I think of the way he
told me I had sullied Lucinda's memory by
hooking up with you. But it's worse than
that. Three separate women are actually
accusing him of rape and assault. Whilst
he isn't here to defend himself, there does
appear to be a lot of evidence stacked up
against him in the form of photographs,
documents and witness statements. I

just wanted to give you the heads up in case it all comes out in the open and friends of yours realise who he was.

What's really upsetting me is that I have an awful memory of Lucinda telling me that Alex had touched her inappropriately. At the time I didn't take it seriously but, when I think back, it becomes clear that she was scared of him and avoided him as much as possible. She even warned me about him again when she was dying but I just thought that she was hallucinating. I am so sorry that I let her down. I'm glad now that he's dead. If he were still alive, I would probably kill him myself.

Please don't hold it against me that I had a monster as a brother. I am nothing like him. Even Barbara has stopped supporting him and says she often suspected that he was up to something with other women. Barbara and Mia both send you their love.

I loved our time together, Patty, and I wish you all the happiness in the world. I hope that Kenneth is taking good care of you.

All the best,
Dougie.

For a moment Patricia felt very confused. Then she noticed a second piece of paper sticking out of the discarded envelope. Again she recognised Dougie's distinctive handwriting.

Patty,

I was talking to my friend, Cameron Ferguson, last night and happened to mention that I had written to you as I didn't want you finding out about Alex from a third party. He looked very shifty and then admitted that he had concocted some story for Grant and Imogen, apparently telling them a pack of lies in an attempt to make you all 'feel better'. I have no idea what he meant and he absolutely refused to elaborate. Anyway, it wasn't true. Whatever it was.

Dougie.

Patricia's mind was in a whirl, thoughts whizzing here and there, competing for pride of place but crashing into each other like snowflakes in a blizzard.

Mia doesn't hate me.

Casey didn't kill an innocent man.

Barbara didn't want me dead.

Casey didn't kill an innocent man.

Cameron must have known all along. He made up that story to protect me.

Casey didn't kill an innocent man!

OK, he still shouldn't have done it. But it's not as if he acted as judge and jury. It was an accident. The man was a monster. There is no grieving widow. She's well shot of him.

Should I tell Casey? He has made peace with himself. Maybe leave well alone, not open up old wounds.

"Are you all right, Mum?"

Patricia swung round to find Jasmine staring at her in puzzlement.

"Yes, I'm fine. Absolutely fine."

"I forgot my handbag," her daughter explained hurriedly, feeling like a bit of a spy. "You'd think I would have more sense after the events of this morning. Leaving things behind. Ah, there it is." She picked it up off the sofa. "Are you sure you're all right?" Her glance fell on the paper in her mother's hand, the discarded envelope on the sideboard. "Is that some kind of bad news?" Patricia handed her the letter.

Kenneth could be heard coming in through the back door. He was talking to someone. And then they both heard little Stevie squealing with delight as he discovered his elusive blue tractor that his grandpa had eventually found in the potting shed, now sitting waiting for him on the kitchen worktop. Sam and Tania appeared in the room first, accompanied by Alastair who had got out of the car on spotting their arrival. Kenneth and Stevie followed them in. Jasmine looked up from the letter she was reading, her face ashen. "They made it up," she muttered, trying to make sense of the situation but feeling crestfallen.

Alastair pulled a face. "Who made what up?" he asked her.

"Imogen. Grant. Grant's father."

"You're not making any sense, Jaz," Sam pronounced, taking the sheet of paper from his sister and perusing it for himself. He read it and then turned to his mother. "What does he mean? Why was he writing to you in the first place? Does he know about Dad?"

Kenneth stiffened. "What's going on?" he asked, dreading the answer. Was he going to prison after all?

Patricia blinked and tried to gather her thoughts. It was too late now to keep this to herself. When Jasmine had taken her by surprise, she had handed the letter to her as though in a trance. The rest of the family had taken them both unawares. But why was no-one rejoicing? Could they not see that this was actually good news? Kenneth had in all probability done the world a favour, albeit unintentionally. And then she looked down and realised that she was still holding the main letter in her own hand. Jasmine and Sam had only seen the postscript.

Patricia went over to her husband and gave him a comforting hug. "Read this," she bade him, easing the sheet of paper into his hand, before scooping up her little grandson into her arms and heading out to the kitchen to find him a treat. A few minutes passed. And suddenly all five voices reached her ears, almost in unison.

"Wow!"

"Gosh, would you believe it!"

"Well, that's definitely you off the hook now!"

"The bloody bastard!"

"His own sister-in-law!"

Patricia smiled to herself. The nightmare really was over this time. She could feel it in her bones. She

290

gave Stevie another chocolate button and revelled in his excited little face beaming back at her. Alastair and Jasmine joined her in the kitchen.

"Some good news at last, Mum," Jasmine gushed.

"I do feel that a weight has been lifted off my shoulders," Patricia agreed.

"It was nice of him to tell you. It shows that he still has a lot of respect for you in spite of everything."

"I'm glad you see it that way. I was just thinking the very same thing."

Jasmine cuddled up to her boyfriend as she addressed her mother again. "We might never have met one another if it hadn't been for your association with Douglas."

Patricia stared at her, wide-eyed. "How do you come to that conclusion?" she quizzed, interested in spite of herself.

Her daughter smiled mysteriously. "I just worked it out one time. I heard you talking to him on the phone and that conversation set in motion a chain of events that led to me meeting Alastair."

Patricia nodded, trying to remember. Then she bit her lip and sighed. "It still wasn't right," she proclaimed. "I should never have betrayed your father. I almost destroyed our family. And you two would have found one another eventually. You're perfect together. Anyone can see that."

Alastair whispered something in Jasmine's ear and they shared a kiss just as Kenneth appeared on the threshold.

"Do you still have his number?" Kenneth asked his wife. "He's been very honest with us and I think we have to reciprocate."

Patricia looked worried. "Is that wise?" she ventured. "He might still go to the police."

"That's a chance I have to take."

"Well, you can't. I deleted his number ages ago."

An awkward silence ensued, broken only by Tania coming in to check on her son. Instantly aware of the tension in the room, she took Stevie by the hand and led him away out of earshot.

"You must have it written down somewhere." Kenneth was calm but insistent.

"No, I promised you I'd make a clean break from him and I've kept my word."

"I appreciate that but I can't do this any longer. I want to speak to the man."

Jasmine gulped, squeezing Alastair's hand tightly. "I think *I* still have it," she declared hesitantly. Opening her bag, she took out her phone and scrolled down through the list of contacts. And there it was. DM. She handed the phone to her dad. Patricia looked daggers at her daughter and started to tremble. Jasmine avoided her gaze. She agreed with her father. It was the right thing to do. They all watched as Kenneth activated the call. He selected the 'speaker phone' option. A ring tone became audible. And suddenly they were all listening to the voice of Patricia's former lover.

"Hello. Douglas McKendrick here."

"Hello." Kenneth cleared his throat nervously. "This is Kenneth Campbell."

"Patty's husband?"

"Yes."

Sam was also in the kitchen now, having been alerted by Tania to an impending atmosphere. He sidled over to his sister and asked her what was going on. Jasmine just indicated with a gesture that he should listen in with the rest of them. As she did so, their father's voice could be heard again.

"Patricia just received a letter from you."

"Yes, I wanted to put her in the picture. There may well be press coverage which she might find embarrassing because of her association with me."

"That was very thoughtful of you and we both appreciate it." Kenneth hesitated for a moment. "But there's something you should know."

Douglas made no response but simply waited for clarification.

"It's about your brother, Alex."

"What about him? I don't think Patty ever met him."

Kenneth tried to remain calm. "No, but I did."

"You knew my brother?"

Jasmine, Alastair and Sam all held their breath. Patricia almost fainted.

"I met him once. The night he died."

Douglas didn't respond. A deafening silence filled the room. Kenneth was struggling to continue the conversation. Patricia decided to intervene.

"Hello Dougie," she said.

"Patty," he sighed. "How lovely to hear your voice. I hope you are well."

"Thank you. Yes, I'm fine. Jasmine and Sam are here too. We all have something to tell you."

"About Alex? About the night he died?"

"Yes."

"It doesn't matter now. Don't give it another thought."

Patricia took a deep breath. "You knew all along?"

"Cam and I kind of worked it out."

Kenneth managed to find his voice again. "I'm so sorry, Douglas. It wasn't supposed to happen. It was an accident."

"Obviously."

Another lengthy silence.

"I just wanted you to know the truth. I should have owned up a lot sooner."

"Water under the bridge, Kenneth. Forget it."

"You're not going to report him?" Patricia asked in desperation.

"No. As you say, it was an accident. End of story."

Jasmine and Sam could contain themselves no longer. "Thank you, Mr McKendrick," they chorused. "Thank you so much."

"There's no need to thank me," Douglas replied. "I would never do anything to hurt your mother."

Kenneth beckoned to his family to leave the room with him, allowing his wife to finish the conversation in private. They closed the door behind them.

"They've all gone," Patricia said into the phone. "It's only me here now."

Douglas sighed. "I miss you, Patty. What a year it's been. Are you happier now?"

"I miss you too, Dougie. But yes, I am happy. I did the right thing."

"I'm glad we've cleared the air."

"Me too."

"I'm so angry about Alex. When I think of the encomium I gave him at the funeral, it makes me sick."

"Give it time. You'll eventually remember the fun you had growing up together. You'll learn to forgive."

"Never!"

"I'd better get back to the family. Bye Dougie. And thank you."

"Keep in touch, Patty. I'm chuffed that you still had my number."

"This is actually Jasmine's phone."

"Aww, you could have pretended."

"No more lies, Dougie. No more lies."

"Bye Sweetheart."

"Bye."

***

Patricia walked out to the car with Jasmine and Alastair.

"I'm glad I left my bag behind," Jasmine chuckled. "This is turning out to be such an exciting day."

"And it's not over yet," Alastair said with a grin.

"You had better get that man's name back into your contacts, Mum. I want him to be invited to the wedding."

Patricia took a step backwards and stared at her daughter, a questioning look on her face.

"We want to be married before the baby is born," Jasmine told her, her face radiant with happiness.

"But that's only months away. It takes ages to arrange a wedding. Just ask Sam and Tania. And what about your

American family, Alastair? It doesn't give them much time to get organised."

"Don't you worry about that. Granny Gertrude knows some people who can pull a few strings," Jasmine told her. "Sam and Tania have their own way of doing things and we have ours. This is important to us and we don't want to put it off."

"But my gran won't be taking over or anything," Alastair reassured her. "You'll still be in charge. She might just be able to get us a venue at short notice. And it'll just be my grandparents coming from America. We're going to travel over there next year to meet the rest of the family."

Patricia gathered them both into a warm hug. "Well that's wonderful news," she gushed, feeling truly delighted. "But you can't be serious about inviting Douglas McKendrick. That wouldn't be fair to your father."

"We've already checked with him. He doesn't mind in the least. Here he comes now so you can ask him yourself."

Patricia swung round and there was her husband, looking happier and more relaxed than she had seen him for years. He didn't need to say a word. The soothing arm around her shoulder, the gentle nod of approval and the loving smile on his face told her all she needed to know.

Jasmine and Alastair got into the car and drove off with a wave. Some children a few houses away were out in their wellingtons, splashing in the puddles and giggling with glee now that the sun was shining. Jasmine had a fleeting memory of happy times with her sister when they were small. Molly should have been preparing now to be her bridesmaid. And suddenly Alastair was talking about his childhood memories too, triggered by a little boy on a bike without stabilisers, cycling erratically along the pavement, under the watchful eye of his father.

"Your dad would have been so proud of you," Jasmine trilled. "And you're going to make a brilliant dad yourself."

"You're going to be the best mum on the planet," Alastair replied.

"I love you."

"I know you do. I love you too."

As he spoke, Jasmine felt a gentle kick from the baby growing in her womb and a surge of happiness filled her heart. "Let's make it a quick visit to your mum," she proposed. "I've had enough excitement today to last me for a month."

"I agree. Fifteen minutes max. Then home. We'll lock up and pretend there's no-one in."

"Sounds like a plan," Jasmine concurred with a satisfied smile, as they stopped at a red light. "And we'll turn off our phones. A candlelit dinner, a romantic film, then bed. Paradise." She closed her eyes and sighed with contentment. But then she spoke again. "Except for Grant and Imogen. We should tell them."

Alastair nodded. "And Bradley and Jillian."

"Maggie and Lawrence."

"OK, you win. Forget the candlelit dinner for two. We'll have an impromptu party instead."

"Good idea. A party it is. We'll have to do some more shopping!"

They exchanged loving glances as the red light turned to green.

"It's been an interesting day," Alastair mused. "We've a lot to celebrate. Things are looking up for your mum, my mum, Maggie's mum."

"It does feel kind of special."

"It does." He paused for just a moment. "It's the first day of the rest of our lives."

Jasmine nodded her agreement. It wasn't just a well-worn cliché; it was perfectly true. "Let's make it count," she said with a smile.